SILVERGLEN

E.A. BURNETT

Copyright © 2017 E.A. Burnett

All rights reserved. This book or any portion thereof may not be reproduced or used in any manner whatsoever without the express written permission of the publisher except for the use of brief quotations in a book review.

Cover By: Leesha Hannigan and Bookcoverworld

ISBN: 1544237685
ISBN-13: 978-1544237688

*For Allie, my little sister.
You will always be my very first muse.*

CHAPTER ONE

EMBER SENSED THE trap before she saw it, like the scent of a cold and unmoving predator.

When she turned the corner into the short, dark hallway, the trap was visible, a crystalline cage that gleamed in front of the oak door. She had caught the rank smell of the fish bait several minutes ago, and had so far done an excellent job of ignoring it. But as she neared the trap, the smell invaded her cat-mind, making it difficult to concentrate on the door behind it.

Behind that door lay clues, answers to her questions. Were there any shifters left alive? What had her father been up to these last months while she was away at the Academy? Power through knowledge.

Change now, she remembered. The hallway was empty, and so was the corridor beyond it. Now was her chance. She focused her cat-mind on her human form and dove into the swirling sensation of shifting skin and bone and muscle, an uncomfortable, unbalanced feeling that jolted her into nausea.

She opened her eyes in a crouch, intensely missing the warm fur and sharp senses of the cat. The stones beneath her feet were icy cold, and a draft crept over her bare skin, raising swathes of goose-pimples. She always felt dumb upon returning, and always felt the need to do some mentally challenging task in order to remember the strengths of being a human.

Planning and reasoning. A powerful intellect, she reminded herself. She evaluated the trap against the door. It was made of wrought iron, just like the ones from her father's study, but the edges of it shone with a vivid silver light—a light that any other person would be unable to see. The light was a type of Blinding spell, a unique twist that made the viewer see what they expected to see rather than what was actually there. A harmless spell, unless you were an animal.

Or a shifter.

A soft footstep echoed down the corridor.

She slid the trap-door closed so that no animals would be tempted to enter, and flashed the hand-signs to undo the Binding spell that kept the study door locked. She turned the handle, stepped into the study, and closed it neatly behind her, motioning again so the door would lock. She listened in the dark for noises from the study and the hallway.

Silence. Her father, Arundel, had left Silverglen today, so she could be sure it wasn't him in the corridor.

Fletch.

Ember's skin prickled along her neck and arms. Fletch was too keen, and far too close to Arundel for her to risk being seen by him. She waited against the door, ready to lunge toward her usual emergency exit—a dingy window over the desk—if she needed to.

After an endless period of silence, she eased away from the door. Whoever was out there had likely been a servant, probably checking the torches along the corridor to be sure they would last through the long night.

The trap worried her. She found it hard to believe that Arundel would be having a rodent problem; he went to great pains elsewhere throughout his castle to eradicate them with his traps. But she never remembered him placing one here, three floors above ground-level, directly in front of his study door.

And on the night of my return. The thought made her stomach twist with anxiety. Was it a coincidence? Or did he suspect that someone visited his study and knew that it was her?

When she left for the Academy in Pemberville nine months ago, he had acted normal. Distant, distracted, and in one of his melancholy moods. He had even given her a new dagger before she left, tipped with a strong freezing spell. There was a possibility he had found a clue of some sort while she was gone, some hint that his daughter was a shifter.

Mother. Ember's heart thumped in her chest.

Her mother was the only one who knew. Or at least, the only one besides her closest friend, Gregory. But he would never tell, she was certain of it, and her mother wouldn't either. Exposure of the truth would mean her mother's death, not just Ember's. But Ember hadn't yet seen or spoken to her mother, Salena, since her return from Pemberville. She wasn't ready to speak to her yet. *That may be another trap, all on its own.*

Ember shivered and walked into her father's dark study, the wood floor cool beneath her bare feet. The space remained the same as always, cluttered on one side with a desk, a stuffed chair, two sofas, and a table, the walls lined with shelves upon shelves of books.

On the other side, the study transformed into a small armory. Glass cases reflected the dim moonlight that filtered through the window, and various weapons glowed with spells on their mounting stands, looking sharp and conspicuous among the shadowy furniture. From behind a closed door in one corner of the armory, she sensed the cold emanating from a hidden heap of spelled traps. The traps were used to capture shifters during the rebellion, but Arundel gave them to his patrols and used them in the castle under the pretense of managing Silverglen's rodents.

On a long wooden table in front of the glass cases lay sheaves of papers and a metallic device.

She crept over, straining to see in the dim light.

The device was a snare, but unlike any she had seen before. The long rope she was accustomed to seeing was replaced with strands of metal, like the ones used in musical instruments. Ember pushed her fear down and picked up the delicate-looking wires, braided together to form a long tether and loop. The snare had been skillfully made, the wires flawless and perfectly wound together: a rather admirable display of Arundel's skills in forming and manipulating metal.

No chewing through this one. She fingered the strands, which had yet to be spelled. She remembered when she was seven, and Arundel had come back from hunting. Ember and her sister had been waiting eagerly for him to arrive, and he had been grinning and happy and proud, and it wasn't until he lifted up his brace of rabbits that she understood. Rabbits could be hunted with a bird, or they could be trapped with a snare.

You see, her father had told them with gleaming hazel eyes, *rabbits like to run. They have powerful legs, and when their neck gets caught in the snare, they try to run. The loop tightens the more they struggle—*

Ember shuddered and forced the memory away.

She set down the snare, went to the glass cases and worked her way through each weapon, careful not to touch spelled areas. She was familiar with all of them—pole axes, old foot and neck snares, lethal body traps, spears, crossbows, steel jaws, and restraint poles. Arundel had welded his own small collection: a sword whose end curved like a scythe, a lance with a spear on one end and a hammer on another, and a staff with two serrated blades protruding from one end. Each weapon held at least one spell. Freezing, Blinding, and weight spells, some simple one-handed spells that were already fading, others highly complex two-handed spells that radiated cold light.

Ember glimpsed her pale reflection in the glass cases. Naked. Uncertain. Vulnerable.

She repressed a shiver and grabbed her first weapon, easing into the fluid motions she had known since childhood. The strong, controlled thrust of the spear, the heavy draw and quick release of the crossbow, the smooth arc of the pole axe as she brought it down and twisted it into a jab at the last moment.

Ember breathed a sigh as she set down the last weapon. There were so many things she was unsure about, but coming here always made her feel better. *Power through knowledge.* Arundel's words, though he had no way of knowing how she would use them. She must always be ready, always alert to new traps and weapons. It was the only way to stay alive and hidden.

A flash of light caught her gaze.

There, on the desk just beneath the window. Ember drifted to it. Papers, quills, ink pots, and books cluttered the desk. Her father was an industrious man, often busy being a Lord of the Council, and if not that, overseeing the smelter or welding some new weapon or trap for hunting. His latest project was still being sketched. It was some sort of tiny guillotine, as beautiful and delicate as any of Arundel's work, meant for quick decapitation of rodents. Another sketch of a smelter furnace, and another of a network of mine shafts delving into the earth. Ember pushed the drawings aside and reached for the item she had seen from across the room.

A chill emanated toward her fingers and she snatched her hand back before she touched it. The small key pulsed with an incredible spell.

No, three spells, woven together as one. A Blinding spell, a Freezing spell, and a Binding spell. Too strongly forged for her own magic to undo. The spell was strong enough to trap her for hours, paralyzing her, making her senseless and stupid while it stuck to her like her own skin. She would have been caught red-handed by a servant. *Or Fletch.*

The length of her hand, the key was rather simple, with a small head and only a few notches at its tip. A slight chain threaded through the key loop and gathered at its base. Like any other key Ember had seen, but why the spells? If her father had created the spells, they wouldn't affect him when he wore it. But they would affect anyone who tried to steal it.

Such a strongly spelled key could only mean one thing. *What are you hiding, Father?* Coins? Traps? Rare metals or jewels?

Ember shuffled through the books on his desk, looking for clues. One fat book opened to a page about Blinding spells. The binding creaked as she looked at the cover. *Spells of Old.* She studied the table of contents, noticing nothing unusual. The book reminded her of the texts she had been required to read at Pemberville, only much older.

She flipped through the first few pages, and a sentence caught her eye. Her heart stopped, then banged in her chest.

"...Ineoc is the god of shapeshifters," she whispered, "that group of people whose ability to shift into animals is passed down through the blood from parent to child..."

Ember read on, learning more about Ineoc but nothing else about shapeshifters. She clapped the book shut, ignoring the dust that billowed into a cloud around her head.

The book should have been destroyed with the others during the rebellion. Arundel himself had ordered that anything with information about shifters was to be burned. Ember had spent her entire life searching for ones that might have been missed, but Arundel had been thorough. How many other unlawful books did he keep? Was that what the key was hiding? Ember stared at the tome, barely seeing the leather cover, barely feeling the rough edges, and blind to her trembling hands.

If what this book says is true, my mother has been lying to me my whole life.

The thought shocked her. Her mind seemed unable to move beyond that single realization, as if it were frozen in a heartbeat that rippled through her past. Memories became dreams from which she was now waking, and it felt terrible.

Scratching at the door broke her paralysis.

Fletch.

The door to the study loomed up before her, candle-light filtering in through the edges, shadows flickering as he made the signs to unlock the Binding spell.

Ember tore her gaze away. She reached across the desk, unlatched the window and shoved it open with ferocity, strangling thoughts of panic into submission. Frigid air gusted into the room, stealing her breath and scattering papers to the floor.

One step up the desk, one step up the sill, she thought while she imagined a mockingbird, light and small and quick. The door handle squeaked as it turned, but she hardly gave it thought as she sank into familiar nausea.

She vaulted from the window.

CHAPTER TWO

Darkness dressed Ember's balcony.

Situated strategically above the great hall, the balcony put her close enough to be within earshot of the doors far below, but far enough away from the torchlight to mask her shifting. The east-facing wall of the great hall held dozens of wide glass panes, each dancing with reflections of shadow and flame that arose from the two rows of torches lighting the path to Mirror Lake. The lake, along with the surrounding Merewood forest, belonged to Lord Arundel, and served as the only entrance into Silverglen.

Ember landed gracefully before her balcony doors, the familiar glass panes framed by ironwork resembling ivy-laden oaks. Savoring the dark, she shifted back to her human form.

The night air leached the heat from her bare skin

and cooled her panicked thoughts. Had Fletch seen her? She couldn't be sure; shifting had the tendency of swirling her mind to the point that she became unaware of her surroundings. And she hadn't been able to risk letting go of her focus to listen or look around — the result would've been an uncomfortable half-transformation at best, or, in the case of jumping out of a three-story building, fatal at worst.

She shivered and unfolded from her crouch.

She always kept her balcony doors unlocked for circumstances such as this. Stuffy air crowded her sparsely furnished bedchamber. A strangling effusion of engraved roses hung from the ceiling, and the cherry bedposts protruded like towers smothered in ivy. The two bookcases and small writing desk were equally embellished with the overzealous floral pattern. Ember had asked for anything besides the wrought iron and hunting scenes that were the life and breath of Silverglen, so her mother had provided her own unique style instead.

At least it's wood rather than iron.

She lit a fire and sat in front of the crackling tinder, watching as the small flames curled around the pine logs and charred them to black. Unlike the rest of her family, she kept no personal servants. Her secret would never stay hidden if servants lurked around. And anyways, she didn't mind doing menial tasks like starting a fire or changing her bed-sheets; they gave her time to think, time to move away from her constant

anxiety of discovery. Time to be normal and ordinary.
Like Gregory.

She hadn't seen him since last summer, before she left for her second year at the Academy in Pemberville. She wasn't sure how last summer had happened. When she had returned from the Academy last spring, he seemed different to her. Older, more mature, more attractive than she remembered him being during their childhood. And she had been gone for such a long time, with no one to talk to who understood her, who knew her like he did.

"Where have you been?"

Ember sprang up and whirled. Salena sat in the corner of the room, half in shadow.

"Mother." Ember grabbed a shift off her bed and threw it on, gritting her teeth against the irritating fact that her mother had been watching her. "I've been out. How did you get in?" The question was futile, as Salena had strong enough magic to open practically any door she wished, but Ember felt the need to say something to distract her mother's perceptive gaze.

Salena gave a cat-like smile and ignored the question. "Perhaps you should learn to check your rooms before becoming human again," she suggested, looking at ease in Ember's stuffed reading chair. Copper hair fanned over her shoulders and flared against Salena's green satin robe. "Have you discovered anything useful in your ventures?"

Ah, the old interrogations. That was why Salena

waited in her room, looking so placid. Ember knew the impatience her mother must be feeling to have come there and waited, on the same night of her arrival back from Pemberville. Ember had grown used to communicating with her by letter and thought she had done a decent job at weaning her mother off her dependence on Ember for information. But now Salena's hunger glowed from cool blue eyes.

"I was in father's study." Ember went there for her own reasons: to find clues about where shifters might be, and to practice using Arundel's weapons. But she knew her mother wanted information of a different sort. "His latest projects are a snare made of metal wires and a miniature guillotine."

Salena's expression remained smooth. They were petty details. Meaningless, according to Salena, but Ember knew better.

"Someone set a spelled trap outside his door," Ember added. Salena's expression shifted—or was it just the shadows cast by the fire?

"And you still went into the study?" A mild disbelief in her tone. Worry hovered behind it, within reach. Ember knew the worry wasn't just for her own safety. Should her father find out the truth, everyone would suspect Salena knew and hid Ember's secret. Would her father torture Salena the way he did shifters? Would he let her live knowing she raised some other man's daughter, if indeed Arundel wasn't her real father?

"Of course. Father is out of town tonight. There is no one else to worry about—"

"You know that isn't true," Salena cut in. A small line appeared between her brows. "You were careless to have gone in there. What if someone had been waiting inside?"

Ember made her tone light, almost teasing, unable to resist disturbing her mother. "He was waiting outside."

Salena gripped the arms of the chair and leaned forward, her face flushing into a scowl.

"That creature? Did he see you?" Her voice was thick. Wheels churned behind those frozen blue eyes.

He is untouchable, mother. You cannot kill this one. Unlike Ember's old nurse maids, who witnessed Ember's odd nightly behaviors of disappearing through windows, Fletch would not be easily ended. He was cunning, and close to Arundel. Besides, Salena wouldn't have reason to kill him, not until she was sure he knew what Ember was.

"No," Ember said with more confidence than she felt.

"But he suspects," Salena said, relaxing a bit into the chair.

"Does he have reason to suspect?" Ember turned to prod the fire with an iron poker. Sparks exploded in the hot air and disappeared a moment later.

"Perhaps he heard something. Perhaps you were careless at the Academy. It wouldn't be unlike you. All it would take would be one small glimpse, or a sound, or an unusual movement on your part. Then the suspicion would take root."

"Perhaps he knows something I don't."

Salena's tone sharpened. "What do you mean?"

Ember turned her back to the fire, feeling her pulse quicken. "Perhaps he knows who I really am. Who my real parents are."

Her mother stiffened and looked away.

"What now?" Salena sounded hollow. "You heard rumors again? I have told you before not to trust them."

And you eat up rumors like a starving cat with a rotten fish.

Ember didn't bother pointing out the irony of Salena's words. "A book informed me that shapeshifting is passed down by blood. Unless either you or Father are shifters, you aren't my real parents."

Salena jerked up from the chair and strode to Ember. "I am your mother!" The fire lit her smooth, perfect face—a face that was not only made beautiful by Glamours, but that was young, and confident, and stern, and knowing. There were other things in that face, things that Ember didn't want to see...love, tenderness, compassion. How could a person lie to someone they loved?

She put a hand up to caress Ember's face, but Ember pulled back.

"You *lied* to me," Ember hissed. She fought the urge to shift and fly away.

Salena's expression hardened. "I birthed you, and you are mine. That is no lie."

"And Father?"

Salena looked into the fire. "What was this book you found?"

Ember crossed her arms. "It doesn't matter. An old tome from before the rebellion."

Salena shook her head. "The book is wrong, Ember. People had their silly notions about shifters back then. The truth is, no one knows how the ability arises. Unless you heard or saw something at the Academy...?"

The researchers at the Academy stayed as far away as possible from shifters. There was no sense in risking funding by angering the Council. So she had seen nothing, and heard nothing. *That's just it, though,* Ember thought. *No one knows the truth about shifters anymore.* If they did, they kept silent. Or they lied.

"Well, then," Salena said. "This argument is over. If you have nothing important to tell me, then I'm away to bed. Welcome home, dear."

CHAPTER THREE

Clang! Clang! Clang!

The unwelcome noise of the smith's hammers woke her at dawn. Twenty blacksmith's hammers multiplied to hundreds as the sounds traveled from the west side of the keep to the east, ricocheting from wall to wall before spilling out over Mirror Lake and bouncing off the cliffs.

Part of Arundel's legacy. Fortunately one that she wouldn't inherit, real daughter or not.

Groaning, Ember clawed out from beneath the sheets and stumbled to the basin of water at her bedside. In the dim light, she made quick work of cleaning up and dressing in her usual comfortable trousers and loose cotton shirt, with a dagger tucked inside one boot. Satisfied, she left her rooms and went to find her row-boat.

She followed the path from the great hall to the lake and took the thick semi-circle steps down the cliff until she reached the last step that rested in the water. Her small row-boat bobbed among the others tied up there, and she started to untie her rope.

"BLOODTHIRSTY BUGGERS!" boomed a voice nearby, followed by a string of equally robust curses.

Ember whipped around to see a large fisherman crouching on the steps several boats down, struggling with a rope line full of jerking fish.

A squelkin had his hand embraced by rows of sharp teeth, with two dozen tentacles winding around his arm and stretching for his neck.

Ember yanked the dagger from her boot and leapt over the steps, blood thundering in her ears.

The fisherman struggled with a tentacle, peeling it away from his throat, yelling profanities at the top of his lungs. He didn't seem to notice her until the dagger sunk into the squelkin's head.

Tentacles and teeth slackened, and Ember removed her dagger. Black liquid oozed out of the opening.

"Thank you," the fisherman muttered, tugging the squelkin from his hand. Tattered flesh clung to his bitten hand, and blood seeped from it as he strung the dead squelkin on his rope.

"I can take you to the healer—" Ember started.

"I have my own healer," he cut in, then gave her a sharp glance that roused a half-apologetic grunt from him. He tossed the rope over a shoulder, but Ember pretended not to notice as she tore a strip of cloth from the bottom of her shirt.

"Here, at least let me wrap it. Please."

The fisherman scowled and hardened his lips, but let her wrap his hand snuggly. He avoided her curious gaze.

"You've been bitten before," Ember said, noticing the scars on both forearms.

"I'm a fisherman," he said with a touch of scorn, as though the scars didn't need explaining and he had only pointed her in the obvious direction because she was the lord's daughter.

Did he dislike her because of Arundel, or was it that she dressed like a boy? Cheeks burning, Ember knotted the cloth, wondering what a normal woman, with nothing to hide, would say.

"I hope it heals quickly—"

The man nodded once and was off, striding up the steps as though nothing out of the ordinary had happened, his rope of fish and squelkin bouncing against his broad, sweat-soaked back. Inky liquid splattered on the steps behind him.

Ember rinsed her dagger, tucked it back into her boot, and nodded at another fisherman who approached the steps. He raised his hand and gave a grim smile.

She stepped into her boat and rowed as fast as she could straight east.

She passed under the immense walking bridge that spanned from the northeast tower to the southeast tower, cutting through one of its three round arches that smelled of fishy moss. Sunlight shimmered off the water and onto the stones as the oars dipped.

Ember redirected the boat northeast, ignoring Arundel's Blinding spells that warped the appearance of the lake, and focused instead on her own internal compass that had unfailingly led her to Gregory's over the years.

She was sweating by the time she neared the small cliffs closest to Gregory's bungalow—or rather, his father's bungalow, which Gregory would inherit along with the horse-breeding business when his father died.

This spot in the cliffs was the lowest on the lake, not an official entrance like the great staircase to the east. Here, the cliffs had crumbled and receded beneath massive pine and cedar trees, one of which had fallen and rested like a ladder along the rocky edge.

Ember threw the boat's rope around the tree, knotted it securely, and scrambled up the log until she reached the dense pines at the top.

She had made a habit of flying to the bungalow when she was younger, when she and Gregory were just friends. And before it mattered that she showed up without clothes on—a rather annoying trait of shapeshifting that she had tried desperately to change. But no matter how much she tried, her mind could only alter her own flesh and bones, not any other material. Gregory hadn't minded her nudity last summer, but now she wasn't sure, and she couldn't take her chances shifting during the day.

Ember broke out of the woods and onto green pastures. Acres of grass spread around a squat stone building and rows of stables. The tree-line lay to the north, where the Merewood Forest rose in gentle hills before reaching Arundel's smelter. Beyond the smelter and the forest clearings lay the rounded Orion Mountains, but Ember had no attention for them today.

Near an opening of a stable paddock, she saw Gregory straddling a leggy mare. His back was rigid, poised, and his mare's ears perked back, waiting...

His trainer, standing ten paces away, made a signal, and Gregory thrust his heals into the mare's flanks. In a flash they were flying toward the forest, the mare's white tail streaming behind her like a brilliant flag in the morning sun. Ember ran to the paddock, breathing in the smell of horse and dung as she watched Gregory. A thousand things filled her head— memories of playing chase with Gregory as a child, of grooming horses and mucking stables and doling out oats. She could recall the sweet smell of alfalfa, how the evening sun slanted through the stable doors and gilded horse hair and dust, and how they glimmered as they danced in a warm breeze.

More than anything, she remembered last summer. Butterflies in her stomach, hay sticking to her sweaty skin, his face like sand against her.

Horse also tried to fill her head. The scent of the lush grass was hard to ignore, and the sudden feeling of freedom as she ran, unbound by fences, with the wind gliding along her nape. She forced it all away, repressing the urge to run on all fours, to toss her head in the air and kick, to let her skin melt and her muscles flex into...

No, she thought, *it's Gregory I want.* He was a distant point at the forest edge. He whirled the mare with finesse, and she bent her head toward the ground as she careened back.

Ember reached the paddock fence and pulled herself up to the top rung. The trainer, Florence, had the copper skin and golden eyes of an Ekesian, with a wiry figure and an ugly patched beard. He had a foul temper, but today he was intent on the race, and his skinny, ringed fingers moved beads rhythmically on his counting-piece.

Gregory flew. He leaned into the mare, crouching in the stirrups, his elbows pointing down and out for balance. Every jolt of the horse rocked his slim figure, but he moved into the jolt fluidly, as if he was a part of the horse and could not be separated from her.

I want to be that horse.

She dug her fingernails into the ridged wood of the fence. Gregory was close now, his brown curls pressed back from his wild eyes. He wore plain clothes, as he always did with the horses: a leather jerkin over a loose white shirt with rolled cuffs, brown trousers and leather riding boots that rose to mid-thigh.

"Ember!" he called when he saw her. He ran full-tilt toward the fence and yanked the mare to a halt three paces in front of her. He grinned and patted the mare's neck with a muscled, tanned forearm.

"You're mad," Ember said, grinning back.

"Me? It's all Pigeon. Did you see us fly?" He whooped into the air and Pigeon rocked her head up and down, wet nostrils flaring. Gregory turned to the trainer. "Well, Flor, what do you think? Am I good enough to enter the contest this year?"

Florence frowned at the nickname and tugged on a scraggly tuft of chin-hair. "The Red Morning?" He sniffed and looked hard at Gregory and his horse. "Yes. Thirty beads this time," he said with a thick Ekesian accent. "No winning. Not with *that*." He waved petulantly at the mare. "You need a stronger horse. Ride Brimestone."

"Brimestone?" Gregory laughed. "He would kill me with his reckless temper. Besides, I would never take a stud to a race. I will take Pigeon. She is the lightest and fastest of them all, not to mention *sane*."

"Of course. I forget you are Lachian, not Ekesian. I am finished here," Florence said. "We race again at sunrise." He threw a silky red sash over his shoulder with a bejeweled hand and trudged off toward the stables, clutching his counting-piece.

"He thinks he's one of the best horse-masters,

and yet I've never seen him ride," Gregory said, amused.

"Perhaps it makes him uncomfortable to ride."

Gregory grinned. "Perhaps. But I'm beginning to wonder if Ekesians feel anything other than pride."

Ember snorted and nearly dropped the reins Gregory tossed to her. She stroked Pigeon's sweaty, milk-white neck as Gregory dismounted, and traced the irregular pattern of blue veins that stood out in soft ridges.

"Will you really be entering the Red Morning this year?"

The prestigious race lasted a night and a day, covering the long distance from Merewood to Kingsbury. Not all the contestants ended up in Kingsbury. Some would be found half-way or only an hour from the start. Others would simply never be found.

"You heard Flor. I'll be sending in a dove today to let them know. The race starts tomorrow evening, but there's no such thing as being too late to enter, if you give them enough coin."

"Tomorrow?" Ember forced a smile and clasped the reins. "You must be really excited. I'm happy for you, Gregory."

"You will be there, won't you?" He fell into step beside her. Pigeon's head bobbed between them as they walked toward the stables.

"I wouldn't miss it," said Ember. "I know how

long you've been preparing."

"My whole life," Gregory said, nodding. "I've never felt more ready." His excitement simmered down as he looked at the ground. "How was the Academy, anyways?"

"Same as usual. Dull, tedious, and I nearly failed my practical." Ember hesitated. She wanted to tell him about the cage in front of Arundel's study, how she suspected that Fletch knew she was a shifter. "I found a book," she said instead. "Arundel isn't my father."

Gregory stopped short and stared over Pigeon's smooth nose. "The book told you he's not your father?"

"No. The book told me that shifters get their abilities from their parents. My mother is not a shifter. Neither is Arundel." Ember had spent enough time spying on them to know they were nothing more than wizards.

"And you think the book is right?"

"It's the only explanation that makes sense to me."

"The wife of Arundel, the man who slew hundreds of shifters, sleeping with a shifter. An act that is not only forbidden but that completely revolts most of society. Makes perfect sense."

Ember swatted him on the shoulder. "If it was that revolting, you wouldn't have done it."

Gregory gave a half-smile and shook his head, leading Pigeon into the stable corridor and tethering her in a grooming stall.

"But it makes sense, doesn't it?" Ember went on as Gregory picked up a hoof-pick. "Arundel and I have never had anything in common. You know who I am and what he does to people like me."

"You aren't completely different from him, Ember. What about your love of weapons?" He leaned on Pigeon's side, and the mare willingly offered him a hoof.

"I don't love weapons," Ember replied, grabbing a curry comb. "You know the only reason I have anything to do with weapons is for my own protection."

She could feel his glance as she rubbed Pigeon down.

He finished cleaning the last of Pigeon's hooves and helped Ember brush Pigeon's shoulders. "Do you have any idea who your real father is?"

"Not the slightest. There aren't any shifters left in Merewood, remember?"

"As far as you know."

A billow of horse hair and dust rose between them.

"I'm watching and listening for them all the time. Don't you think I would've heard by now if someone was like me?"

Gregory shrugged. "There's always a chance you missed something. Or that the shifter is in hiding. Maybe he's a cook in Lord Arundel's kitchen, or a groom in his stables. It's just like with the book. You've been reading them practically your whole life, and just now you find one with information about shifters. Where did you find the thing, anyways?"

"Tucked away in a corner at Silverglen. It was an old dusty tome."

Gregory took the grooming comb from her and tossed it in a bucket. "You're being carefully ambiguous. What are you not telling me?" He raised his eyebrows at her as he untethered Pigeon.

Ember sighed. "I found it in Arundel's study. It was open on his desk."

Gregory paled. "You didn't shift there—"

"I did, and I'm fine."

"Ember... What if Arundel—"

"He was gone from Silverglen last night. He's likely not even back yet."

"And Fletch, was he gone?"

"He's never gone. I made sure the study was empty first." *And that I had an escape route.* "I'm not afraid of him, anyways."

"You should be," said Gregory. He gave Pigeon a tug toward her stall and locked her in. "He's Arundel's pet."

Ember didn't want to think about Fletch anymore.

"It seems like forever since I've seen you. You look older, like a seasoned horse-master."

Gregory shook his head and sighed, giving up on the argument. "That wrinkly, huh? And here I thought I was aging well."

You are, she wanted to say. *Just looking at you makes my chest hurt.* She laughed instead. "Have you been practicing with your throwing knives?"

"Every day," he said, patting the thick belt on his leather jerkin where a small, metallic hilt poked out of a sheath on each hip. The pair had been Ember's gift to him before she left for the Academy last fall. "I'm still best with a quarterstaff, but I haven't had much of a chance to practice this winter, for lack of willing opponents."

"If that is a challenge, I accept."

"Excellent."

He grabbed the two quarterstaffs that leaned against the wall with the brooms and pitchforks and hanging bridles.

Ember rubbed the dust off of hers and hopped the fence into an empty paddock. Sweat prickled along her back as she strode out to the center of the grass. Gregory followed and stood a few feet from her, grinning and tossing his quarterstaff back and forth. His staff was as long as he was tall, which wasn't very long because he was nearly of a height with Ember. Her own staff went a few inches over her head, and it was hard and heavy in her hands.

Heavier than I remember.

Gregory twirled his staff with lithe arms before swooping it toward her. She parried the attack clumsily, letting the impact jitter up her arm. She tightened her grip on the staff, and swung it up and over with full force.

He recognized her intent and barred her blow, knocking her staff away from him. He attacked and she parried again, and again. Her arms burned as she moved the staff faster. High, low, low, high. The quarterstaves clacked each time they met. She swung high once and he ducked, bringing his staff up to throw her off. He was quicker than she, and had better balance. She knew he moved slowly for her, that he was withholding his best moves.

Typical Gregory, she thought as the staffs clapped together. *Polite even in combat.*

She lunged at his midsection, and quick as a snake he parried, grinning. She swung at his left, at his right, above, and below, pushing him toward the fence. He leapt back to give himself room, and glanced down in surprise when he stepped in fresh horse dung. She used the distraction to feint another lunge, and as he went to meet it, she twirled her staff up toward his head.

Gregory's staff disappeared for half a moment, and then pain cracked through her hands as their staffs met. Her surprise gave him all the time he needed to swing his staff to her side. The quarterstaff hit her ribs and knocked her to the ground.

"Are you hurt?"

Dazed and wincing with every breath, Ember sat up. "No, of course not."

"Sorry. I shouldn't have swung so hard." He proffered a hand to help her stand, his lips curled in a half-smile.

"It's to be expected," she said, taking his hand. "I wouldn't have accepted the challenge if I wasn't prepared for injury..."

Gregory pulled her up, and his sweaty, sweet clove scent warmed her so much that she forgot what she was talking about. The sun lit the gray flecks in his eyes, and a brown lock of hair curled against his temple. Ember was drawn to his soft lips like a butterfly to nectar.

His smile disappeared. He dropped her hand and stepped away to rub his boot over the grass.

Dizziness rocked her, and a broken-winged sparrow beat inside her chest.

"Well, I should probably get back," she said, turning to go. "Good luck at your race. I will be waiting at the finish line."

Gregory picked up the quarterstaffs, red tinging his neck and cheeks. He wouldn't look at her. Not even a glance.

She walked away.

"Ember," Gregory called. He held the staffs with hunched shoulders and a line creasing his forehead. "Thanks."

Ember nodded and let her feet carry her back to the lake.

CHAPTER FOUR

Ember tackled each side of the boat with her oars in equal rhythm until she reached the stone steps of Silverglen.

With aching arms, she tied the boat up to one of the twisted iron stakes along the base of the steps, and sluiced cold mountain water over her hot face.

She couldn't seem to make sense of Gregory. Why was he so distant? Perhaps he was simply nervous for the race, or had other things to think about. *Or he regrets last summer and no longer loves me.*

She pulled away from the water when it started to ripple. *A curious squelkin.* She climbed up the stone steps and walked beneath the iron arcade that bent over the main path leading to the great hall. Curving shadows simplified the slender twists and arcs that were Arundel's handiwork. Four servants worked at one end of the arcade, scraping off rust and rubbing linseed oil into the iron with emery cloth.

Gregory would always love her, but perhaps not in the way she wanted. *Not like last summer.* She couldn't help but wonder if his distance had anything to do with who she was. But Gregory had never before cared that she was a shifter. *Perhaps something made him change his mind, but what?*

Her thoughts were broken by the sound of voices rising from behind a screen of tall conical evergreens. The shrubs rose up in the gardens on either side of the arcade, forming alcoves and screens to hide parts of the gardens. Salena's handiwork. Ember crept along the nearest garden path to hear better.

"Mother, you're being unreasonable. I'm only asking for one summer. I did well at the Academy, and I deserve a break."

"Just because you passed your practicals—"

"I did more than just *pass* my practicals! I had perfect scores. Do you want to test me yourself?"

"Don't goad me, Finn. Your father will be the one to test you when he returns, and you know perfectly well that you need his consent to leave."

Ember hovered on the other side of the screen before deciding to rescue her brother.

"It's like being in a dungeon," Finn was saying as Ember entered the alcove.

He stood to one side of a small table, tall and lanky, grasping the top of an iron chair. A mop of dark brown hair was topped by a round red hat, and a sparse crop of brown-gold hairs formed a patchy beard. His clothing was immaculate as always: a pressed red tunic, seamless dark hose, and pointed leather shoes that gleamed with oil. His violin sat on the table, looking worn and soft compared to the iron on which it sat.

Finn revealed his sharp, pointed teeth in a grin.

"Sister, I hate to tell you this, but dressing like a man doesn't make you a man."

Ember smiled wryly. "I'm not trying to be a man. I only want to go unnoticed."

"A man with a bosom and curves is strange enough to draw a blind man's gaze. If you're looking to make yourself unremarkable, throw on some Glamours."

Finn knew Ember couldn't cast spells very well. *He's in a sour mood.*

"Thank you for your advice, little brother. Perhaps you can help me practice over this long summer. In the dungeon, if you like."

"Ember," said Salena, lounging in a chair on the other side of the table with her modest green dress gathered around her. Her vibrant copper hair was twisted and braided a hundred different ways and coiled over her head like rope netting. "You know how I feel about those clothes. And why are you so sweaty?" The Glamours on her face failed to hide her irritation as she waved a pomander beneath her nose. "I insist that you bathe before supper. Your father will be home by then."

He's not my father, Ember wanted to argue. She smiled politely instead.

"I don't wish to change the subject. I think Finn should be allowed to go to Edlen for the summer."

Salena sighed. "There is nothing further to say on the topic, Ember."

"He is only seventeen, Mother, old enough to travel on his own. And he's a lord's son. It's expected of him to travel."

"Yes, with his father," Salena pointed out. "To learn the politics of Lach. You know your father's plans for him."

Finn slammed a fist onto the chair. "I don't give a damn about the politics, or about Father's plans for me. There are still years before I would ever have a chance of obtaining a position with the Council."

"You have to work your way up, as you know," said Salena. "And you have the smelter and mines to think about, as well."

"They are a bore, Mother—"

"They are your family's legacy."

"I have no intention—"

Salena's expression hardened. "You can travel with your father or not at all."

"He still has two years left at the Academy," Ember said. "There is plenty of time for him to learn everything and work his way up."

Salena pretended not to hear. "You will not go to Edlen. This argument is over."

Finn's face reddened. He grabbed his violin and stalked out, fury rolling off of him like clouds of smoke.

"You know this would be good for him," Ember continued. She empathized with her brother's need to leave, wanted him to be able to do what he loved. "It would give him time to grow up. He could indulge in his music."

"Drinking, you mean. And falling in love with whores. That city is tainted."

Ember had never been to the city, but she had heard plenty about it. "That city is all he's ever dreamed of. Music, dancing, artists." She longed for him to go there. If what she had heard was true, she was certain he would love it.

"Yes. He will come back married to some Ekesian who can't speak Lachian. His prospects would be ruined forever."

"That's ridiculous, Mother. Ikish and Lachian are both common languages. If you're worried about him getting married, make him vow not to marry while he's away."

"Words mean nothing to someone of his age. Too young and stupid."

Ember, only a few years older than Finn, chose not to take offense at this comment. "But that's exactly why he should go to Edlen."

"I know," Salena said wearily. "He may come back a man. He will drink, fight, likely fall in love. He might have more focus when he returns. He might even discover he dislikes Edlen and that his dream was a delusion."

"So you will let him go?"

"No. That decision is your father's."

Arundel would never allow it, unless Salena could convince him. She had surprising influence over her husband's behavior. Except when it came to shifters.

"Where have you been?" Salena asked, evaluating every smear of dirt and drop of sweat with sharp eyes.

"Visiting Gregory. He's entering the race tomorrow, and I promised I would—"

"Tomorrow? Yes, the Council is coming here tomorrow." Salena spun the pomander on a strand of green ribbon. "It's absolutely essential that you attend their meeting—in secret, of course."

Ember felt faint. "But I promised I would go. I said I would be there..."

She didn't try to explain how important the race was to Gregory, or how important going to the race was to her. Salena would never understand. Nor would she care.

"You have duties here, Ember," she said in a low tone. "You know just as well as I do how essential it is for us to know what the Council decides regarding shapeshifters."

Heat rose to Ember's face. Salena was not a member of the Council, and was therefore forbidden to attend meetings; Ember had grown up attending the meetings in her stead, usually in the form of a mouse. But she knew Salena wasn't just interested in news regarding shapeshifters. She wanted it all: the gossip, the laws, the beliefs of the Council members. Any scrap of information Ember brought back Salena hastily gathered up, to sew into some hidden quilt of intrigue.

Ember straightened her back. "I made a promise to him, and I intend to keep it. You can't go on using me for the rest of your life."

"I can, and if you refuse to do your duty—" Salena's eyes grew flinty, and she grasped her pomander in one hand, "you will no longer be welcome here."

Ember's voice quaked. "You would throw me out?" *I'm getting too old to be ordered around. How have I let her have so much control over me?* She felt as though she was being stuffed into a drawer. *Too small. Too suffocating.*

"I would have no other choice. Your place is here with me. You were meant to be a spy, Ember. You have nothing else to offer beyond your female parts. Do you want to be reduced to such filth?"

Salena didn't typically stoop to such insults. This one hurt, not because what Salena said was true, but because Salena still thought Ember was childish enough to believe it.

Ember crossed her arms. "You know as well as I do that there are hundreds of things I could do before selling myself like—"

"Devondra."

Yes, like Devondra, Ember was about to reply when she realized Devondra had walked up behind her. Her sister, two years her elder, wore a flowing white gown so bright and pure that it made the apple blossoms appear yellow.

"Mother, I hope you weren't referring to me," Devondra said in her lilting voice as she floated into the alcove. Devondra's handmaid followed at her heels. "And really, why wouldn't you put up silence wards if you wished to speak of such delicacies?" With a flutter of her hands, she cast a ward to the alcove entrance. Her copper hair matched Salena's, but hung loose down her back and shoulders, crimped from drying in plaits.

"Sister," Devondra said, pecking Ember on the cheek with a moist kiss. A heady scent of rose and mint fanned over Ember as she swept away to give a similar greeting to her mother. Before they had left the Academy, Devondra had spent days locked in her rooms, crying about some lover who had been a researcher and twenty years her senior. Today, not a dint of remorse showed on her soft, smooth features. A simple Glamour brightened her large hazel eyes and reddened her fulsome lips.

"I wasn't expecting to speak of such things," Salena said as Devondra sank into the chair opposite. Her handmaid stood a few paces behind, her calm dark eyes resting on the back of Devondra's head. "But we are finished now, aren't we, Ember?"

It wasn't a question. Ember pursed her lips and began to turn away.

"I take it from your outfit that you visited Gregory today," Devondra said in her innocent, silvery voice. "Tell me, did he seem distant? Distracted?" Devondra regarded her with placid eyes as she twisted a golden necklace laced with emeralds. "I've heard rumors about a woman who dresses very finely, with very lady-like manners, and who is an excellent horse-woman. Have you heard? It seems that she's befriended your Gregory."

"He mentioned nothing about her." Gregory would never be interested in someone so refined.

"Of course." Devondra tilted her head down a fingernail-width. Her gaze took on a feline quality. "Did you really think he'd continue to be interested in a girl who dresses like a boy? Really, Ember, you're covered in mud and smell of sweat. I can't imagine how he ever found you attractive—"

"He works with horses all the time," Ember said, trying not to yell. "He's used to bodily smells."

She gave a pleased smile, caressing the necklace that was probably some payment from the old researcher in Pemberville. "Oh, so you wish you were his horse."

The comment hit too close to her heart. Her chest tightened.

"I—"

"Enough," Salena interrupted. "Devondra, we need to speak about Lord Wincel Bourke and your scores from the Academy. Ember, you may leave us."

Ember jerked away as Devondra began making up excuses for missed classes. She knew Devondra would go on to explain how Lord Wincel, with his hunchback and drooping face, was a pathetic prospect for a husband, and that eventually she would wheedle her way out from Salena's pressure to marry. Somehow, her sister always seemed to get what she wanted. *Nearly any man in her bed, jewelry, and freedom from marriage.* Even with all her missed classes and low scores at the Academy, Devondra had somehow managed to graduate in the spring.

Yet Ember wanted none of those things. Jewelry was pretty but boring and useless; marriage was something neither she nor Salena wanted for herself; attending the Academy at all seemed pointless. But having any man in her bed...

Gregory. Was he interested in another woman now? *An excellent horse-woman. And I wanting to be his horse.*

Her face burned as she headed toward the great hall. The wide iron doors showed twisting vines that seemed to strangle birds and beetles and butterflies.

Two guards opened them for her and she nearly ran to the back of the great hall, focusing her gaze on the doors that led upstairs to the keep. The murals of the great hall would be too much just now. She didn't want to be reminded of hunting, or of Arundel. She didn't want to see or think of animals.

    She must go to the Council meeting, and she must keep her promise.

    I will find a way to keep it.

CHAPTER FIVE

EMBER CREPT INTO the cellar when no one was looking. The deep, cold passages ran beneath the great hall and extended directly under the solar where the Council would be meeting.

She went to the darkest corner of the cellar, where she knew the crates stood empty and the braids of garlic and onion were long gone. She tucked her clothes behind a crate and shifted into her smallest form, a mouse. She was more like a small rat, fat and plump, but forcing herself into something smaller was akin to being stuffed into a jar. At some point, there wasn't enough room for all of her, as if her limbs were detached from her body, and it was too uncomfortable to bear.

At once she could hear voices from above, thin as strands of hair weaving their way through the stones.

Ember hopped and crawled her way over the crates and shelves, smelling the residue of jarred peaches, plums, and pickled goats-feet. At the end of fall harvest, the cellar was always packed full, either with food grown, hunted, or caught in Merewood or with food from Ekesian traders. Arundel had a distinct appreciation for rich and exotic foods, a fact that earned him a bit of respect from Lachians who lived a sumptuous, lavish lifestyle.

Ember squeezed through a sliver of space between the stone ceiling and the stone wall. She entered the solar near the middle of the room, just under a giant circular table.

Dozens of candles lined the walls, each held captive by an iron sconce that twisted and bent to form a sun. Flickering sun-shadows stretched up to the ceiling. More candles rested on the table, a giant circular slab of stone. Inlaid into the stone were yellow, orange, and red pieces of glass: a gift from Lady Dell of Glaspell in honor of Yathe, the god of Lach. The room smelled of the candles: a soft beeswax scent mingling with sharp mint and flowery bergamot. She could smell hundreds of other things in that room, even the ones that were nearly gone. Clothes rustled nearby, and Ember crept to the stone base of the table to wait.

The door to the solar swung open.

"Lord Arundel will be here shortly," said a man Ember recognized as the castle steward. "We have refreshments. *Sumbac*, for those of you who enjoy the orange liquor, hot coffee spiced with Ekesian cinnamon, mint-lemon tea fresh from our own gardens, and chocolate warmed with Ekesian cinnamon, vanilla, and sugared hazelnuts."

Behind the steward trailed six members of the Council. Ember recognized them all, this being the twentieth or so meeting she attended. At first she had distinguished them mostly by what they wore, but now she felt she knew them quite intimately.

Lady Dell entered first, wearing her usual white and yellow silks, tailed by a young boy acolyte in similar garments. Her stiff expression transformed into one of adoration at the site of the table.

"Oh, Gerald, would you look at this table! This was the gift I was telling you about. A splendid honor to Yathe," she said reverently, ignoring the steward as she dragged the acolyte by the hand to the table. The acolyte smiled with equal adoration, crimson tinging his cheeks.

Lord Histion, a strapping man whose clothing *clinked* and *tinked* with pearls, starfish, and coral pieces from the east ocean, scowled at Lady Dell as he came in behind her. "Let's not confuse Lord Arundel's solar with a sanctuary, Lady Dell."

Lady Dell lifted her nose at him. "They might be seen as the same thing, Lord *Histion*," she retorted, emphasizing his name with a hiss.

"It's far too early to be arguing already," called out Lady Ashlin as she entered behind them. She wore a jutting masculine jaw and a simple blue gown with bodice pulled so tight it flattened her chest. "Let's try to be civil, shall we?"

Lord Histion turned his scowl on Lady Ashlin, a snide comment ready on his puckered lips. Before he could speak, Lord Wincel bumped into him.

"Oh!" Lord Wincel exclaimed in a frail voice. "Do pardon, do pardon." Lord Wincel's stooped back and sagging face did little to shorten his height, which was extended further by a ridiculous hat made of rabbit fur and long tufts of feathers. His garments were of velvet and fur, all soft and supple and white, belonging to ermine and rabbit. The lord had no exceptional qualities, and ruled over Kingsbury, a city not known for anything in particular.

Lord Jeriel stalked around the them, looking hard and quiet, his thick hands hanging heavy beside him. He was stockier than the others and had a generally dusty appearance, having come from Masonshire, where the primary business was masonry. A dog stalked in beside him, a scraggly, dusty female with a bristly snout.

Ember wedged herself against the table pedestal.

Last arrived Lord Thurstun, an elephant of a man wearing sumptuous purple and orange robes, nearly in the Ekesian fashion except that no Ekesian in their right mind would wear so many or such *long* sashes. The sashes, dyed bright orange or yellow or blue, were all the rage in Ekesia, where Lord Thurstun liked to vacation when his presence wasn't required in Pemberville. Ember knew him better than the others, as his lack of interest in the Academy was well-known. *And his fat appetite much spoken of.* The lord liked to eat and drink, a fact that was apparent in the rolls that the robes couldn't hide, his beady eyes and wet, red lips. A sheen of sweat glimmered on his forehead and upper lip. In Pemberville, his home was famous for its gaudiness and abundance of Insulating spells that gave it an Ekesian-like heat.

They sat at the table in a dizzying swirl of aromas, rustling cloth, and heavy breathing. Lord Thurstun took several moments sitting, as he rocked his weight back and forth indecisively between two chairs, preventing the others from occupying either one.

"Where is Lady Rina?" he asked, not sitting down until the others already had.

"She is likely on her way," the steward said as he served drinks.

Tea for Lord Wincel and Lady Ashlin, coffee for Lord Histion and Lady Dell, chocolate for the acolyte who hung back, *sumbac* for Lord Thurstun, and nothing for Lord Jeriel or his dog.

"I hope Lord Arundel won't be too long," Lord Wincel muttered to no one in particular. His rabbit-fur feet tapped the floor, exposing a strip of thin, pale leg.

"What's the rush? Do you have a wife to get back to?" Lord Thurstun asked, chuckling.

"While we are here, there are other things I must do—"

"Women, you mean," Lord Thurstun pointed out. "Is it true you have interests in Devondra Thackeray?"

Someone gasped, but before anyone could speak, the solar door opened again.

"Lady Rina," Lord Thurstun boomed. His cushioned iron chair scraped the floor as he stood. "I have saved a seat for you. Would you like some refreshment? I will serve you myself."

"No need," said Lady Rina. She walked gracefully into the room with sandaled feet, the copper and silver bangles tinkling along her arms and ankles. She was a slender young woman with a taste for both Ekesian and Zarian cultures. Her dark hair coiled on top of her head in the Zarian way, and her colorful robes and sashes were adorned with strips of fur, teeth, and bones. She came from the city of Edlen, which bordered Ekesia and welcomed any immigrant who had a talent for art. "My hands are perfectly capable."

"Yes, of course," said Lord Thurstun. He sighed loudly as he sank back into his chair.

The solar door banged open.

"My Lords and Ladies of the Council!"

Lord Arundel Thackeray's voice startled Ember into squeaking. The dog pointed her floppy ears toward the table.

"Welcome to Silverglen. Please forgive me for not being here when you all arrived," Arundel said. "A matter at the smelter required my attention."

"Any casualties this time?" Lord Thurstun inquired, his massive form blocking most of Arundel.

Arundel wore his riding boots still, which meant he most likely told the truth about being at the smelter. He walked with purpose to the table. *He is in a good mood now.* He wouldn't drink, Ember knew, but he would talk instead. As he settled into his seat, a metallic scent underlain with horse and leather blended with the other scents under the table. Arundel nearly always smelled of the iron he often worked with, and it was a colder, sharper smell than that of blood.

"Three," Arundel replied, as though remarking about how many apples were stored in the cellar. "A furnace collapsed."

"Unfortunate," Lord Thurstun murmured.

"Yathe's mercy," gasped Lady Dell, while the others muttered equally remorseful phrases.

Lord Arundel cleared his throat. "Their families will be more than adequately remunerated. Shall we begin?"

Ember doubted coins would make up for the loss of a family member, but she knew that the family would stay in the mines or smelter where they worked, for the coin and for fear of punishment should they leave.

Trying not to be too distracted by this and smells, Ember memorized every word of what the Council said. The meeting began with the usual tedious discussions of money, land acquisitions, trading agreements, laws, and research findings from the Academy.

"Lady Ashlin," Arundel said. "You purchased two hundred swords from me last month. I hope you are pleased with them."

"They have proven to be of excellent quality, Lord Arundel. I may be purchasing two hundred more. I've made a decision to form a new garrison of women—"

Lord Histion's sea-squelkin shoes jerked in surprise.

"*Women?*" he sputtered. "You're allowing them to fight? Are you mad?"

"I've consulted with my husband on the matter. If I am mad then so is he."

Lady Ashlin's husband was a renowned trainer of the Lachian garrisons. He personally oversaw the testing of the Escort, who were only hired for the Council members and their families.

"But... This is outrageous! How can a woman fight a man? She has neither strength nor skill in fighting—"

"That is why we teach them," said Lady Ashlin, impatience tightening her voice. "We decided it would be best to train them separately from the men, as they have differing needs. You might do well to remember that the city of Wicksburgh belongs to *me*, Histion."

"Yes, and *my* city of Lyn needs garrisons to man

its ships," replied Lord Histion. "Do you expect me to hire *women* for this task?"

"I would hire women," Lady Rina offered in a low voice. Her legs were crossed, and her orange and green skirts parted to reveal a slender leg. A sandaled foot bobbed up and down, dangerously close to Lord Thurstun's purple sashes.

The pungent smell of sweat doubled.

"Perhaps more would be convinced to hire women once their skills are tested for us," Lord Arundel suggested.

"It will be a year or more before they are ready," said Lady Ashlin. "When the time comes, I will bring them to the Council. Lord Wincel, I've brought the three men you requested to add to your Escort."

"Yes, very good," Lord Wincel tittered. He tapped his rabbit-fur toes against the floor.

Ember was beginning to get cramped in her stone nook. The dog had refused to lose interest in her, and stuck her head under Lord Jeriel's chair, wet nose twitching. Lord Jeriel didn't seem to mind. He had hardly said a word during the meeting, hadn't moved his dusty leather shoes even an inch, but only fiddled with a small stone token, round and worn from years of fiddling.

"Lady Rina," said Lord Thurstun. "Any news of Ekesia? Zari?"

"I have heard that King Richaro of Ekesia has raised taxes again. A dozen or more immigrants arrived in Edlen only last week." Her sandaled foot bobbed in smooth rhythm.

"That king is a fool," said Lord Histion. "Is he looking to raise a rebellion?"

"He is young, and in need of better council," Lord Thurstun put in.

Lady Dell spoke up. "Perhaps if we invited him to visit Lach, and impress upon him the values of Yathe—"

"The Ekesians don't care for Yathe," Lady Rina stated.

"Simplicity, order, beauty, and perfection," Lady Dell continued. "Perhaps he should focus on those instead of sowing disorder by being cruel to the poor."

"Not everyone is able to be as generous as you to those beneath us," Lord Histion said with a hint of scorn.

Lady Dell sniffed. "I don't believe it's a matter of ability. Only willingness."

"I think it would be unwise to upset the new king of Ekesia," said Arundel. "We have certain alliances with him that must be maintained for the safety of Lach."

"You mean the agreements about shapeshifters," said Lord Thurstun.

The dog had crept closer. She crawled on her elbows under Lord Jeriel's chair, her nose dripping as it waggled. Ember couldn't stop her mouse-body from trembling. Her only escape route, the slit in the floor, was close enough to the dog that she could snap Ember up if she dove for escape. *She can't see me,* Ember told herself. *If I hold still enough she will soon forget I'm even—*

The dog saw her. She could tell by the way her eyes grew huge and her muscles bunched. Instinct overtook her. Ember dove into Lord Thurstun's thick garments just as the dog pounced. The dog barreled into Lady Rina, pushing the woman into Lord Thurstun, who moved barely an inch from the impact.

"Get that damned bitch out of here!" Lord Thurstun bellowed, tugging his sashes out from under the dog.

Ember burrowed into a particularly thick sash hanging close to Lord Thurstun's knee. She glimpsed Lady Rina's amused expression as Lord Thurstun patted her all over to make sure she was unharmed.

A sharp command came from Lord Jeriel. The dog, ears pressed back in submission, sulked out from under the table, mouse forgotten.

Ember sprang back to her nook. Lord Thurstun had re-arranged himself so that he sat closer to Lady Rina. Her bobbing sandaled foot now stroked his lower leg.

"I do wish to keep the agreements with Ekesia," Lord Arundel went on as if there hadn't been a disturbance. "And I'd like send out another patrol."

The room erupted with voices.

"Ekesia?"

"*Another* patrol?"

"Lord Arundel, do you really think it's necessary—"

"There have been rumors," Lord Arundel cut in. "Of another faction in Ekesia. I can't be confident that this King Richaro will be as loyal as his father was to our agreements."

"But there are rumors that shifter factions are everywhere," Lord Wincel said. "The commoners who spread them must be mad."

"Commoners are like dogs," explained Lord Histion. The shells on his feet clacked as he shifted. "They'll say anything you wish them to in hopes of a reward."

"*My* commoners do no such thing," said Lady Dell, crossing her silken feet demurely.

"I agree with Lord Wincel," boomed Lord Thurstun. His great stomach jerked as he spoke. "I've been hearing all sorts of madness about how shifters have been helping commoners forage for food, how they save their children from harm."

"It happened in Masonshire."

The quiet, rough-edged voice came from Lord Jeriel, who had ceased fingering his token.

"A lost child," he continued. "Said to be dead. A great wolf was seen guiding the child home. I've heard the account directly from the parents."

The disbelief was palpable. Everyone's feet shifted at once.

"You can't possibly believe them," said Lady Ashlin in a shrill voice.

"I had no reason to disbelieve them."

"Perhaps the wolf hunted the child rather than guided it," suggested Lord Thurstun, rubbing his belly absently.

Lady Rina's sandaled foot slid over one of Lord Thurstun's purple sashes. "I believe," she said, "a better point to make for Lord Arundel is that none of his patrols have seen sign of shifters in years. How many do you have out just now?"

"Less than there have ever been. Three patrols in Orion, five in Lach, and only two in Ekesia. There is one returning shortly from Zari."

"Eleven patrols in four countries, then." Beneath the table, Lady Rina's toes dipped under the sash, causing Lord Thurstun's jeweled hand to flutter toward her lap, where a sliver of tanned thigh lay exposed from a slit in her dress. "What do you think, Lord Thurstun? Should we pay for another patrol to be sent out? There is a good chance we will pay to find nothing."

"We pay...?" Lord Thurstun's thick fingers twitched, brushing Lady Rina's leg. "But it's been nearly two decades since the rebellion, and as you said, no sign has been found of shifters. They are likely all dead."

Lord Arundel's leather boot moved back an inch, but otherwise he maintained a relaxed posture.

"There have been other rumors, as well," Arundel said. "Rumors about shifters speaking with peasants, stealing food from our forests. They pose a threat to all the wizards of Lach. Shall I remind you of the rebellion? Lord Thurstun, have you forgotten your mother-in-law? Lady Ashlin, your young cousin? And I'm sure you haven't forgotten your own brother, Lady Rina...?"

"Mauled to death by a stag," Lady Rina stated. Her foot stilled.

"His own shifter," Arundel pointed out.

"My brother was a foolish wizard and a heartless man."

Arundel's hand, which had lain composed in his lap, curled into a fist. A wavy whisper of prayer came from Lady Dell, and Lord Wincel's rabbit-lined boots tapped against the stone ground.

Lady Ashlin drew herself up. "My young cousin was no such fool, and he never lacked compassion. I say we send out a patrol. What's the harm?"

"For how many more years will you ask us to send them out?" Lord Histion said, straightening in his chair. "How much use will it be sending out another patrol when none of the recent ones have brought anything useful back? We could be putting more coin toward trading galleys, garrisons—"

"Feeding the poor," Lady Dell added.

"You can keep your coin," Lord Arundel snapped. His fist relaxed. "I have had every success I've hoped for this spring. I wish you to share in my bounty."

There must have been a signal, for the door to the solar opened and servants carried in heavy chests, which they set at each of the council-members' feet.

A bribe, Ember realized. What was this success he spoke of?

"For you, Lord Histion, a rare horn-shell from my own Merewood Lake."

The twisted horn-shell gleamed pink and coral and burnt red, as large as Lord Histion's hands.

"Lady Ashlin, I gift you a small priceless dagger to carry on your person. Forged using the best steel and the strongest of Blinding spells."

Knotted patterns of gold were inlaid on the hilt. The blade was long and pointed, and the metallic scent of the spell permeated the air.

"For you, Lord Wincel, a feather from the extinct firebird."

A servant flourished the plume from the chest like a bout of flame. Scarlet, orange, and gold melted together, looking more liquid than feather. No doubt Lord Wincel tucked it into his hat.

Lord Arundel presented other gifts: exquisite furs of ermine and snakeskins for Lady Rina, a jeweled box of gold for Lord Thurstun, and a sun made of rose-quartz for Lady Dell.

"Lastly, Lord Jeriel's gift. In my spring fortune, I've hit a rare spot of stone that I'd like to give you access to."

Lord Jeriel's fidgeting fingers quieted. "The type of stone?"

"Sunstone. There isn't much of it, but I've no use for it and I know of its value to masons."

Lord Jeriel pocketed his token and stood. "It is beyond value, Lord Arundel."

Ember watched as the shadows cast on the floor shook hands. Each one followed in turn, grasping and shaking heartily.

Another patrol mission approved by the Council.

She dove for the hole near Lord Jeriel's chair before the dog could see her again, and clambered back through the cellar. Night had already folded over Silverglen, and dawn would rise soon. She was weary, and slipping back into her human form was like dipping into a cozy bath. She would be pushing herself by not sleeping, but it would be worth it. Gregory's race, his dream. She couldn't, and wouldn't, miss it.

CHAPTER SIX

SHE FOUND GREGORY at the edge of the swampland, shrouded by black waters and shadowy ash trees. Ember saw them easily in the yellow moonlight with her owl eyes, and the squish of Pigeon's hooves in the muck resounded through thickets and up to the branch of a half-dead maple where she perched.

Bone-weary, she thought as Pigeon's head drooped. *But alive.*

Unlike his mare, Gregory sat erect and attentive. He guided Pigeon around a large ash and paused occasionally so he could listen.

Ember followed them, gliding soundlessly from one ash to another, scouting from above. He had only to emerge from the swampland and travel a short distance through forest before arriving at Kingsbury.

And yet he is taking his time.

Restless, she flew up above the canopy. Already the moon's edge was fading and the sky softening to the east. A rank stench rose with the wind as she circled Gregory overhead. As an owl, she could easily avoid thinking of the dead, or the dying, or whether they had died by Gregory's hand. It wasn't so easy to ignore the sheen of blood and the gleam of a sword through the canopy.

One of the dead.

She dropped down to a long tree limb some distance behind Gregory and Pigeon, and saw that she was wrong.

A rider and her gelding moved as a shadow in the brackish water. A simple rope bridle quivered on the gelding's snout, and the rider rose from his bare back, darkness melding with darkness. A bloody sword hung at her waist, opposite a quiver of feathered arrows. She held a curved bow in one hand, and sat with loose shoulders as her body swayed in the moonlight.

She twitched her head when Ember landed, exposing a long scar that twisted over cheekbone and curled into her upper lip. Obsidian eyes hammered into her.

Ember jolted off the tree before the woman could lift her bow.

The archer neared Gregory, and soon the dark wouldn't hide him anymore. Already it seemed to

Ember that his white mare might be visible to the archer. She merely needed to wait until he was within bow range before picking him off, just as she had likely picked off others before him. They were in the last leg of the race, and it wasn't unheard of for there to only be a few riders left at this point. Usually there was only one.

A few moments more, and there may be.

Ember landed on the ground in a flurry of leaves, between Gregory and the archer. The still air would allow her scent to go unnoticed by the horses, at least for a short time.

Queasiness gripped her as she shifted, forcing her bones and muscles to grow into a wolf. The tiredness in her limbs carried over into her new form. She shook herself, allowing the thick black coat to ripple over her, and sniffed.

Scents flushed into her. Decaying leaves and wood, the wet smell of frog, the heavy stench of carcass some ways behind her. She followed the sweet smell of horse dung, skirting the deeper waters and keeping her distance from the horses.

Pigeon whickered ahead as Ember rounded a stump. Barely audible, a feathery noise that the archer might not have heard—

A soft rasp of wood against wood resounded behind her.

Ember lunged toward the noise, leaping over water as if her wolf-body could fly. The ground and water became the same dark fluid mass.

She reached the gelding as the archer released the bowstring. A scream erupted in the swamp.

Ember grasped one of the gelding's legs in her mouth, digging her teeth until she tasted blood.

The horse reared, screaming, and punched the air with his hooves, but the archer clung to him. Her hard eyes bored into Ember and the scar on her lip deepened as she smiled.

Somewhere nearby, hooves thudded the ground, growing louder—

The archer's sword slithered out of its scabbard and slashed toward Ember as the gelding came down.

Silver flashed by out of the corner of her eye. The archer cried out and dropped the sword mid-swing. Blood pulsed from where a knife hilt now grew out of her shoulder.

Gregory's throwing knife. Already Pigeon's hooves careened away from them, but Ember didn't waste time looking back. He had come to save her from the archer's sword. He had shortened the distance between him and his enemy. And the archer saw that, too.

Twisting her lips, the woman grabbed the hilt, tugged it out, and flung it at Ember.

Ember flinched. The weapon sailed harmlessly to the side.

The rider dug her heels into the gelding's flanks as Ember nipped at another leg, but the archer gripped the reins tight and shouted at the horse to prevent him from rearing again.

With a strangled sound, the gelding shook his head and stomped his front hooves, his injured leg bloody and trembling. He wouldn't tolerate putting his weight on it much longer. The archer pressed him forward.

Ember leapt in front of him, snarling and snapping.

I must give Gregory more time.

Again the archer thrust her heels into the gelding's flanks, but each time Ember pushed him back with teeth and her most vicious growls.

The archer picked up her bow and notched an arrow, but she couldn't hold it up while grasping the reins. Cursing, she dropped the reins and jerked the bow toward Ember. Her wound wept blood as she pulled back on the string.

The gelding reared again, and the archer cried out, letting loose the arrow even as she dropped the bow to cling to her horse. The arrow disappeared into the canopy, and the gelding took off with his rider, splashing wildly through the muck.

The archer craned her head back, the scar on her lip stretching into a smile that didn't reach her cold stone eyes.

She knows. She knows what I am.

The fur on Ember's scruff stood on end, and she bared her teeth in a growl until the woman and her horse disappeared into the trees.

CHAPTER SEVEN

Pigeon's tail rippled with speed as she ran to the northern gates of Kingsbury.

Thousands of people pressed together there, cheering as the dawn sun cleared the horizon. Golden light spilled over the gates, gilding fruit stands and shops and colorful garments.

Ember flew too high to see faces, but the only one who mattered was the man who rode the white horse below. She dropped out of her warm air current and circled down, checking behind one last time for the archer. Still no sign of her or her gelding. Ember's talons tightened around the hilt of Gregory's throwing knife.

Pigeon and Gregory burst from the edge of the forest, and for a moment horse and rider blazed in the dawn light. A roar rose from the gates and the people pushed forward with welcoming arms. With her hawk eyes, Ember saw that Gregory grinned, and that a long gash reddened his left sleeve.

The arrow got him after all.

They came up the road at a canter and broke through a long scarlet ribbon, the fabric streaking over Pigeon's chest before fluttering to the ground. In a moment, they were swallowed by the crowd.

Ember didn't dare drop any lower. Doing so would only draw notice and an artful attempt at killing. She had seen it before, and with so many people there were bound to be a few who hated shifters, who would try to kill a hawk just on the fact that it *might* be a shifter.

With Gregory safe, the weight of tiredness she had been keeping at bay pulled her down, and each beat of wings took almost too much effort. She flew north to Silverglen castle, nestled so deeply in the Merewood Forest that she couldn't see it from her height. With her hawk's sense of direction, Ember knew that if she flew straight north toward the endless Orion Mountains, she would find Silverglen.

And the deliciousness of expanding back to her human form, of crawling under the sheets, and slipping into slumber...

And perhaps I will seek Gregory when I wake.

CHAPTER EIGHT

Finn's voice rose above the explosive hammering of the Iron Fist. Their father must have dragged him to the smelter again, to learn about the family business he would inherit. Ember didn't blame Finn for hating it. She spread her leathery wings and fluttered toward his voice as the hot, rank stench of iron clawed into her belly.

She found them by a huge stone furnace, two silhouettes against the blinding white of molten slag. Clinging to a rafter, she strained to hear beneath the roar of the furnaces and bellows and the banging of the Iron Fist. Finn hunched and clutched his violin to his chest while their father towered over him, a straight pillar of dark. His stillness made Ember forget the noise and tremor of the smelter.

The pillar snapped, and in the breath of a

moment their father ripped the violin from Finn's arms and tossed it into the furnace.

Finn's wail tore through her.

"You will not be a useless musician!" their father's voice boomed. "You are a Thackeray. This will all belong to you," he gestured around the smelter. "In addition to the mines. You are too smart and highborn to be a musician. Do you understand?"

Ember wanted to scream at Finn to answer, because again a breath of stillness solidified their father, and it was the same stillness he held before hitting the dogs.

But Finn cradled himself with lanky arms and cried as the violin smoldered and shrank in the vast furnace.

Their father grabbed Finn by the arm and dragged him to the Iron Fist.

The great iron hammer, like a giant's fist, pounded a bloom of iron the size of a piglet. Sparks sprayed over Finn as their father gripped him by the wrist.

Cold dread seized her.

"Perhaps I should take off your hand?" their father shouted above the hammer. The sparks flashed orange in his gaze. "Would you like that? You would no longer have the option to be a musician. Do you want me to take away your choice?"

Finn struggled to pull away as their father forced his hand close to the Iron Fist, strong and unheeding of

Finn's resistance.

Ember dropped from the rafter and dove at her father's head.

He shouted, and his huge blacksmith's hands pummeled the air to try to hit her. With a bat's wings and high-pitched chatter, Ember darted between his flailing arms like a needle through fishnet.

Livid, he reached for an iron bar, half-hammered into a sword and hot enough to turn his hand red as he swung it. A familiar fury colored his face; he knew she wasn't really a bat, and he would kill her for it.

Ember zipped out of reach and squeezed through a smoky opening in the ceiling. Outside, Finn hunched low on a galloping horse as he drove home to Silverglen.

Good. He is safe now.

Her father rushed out the door of the smelter with the iron bar still gripped in hand. He stared after Finn, fury and madness darkening his expression. A moment later, his quick gaze darted around the sky.

Ember veered east, away from Silverglen, speeding over the hills of mangled stumps toward the dense forest edge. Her father would be more interested in the shifter attack now, not his son's disobedience. Once hidden in the oak leaves, she would shift to a falcon and make haste to Silverglen before anyone noticed her absence.

No one must know. Her father must never suspect.

CHAPTER NINE

Ember's chamber door crashed open, jerking her out of the darkness beneath her pillow and into the bright afternoon light swelling into her room.

"Ember! What are you doing in bed?"

Dreaming memories. Her stomach clenched as she wiped the sweat from her face, feeling as hot as if she had just stepped out of the smelter. Finn's scream echoed in her heart, and she took a breath to loosen the sudden tightness of her throat.

Devondra swept into the room wearing a loose chemise, followed closely by her handmaid, whose arms brimmed with garments, and went straight to the small room that held Ember's tub and wardrobe.

"I presume you heard about the race? The Red Morning? Your little man won, and now father is holding a feast in his honor." Ember heard water splashing into the tub, and the creak of her wardrobe door opening. "So of course Mother sent me to get you ready. Always babysitting. Really, Ember, I don't understand why you refuse to have servants. Holly, bring her here."

Devondra's handmaid dropped her load of garments on the end of the bed, yanked off Ember's covers and grabbed her wrist.

"Don't—"

"Come here, Ember. No excuses now," Devondra said.

"You sound like Mother," Ember replied, pulling her wrist away from the handmaid, who only smiled and held tighter, her eyes skimming over Ember's nudity with mirth.

Horrified, Ember jerked out of the handmaid's grasp and hurriedly pulled on a chemise.

"What do you think of this?"

From the wardrobe, Devondra flourished a bell-shaped mound of taffeta with deep cuts in front and back and stays pulled tight at the waist. The explosion of material looked ridiculous, like a child's cake with too much frosting, layer upon layer of silkiness the color of dried blood.

Devondra pushed it against Ember, assessing. "Yes, this will do quite well."

Ember shuddered. "I'm not wearing that thing."

"You will. Mother ordered the fabric from Zari, you know. It's been sitting in your wardrobe for ages, and we've never seen you wear it."

Ember had left the dress behind when she went to the Academy. She hadn't opened her wardrobe since she'd been back, and likely wouldn't ever have opened it. The trousers and cotton shirt were enough for her.

Devondra sighed and glided past Ember, pecking her handmaid on the cheek and whispering something in her ear. The handmaid let Ember go and followed Devondra out, closing the door behind her.

Alone in her bathing room, Ember peeked into the wardrobe. Ruffles, sashes, and silks of all colors bulged against the doors, straining to get out of the musty, dark air—

Ember rammed the doors closed and sagged against them. She was still exhausted from her night out, and the idea of wearing a frilly expensive dress and acting as a demure lady for the rest of the evening made her head ache. She went to the tub and sank into the hot water, rubbing the heat into her temples to assuage the throbbing pain.

A feast for Gregory, she mused. It didn't surprise her; many of Arundel's best horses were bought from Gregory's father, but Gregory and Arundel were by no means friends. Still, Gregory would accept the invitation to his own feast and would politely pretend to enjoy it, if only for the benefit of his family's business, which he would inherit once his father died.

She glided a hand down the wall next to the tub and felt for the gap in the stone.

There. A slit of the perfect width, hidden from view by the massive tub. The dagger was still there. Not Gregory's knife, but one of her own.

She pulled it out. The skinny blade tapered to a hand-span's length. A heavy columnar handle wound in leather formed the simple hilt, worn from her years of practice fending off the worst of enemies. Zealous squelkins, mostly, with the occasional, equally zealous street-cat. She had never had to use it on a person, but there had been a few times she had brandished it to ward off men with too much curiosity.

She brushed her thumb over the blade's edge, hoping for the hundredth time that she would never be forced to use it for its real purpose. Had Gregory thought the same about his daggers before the race?

A sigh of pleasure filtered under her door.

"Dev?" Ember nearly shouted her name.

No response.

Ember scrubbed her skin with haste and stepped out, wrapping the blade and strapping it to her lower leg, trying not to think about what Devondra could possibly be doing with her handmaid... *In my room, on my bed...!?*

Wearing a clean chemise and smelling of rose and elderflower, she rushed out of the bathing room. Her headache radiated to her forehead.

Devondra lay languidly across the stuffed armchair while she peered into a hand-mirror, watching herself as she combed her copper hair. The handmaid stood at the bed, complacently folding garments. Ember didn't miss the flush on Devondra's face or the way she breathed with lips partly open.

"What were you doing?"

Surprised, Devondra looked up and gave an innocent shrug. "I've been sitting here, what do you think?"

"I heard a sigh."

"I was getting bored. Don't you ever get bored, Ember?"

Disgusted, Ember sat at her vanity table, glaring as the handmaid tugged her hair into submission. *I am doing this for Gregory,* she told herself stubbornly. *Only for him.*

After a few moments of silence, Devondra's silk-covered foot bobbed into view as she crossed her legs.

"Honestly, Ember, I don't understand what your issue is with the dress. It's perfectly exquisite Zarian material."

Ember didn't give two silvers where the material was from, or what her sister had to say about anything.

"Why are you here, Dev?" *In my bedchamber rather than your own lair?*

"You know why, silly. You're completely useless at Glamour spells."

"I can do them well enough," Ember said, feeling the heat rise to her cheeks.

Devondra pursed her lips and said nothing.

The handmaid finished Ember's simple plait,

which gleamed black in the dim light. Bangs swooped down to her eyes like the wings of a starling, the dark contrasting her pale skin and brightening blue eyes. They were pretty eyes, with dark lashes and healthy brows, but today there were bags beneath them. Beyond that stood a plain nose and a plain set of lips, surrounded by slender cheekbones splashed with pink blemishes.

She focused on the signs for the Glamour spell, motioning with her fingers in places around her face where she knew Devondra would be the most critical. As she finished, Devondra rose from her chair, resplendent in a sleek silk gown that reminded Ember of spruce, the deep green accentuating the red tones of Devondra's loose hair. Copper bangles clinked as she stalked to the mirror, looking like a goddess in commoner's jewelry. A copper circlet sat like a crown on her head, and from it hung a small coppery pendant, resting naturally between two doe-like eyes.

"Let me see what you've done," Devondra said. As she came up behind Ember, smelling of heavy Ekesian spices, the Glamours around her became apparent. She had one accentuating her hair, another accentuating her eyes, and a third disguising her crooked teeth.

They'll know the truth once their tongue is in your mouth, Ember thought with distaste.

"Oh, Ember... Let me see. You do look *so* tired. Those dark circles don't help your looks much. Do you mind?"

Without waiting for an answer, Devondra's fingers flicked before Ember's face, quick and light as though playing an invisible instrument. A moment later she finished, and gazed at her handiwork.

With layers of Glamour, Ember's skin glowed with a healthy blush and her lashes stood out darker than before. The effect, as it always did, stunned Ember to silence.

She was saved from showing her gratitude when the chamber door opened.

"Mother!" Devondra sang. "Isn't Ember pretty?"

Ember jerked to her feet.

"Congratulations, my dear," Salena purred, coming up to kiss each of Ember's cheeks. The heady scent of rosewater floated over her. "Your man has earned the admiration of the Council, and especially your father."

Your father. Ember met her mother's blue, perceptive gaze and kept her face still. It helped that she felt a bit consoled by the fact that she had gone to the race despite Salena's orders.

"I do hope you like the dress," Salena went on. "It will go well with your hair."

They helped her into the vile garment, and when they were finished, Devondra affixed a simple band with mauve feathers to the side of Ember's plait. With all the Glamours between her mother and Devondra, they could almost be twins except for the modest hair plaits and dress worn by her mother.

Standing in front of the mirror, Ember felt incredibly exposed. It wasn't just the way Salena looked at her, searching and pleased and knowing all at once, but the way Ember could see her own chest heaving, the way the bodice tightened against every womanly curve she had—*a blessing we received from Mother*, Devondra always said—and the feel of air brushing the skin between her shoulder blades. She looked older, more refined, and more like Devondra than she could ever remember.

"There. You look stunning," Salena announced.

Stomach churning, Ember lifted her chin to hold her mask of composure.

"Thank you for helping me prepare," was all Ember could manage to say before turning away.

"Devondra, you may go," Salena said. "Your sister and I need to discuss her scores from the Academy."

Despite Salena's tone, Ember knew there was no point in arguing to have the discussion later. Salena's hunger for information was never so easily put aside.

"Don't be late," Devondra said with her cat-like smile pointed at Ember.

Ember shivered. That smile had only ever meant mischief, and not mischief of the childish sort.

Devondra grabbed her handmaid's arm and sauntered out.

Salena shut the door and signed Binding and

Silencing spells around it, her fingers pulling and twitching at the air to bind it to her command. No one would enter or listen at the door. The spells took only a moment to cast, and left a residue of silvery filaments that pulsed with cold life.

    Silent as an owl, Ember grabbed Gregory's dagger out from under her featherbed, where she had hidden it upon returning in the late morning, and slid it securely into her sleeve. She hoped to return it to him before the feast was over.

    Salena's blue gown rustled as she turned back to Ember with folded hands.

    "Tell me."

    Ember sat on the bed's edge, wincing as the bodice constricted her lungs.

    "What would you like to know?"

    "Don't play games with me, Ember. I don't want to draw attention by being late for the feast."

    "Then perhaps we can discuss this after the feast."

    Salena's face tinted pink.

    "We discuss it now."

    Ember forced her shoulders to relax.

    "Lady Ashlin has formed a new garrison. Women only. Lord Wincel is adding three men to his Escort. The new Ekesian king raised taxes, and now immigrants are flooding into the city of Edlen."

    "I always thought Richaro was too young to take his father's place," Salena said. "What else?"

"There are eleven patrols out now. Arundel requested to send out one more."

Salena turned away, the silk of her blue gown rippling gold in the evening light as she began to pace.

"Where?"

"He's heard of factions in Ekesia. He doubts Richaro's loyalty to their agreement about shapeshifters."

"What about Orion?"

"There are three patrols in the Orion Mountains already."

Not long ago, there had been rumors about Orion. Ember had heard someone from Merewood mention that he had seen a shifter there, and that he had heard the same thing from other travelers. Ember thought it the likeliest place for shifters to hide, with caves and valleys and few peoples beyond the hunting clans that roved with the seasons.

She had never mentioned these bits to Salena.

"He's arrived," Salena said now from the balcony doors.

"Who?"

"Gregory."

Ember rushed out onto the balcony just in time to see Gregory, dressed in a fine red tunic and cap, disappear into the great hall below, followed by several others. His father, his younger brother, and a young woman wearing a gown of green brocade with hair the color of wheat...

An excellent horse-woman.

Ember spun away from the railing and went back inside, closing the doors behind her. Salena paced, a line creasing her forehead.

There is something else she wants to know. Something about Arundel.

"He mentioned his recent venture," Ember offered.

A flicker of worry in Salena's blue gaze.

"Yes, he was gone for nearly twenty days. It was successful, I've heard." A hand fluttered up to her throat, where a heavy blue sapphire hung from a ribbon of gold. *Another gift from Arundel. But Salena will never sway as easily as the Council.*

"He offered sunstone to Masonshire."

"A new mining site, then. He's been searching for years." Salena nodded resolutely. "Is that all?"

"He mentioned three deaths at the smelter. A furnace collapsed."

Salena exhaled with closed eyes, and when she opened them, they were heavy with weariness. "I will see that the families receive extra care. Is there anything further?"

"Nothing of import."

Salena stretched her hands toward Ember. "Come, then. Let's not be too late. Your father will note our absence."

They descended the twisted iron steps that led three stories below, edging around a hoard of servants who rubbed goose grease into the balustrade. At the bottom, they entered a corridor that ran behind the great hall.

More servants opened a pair of doors to the great hall dais. Deep, warm laughter rose from the largest of three tables. Arundel. He was in a good mood tonight.

Salena gave Ember's hand a squeeze and glided to the largest table, where the family usually sat. Arundel stood to take Salena's hand and seated her on his right.

Ember's headache throbbed when she spotted Gregory on Arundel's left.

The seat of honor. Of course Gregory was the guest of honor for the feast, and she should've expected him to be there, but the sight of him so close to Arundel chilled her.

She forced her legs to move. *One step. Two steps...* She heard a throaty giggle that could only be Devondra's, and smoothed her movements. *Tonight is Gregory's night.* She would be pleasant and confident and refined. She would breathe through the headache that crept down her neck.

Gregory didn't see her approaching the table, but Arundel did. He didn't seem to recognize her at first, but in a moment he was smiling and looked pleased, even prideful. He stood tall and strong, his hair the color of bitter Ekesian chocolate, and offered her his hand, the palm scarred from the heat of an iron rod.

Her heart reached for her throat. She took it.

CHAPTER TEN

The great hall had a vast, high ceiling. The eastern wall, filled with leaded windows, usually looked out to Mirror Lake. Now, it stood as a molten black wall, reflecting thousands of candles that burned from twisted iron chandeliers and sconces. The reflection made the hall look larger, with perhaps thousands of people rather than hundreds, a swarm of reds, blues, purples, and greens seated at iron-legged wooden tables. The staff of Silverglen was quite large, and others from Merewood and Kingsbury had come to celebrate.

Ember sat at the head table, which seemed too full by far. The large, rectangular table occupied most of the dais, but with her family, Gregory's guests, and the Council, there was hardly room to breathe.

Not that I could breathe if I did have room, Ember

thought as she rubbed the stays that dug into her ribs.

"Did you say something?" the young man next to her asked through a mouthful of sweetbread drizzled with honey, his arm rubbing hers as he prepared another mouthful.

They were on the third course of the feast, and she had spent the time avoiding looking at the young man, whose name was Eawart, and whose relationship to her own family was unclear. Why she had been seated next to Eawart was a puzzle she had as of yet to solve. She wished she had been seated near Finn. She missed his joviality and his inevitable support should she send him a look of misery. But Finn sat near Gregory, too far to speak to and out of sight behind massive Lord Thurstun.

"No, I said nothing." Ember pressed a finger over her right temple, hoping to squelch a throbbing vein, and tasted the dish in front of her. Sweet currants, cinnamon, and cloves mingled with the delicate fowl-like flavor. They aligned perfectly with the red wine.

"This fish is perfection," Eawart went on. "Just like chicken. I now believe the rumor that your father has the best cook in all of Lach."

"Not fish, but squelkin. A delicacy here," Ember stated, and smiled as Eawart stared down at his plate, a look of disgust curdling his gaiety. She allowed herself a glance down the table to where Gregory sat. He was still preoccupied with re-telling the tale of the race, probably for the third time, to the others at the table.

Ember hadn't gotten the entire story, as Eawart showed a propensity for talking in her ear. She didn't think Gregory would speak of a wolf helping him, but then again she wasn't sure he even knew that the wolf had been her. If he mentioned it, the few people who knew they were friends might start looking at her more suspiciously.

"What do you think about the Ekesian boar?" Eawart asked, disgust apparently forgotten as he waved a greasy spoon toward one of the walls.

The painting that covered the wall resembled an Ekesian landscape—a deep green jungle with palm fronds, thorn-covered trees, and jagged leafy shrubs, all depicted in such fine detail that the wall seemed like a window looking out into another world. The boar Eawart spoke of was a Glamour, and it currently rooted its way around a brushy clump of palmaro, probably looking for fallen nuts.

Before Ember could answer, Eawart spoke again.

"Oh look! There's the hunter, behind that strange vine."

"Hook-vine," Ember corrected. Had the man never learned Ekesian botany? "You might not want to watch this part," she added, hazarding a look at Eawart. Thick lips shone in the candlelight as he stared at the mural.

Knowing what would happen to the boar, Ember lost her appetite for the squelkin and focused instead on the sweetbread. Down the table, Gregory's female friend laughed musically at one of Arundel's jokes. The hum of talk from beneath the dais drowned out most of what was said, although it helped that on her other side sat Lord Jeriel of Masonshire, who hadn't said more than four words to her.

Ember had trouble not staring at Gregory and his friend, though when she did the heat rose up her neck and she was sure someone would notice.

Perhaps the Glamours are hiding it. She watched from beneath her lashes as Gregory spoke into the woman's ear, his teeth flashing white in a grin. *They certainly look like lovers.* Trying not to think about how well they appeared together—him with bronzed skin and a satiny red tunic, her with a head full of spun wheat and a pale, smooth complexion—Ember looked down to her lap, only to be surprised yet again by the sight of her own bosom, looking alarmingly ample in the low-cut gown.

More heat crept up her face.

Eawart gasped at the mural, undoubtedly enjoying the scene of the boar being ruthlessly trapped and gutted. The two other murals in the great hall had more satisfying Glamours at the moment. In Zari, a herd of horned drogons basked in the desert heat, each of their scales melting from cobalt to plum. In Orion, a firebird glided over the mountains like a spark of sun, leaving behind a glittering streak of orange and red and gold that fell like dust through the sky. A magic dust, it was said, that could make any wish come true.

Silent song, wishing dust, from the firebird life is thrust...

"...honored if you would dance with me tonight," a voice said. It was Lord Wincel who spoke, seated on the other side of Eawart, and for a moment Ember was afraid he had been speaking to her. She heard Devondra's lilting response.

"I will be occupied elsewhere tonight," Devondra said from Lord Wincel's side, hardly a note of apology in her tone.

It had taken Ember some effort not to laugh aloud when she saw Devondra, perched like an angry green cat next to the hunched, saggy-faced Lord Wincel. The repulsion on Devondra's face at having to be so close to him had made her insides quake with glee.

"There will be dancing?" Eawart asked suddenly.

Ember stared at him.

"There is always dancing after a feast with Lord Arundel," Lord Wincel replied, his white eyebrows raised like two floating feathers.

"Excellent," Eawart replied, sucking the last bit of honey from his fingers.

"I thought you said you had been to my father's feasts before?" Ember asked.

He glanced at her in surprise. "Yes, but it was a long time ago. I was a child, maybe five or ten."

Eawart looked to be about Ember's age, possibly a couple of years older. That long ago, the rebellion was still active, and Lord Arundel never held feasts or celebrations of any sort. He had been in a dark place, Salena had always said, grieving over his parent's deaths and assuaging his need for revenge.

He had never really satiated that need for revenge, Ember thought. Killing shifters only seemed to make it worse, at least for a time. He was forced to stop when all the shifters were gone, and even now he still tried to find them, nearly two decades after the rebellion began.

Ember glanced to where Arundel sat, Salena on one side and Gregory on the other. He seemed bigger than anyone else, taller and stronger and brighter. He looked happy, for the moment, but Ember knew that with a few more drinks, he would begin his descent. Salena, composed and placid, spoke mostly to Lady Ashlin and hardly at all to Arundel. *Another piece of the puzzle that will bring him down. Always.*

"Will you dance tonight, then?" Eawart said.

Ember found that her wine glass was full again, and she took a long sip.

"I'm not a very good dancer," she tried.

"I don't believe that. I've already noticed the way you move. Very graceful. I am sure we'd make an excellent dancing pair. You should at least promise me one dance."

"Of course," Ember said, resorting to politeness. Her face flamed. *One dance with the lying stranger, and perhaps one with Gregory.*

She was confident that Gregory knew she was there, and yet she had been unable to catch his eye. He seemed preoccupied with the food, and the wine, and the fine woman seated so close to him that she almost looked to be in his lap.

Sickened, Ember spent the fourth course watching one of the Glamours of a Zarian drogon rise, stretch, and rub one long horn into the ground. A Glamour of dust rose up along the wall, heading toward an endless blue sky. She watched until she spotted the hunters creeping in as rocks, inching their way toward slaughter.

By the fifth and final course, her headache had transformed into fuzziness and the chandelier candles above seemed to be casting their warmth down on her. She was satiated, and was growing accustomed to the pressure of the bodice stays, though the same could not be said about her exposed chest.

Voices, interspersed with clapping and hoots, grew below the dais. There were the usual jugglers and acrobats and singers, along with Arundel's famous hired Zarian dancers who mimicked the way animals moved. Their black skin shone in the candlelight as they told a story of a lion taming a lioness, the furs and teeth and claws they wore spinning and clinking as the smell of anise and jipsom flower floated over the dais.

"I should have dancers like those," Eawart was saying, not noticing Ember's silence for the entire last course. "Five, I think, for my castle."

Ember nearly choked on her wine. "Your castle?"

"Yes, well it's a smaller castle than this one, but a

place I can call my own. Have you heard of Witherington? It's in Pemberville, which is quite far from here—"

"Yes, I attended the Academy," Ember replied briskly. She had never heard of a 'Witherington,' though she knew of everyone important in Pemberville and knew that only the Council members were allowed to own castles in Lach.

"Perhaps you've seen it, then," Eawart continued, a pink blush forming on his round cheeks. "A grand thing, beautifully built with four fountains, ten sculptures, and two dozen horses. I've also recently purchased three of the finest gilded carriages in Pemberville."

Ember could just picture him riding in one of the Pemberville carriages, peeking out with his slightly upturned nose, the multitude of Insulating spells forming a sheen of sweat on his bare upper lip.

"Are you a researcher, then?" Ember probed.

"No, but my father was. Hardly ever see him." He took a few loud gulps of wine.

"And what brought you out to Silverglen?"

"Business with Lord Arundel. My father and he were friends a long time ago. Old connections."

Before Salena and Arundel had met, Arundel had been a well-known wizard at the Academy, and a renowned researcher. Unfortunately, the Academy kept their historical documentations under a mass of Binding and Blinding spells, so Ember had never been able to find out what exactly Arundel had researched.

Ember wondered fleetingly if, by seating her next to Eawart, Arundel had been hinting at a marriage prospect.

"So you didn't attend the race?" Ember asked.

"The race? Oh, the Red Morning. No, I wasn't able to see it. Did you?"

"No."

"Do you know the winner? He seems to be having a good time with that lady friend of his. I suppose I would be too, if I'd just won a famous race. I'm willing to bet women will be pouring over him by the end of the night."

Eawart called over more wine with a wave of his hand.

Ember left her filled glass untouched. She was beginning to wonder whether it would be appropriate to leave when Arundel announced that dancing would commence.

The musicians gathered to the side of the dais, and hordes of servants dressed in violet livery cleared and moved the tables. Finn sprang up to join his violin to his fellow musicians, looking about as antsy as Ember felt. She envied his escape into music, but gave a weak smile when he winked and wiggled his brows at her.

As the music began, Ember, like many others in the hall, couldn't help but stare at the sight of Arundel and Salena dancing together. She had seen it at other feasts before, but the sight of them holding one another, of Salena's satiny blue folding into Arundel's deep purple arms stirred an odd feeling in her stomach. They didn't look at one another as they danced, but they swayed and twirled together, the rhythm of one matching that of the other. Salena responded gracefully as Arundel led the way around the floor.

"Exquisite," Lord Wincel uttered.

"I'm envious, too, Lord Wincel," Eawart said. "But I'm certain that Lady Ember and myself would make just as riveting a pair. My lady?"

Eawart stood and held out his hand. His fingers trembled. Ember noticed Devondra watching her over Lord Wincel's stooped shoulder, challenge and delight flaring in her gaze.

Trying not to scowl, Ember accepted Eawart's clammy hand and let him lead her down from the dais.

He held her close, or at least as close as he could given the voluminous mound of taffeta she wore. Bodily heat swallowed the air between them. She found herself looking over his shoulder rather than at his face, and his heavy breath spread over her nape.

The music began and he led her into the rhythm. He kept a steady hand on her back, his steps sure and practiced. He swung her in a twirl, gliding with her around and around the floor, his confidence boosting her own careful step.

Perhaps he does own a castle. A smaller, more comfortable castle than this one.

He guided them past the glass-paned wall, astonishing Ember with her own reflection. She hardly recognized herself—a young, radiant woman looking refined and confident and self-possessed, a small smile curling her lips.

We look as though we've done this a hundred times before.

And it was easy. All the training she had as a child had been difficult; it wasn't the steps she found challenging but aligning the steps with musical rhythm. But with Eawart leading her, moving with the music was effortless, even enjoyable.

Gregory's eyes met hers in the reflection.

"Steady, now," Eawart breathed, as she started turning the wrong way. He guided her back into step. "You're doing beautifully."

She forced herself to retain her mask of composure, knowing everyone watched. Hundreds of people gathered along the walls waiting to dance their turns.

So he does see me. He knows I'm here. Does he know I was the wolf?

She tried to find him again, and did, and saw with disappointment that he danced with the woman in green brocade, and that he held her close. Too close.

Her mind spun with each turn, her gown tugging out with each swirl. *I'm unraveling. How many more spins?*

Eawart's hand on her back kept her going.

They finished the dance, and she let Eawart guide her back to the dais for another glass of wine. She let him talk at her, a constant stream of noise about his castle and his dogs and how beautifully she danced.

They danced again, and had *sumbac*, the orange liquor sharp on her tongue. She tried desperately not to think of Gregory, or where he was, or who he danced with. She tried not to feel like she waited.

By the third dance with Eawart she began to feel carefree, and did a better job at trampling the pain in her chest. She wouldn't let it overcome her. She wouldn't let it ruin her dance with this strange man.

They wove between other couples, past the murals of plants and mountains and desert, past the gazing faces and through scents of roses and spices and jipsom flower. Eawart's hands were hot on her, and his clothes dampened with sweat. He spoke loudly in her ear as they danced, and she could smell cinnamon and orange on his breath. They danced by the murals again, and this time Ember didn't miss the Glamour of the boar writhing on the trap, red running in rivulets down its side.

Her stomach flipped. She focused on Eawart's shoulder, the fine pattern of stitched gold filaments there, and breathed.

When she looked at Eawart—really looked at him for the first time while they danced—she found him staring at her chest, heat in his eyes and a flush darkening his face.

"Eawart!" she snapped, nearly tripping in her haste to put more distance between them.

Somehow his dance steps remained adept and smooth, even as he stumbled through an apology.

"You are just so beautiful," he said. The dance was finishing, and he hesitated before speaking again. "I just wish, or rather, I'd be honored, if you let me show you how beautiful I think you are. The way a man shows a woman—"

She pushed away from him and brushed her hands down her gown.

"No, thank you." An insufferable heat clawed up her neck. "I would like to sit and drink some water."

He bobbed his head, compliant, and she turned on her heel, repressing the urge to run up to the dais.

She wasn't sure what she felt more about his blatant request—mortification or pleasure. Mortified because she didn't know him, pleased because it felt good to be wanted. But she could only imagine sharing such intimacy with one person.

Ember sat at the table, where Arundel and Salena and the rest of the Council sat, and called for water. The liquid cooled and refreshed her mouth. Relief washed over her when she saw Eawart dancing with someone else.

The scent of rosewater weighted the air as Salena sank gracefully into Eawart's empty seat.

"Who was that man?"

"He called himself Eawart," Ember said,

straightening in her chair. "I thought you would have known him. He said he was here on business."

"With your father? How odd. Eawart, you said?" Salena raised a pomander to her nose, thinking. Her eyes lit with understanding. "Ah, yes he is a friend of Devondra's, I believe. From the Academy."

Ember's heart sank. More than likely, he wasn't from the Academy at all. He was likely some stable boy hired on by Devondra to fool Ember into doing something stupid. It wouldn't be the first time Devondra did such a thing. *All those words, lies. There is no castle, and there might not even be an Eawart.* She had half-known it though, after hearing him talk of Arundel's non-existent feasts when they were children, and she had found the castle story to be a bit far-fetched.

And he had said he wanted her. Had that been a lie, too?

She shuddered.

"You two looked quite the pair down there," Salena said. "He seems to be a very skilled dancer. Half the hall watched, saying how beautiful you were. How grown up."

All that attention, Ember thought with alarm. All those eyes watching her, witnesses to any wrong move she made. She hadn't even thought of the danger. The skin on her neck prickled.

"Did I draw too much attention tonight?"

Salena looked at her in surprise, a slight raising

of her delicate brows that hardly altered her mask of composed calm.

"No, I think you did perfectly well. This attention is good. The attention you don't want is the kind you receive from sitting here not speaking or dancing."

"Those two things happen to be very conducive to eavesdropping."

Eavesdropping during feasts was one of the most efficient ways of figuring out anything useful regarding her parents. As hosts, they were always the talk of the guests, and their words had been her gateway to discovering Silverglen's past.

Salena was about to reply, but winced as Arundel's voice suddenly boomed across the great hall.

"Guests," he said. "I would like to present to you my latest find, a treasure I discovered on my journey north."

He sat back in his seat, saying nothing else, and took a deep drink from his chalice.

An ornate piece of ironwork, Ember guessed, or perhaps a sunstone statue. At the last feast, Ember recalled that Arundel had presented Salena with a replica of the rare gold-slippered orchid, bent, curled, and welded to form a fountain that she had then placed in one of her garden nooks. Ember had heard only compliments about Lord Arundel for weeks after that.

But tonight, Arundel's mouth formed a grim line beneath his steady, brooding gaze.

Her chest suddenly heavy, Ember looked to the

double iron-clad doors that stood beneath a painted Ekesian tulepo tree. The loud talk of the hall had subsided to an excited murmur, a sound that made the tips of her fingers tingle.

The great doors began to open, and she felt the cold of a spell touch her mind. Many spells, she realized.

Six Escorts in violet marched in wielding heavy spears. Wizards, all of them, trained and tested until they were deemed of high enough skill to protect a Council member, or anyone of a Council-member's choosing. They were different from patrols. Quieter, more observant. An iron loyalty to those who paid them. They pushed back the crowd using only a tilt of their spears and stern expressions.

She saw the shadows first: great, bulky things cast by the torches just outside the hall. She heard scuffling and the clink of chains, and slowly, the dark form of a bear emerged.

Cold flushed down her sides.

The crowd gasped and whispered, but the noise quickly grew to shouts and whistles of excitement as the animal came into the hall, followed closely by six more Escorts.

The bear's ribs and hips stuck out unnaturally from his patchy cinnamon coat. Small black eyes looked around as he swayed in, dragging iron chains with links as thick as Ember's fist. Iron cuffs had chafed the fur from his skin. He didn't seem to mind the people, or where he went, or the fact that he dragged chains behind him. All the notorious aggression of the bear, all the strength and energy Ember knew every bear claimed, had been stripped from him. How many men had it taken to pull him down? How many spears to repress his fury at being captured? He must have been enormous once, with his large frame and giant paws. How many days of starvation had it taken to cow him?

A flicker of candlelight illuminated the spreading marks the bear left in his wake, like carmine sponge prints over the smooth pale stone of the hall floor. Looking more closely at the cuffs, she saw that there were spikes on the inside that had been tightened against the skin.

Ember stood and pressed trembling hands against the table.

"Sit down," a voice ordered. Salena, stiff and tight-lipped.

"No, I..."

When an Escort jabbed him to move, the bear moaned and sagged his head, revealing an iridescent spelled collar around his neck. Ember couldn't tell what the spells were, not from such a distance, but they felt complicated. Perhaps if she went closer—

The key.

Her mind recognized the spell pattern first, nearly buried by the spells of the collar, and when she glimpsed it hanging from a man's neck, she found Fletch's handsome, dark eyes watching her.

A shiver slid down her spine.

She calmed her expression and lifted her chin, pressing the sides of her gown as though to smooth them.

"Where are you going?" Salena asked, impatience edging her tone.

"To take a closer look at the bear." *And the spell.*

"You'll do no such thing," Salena said, just low enough for Ember to hear. Her face had gone pale, and her eyes shone like polished granite. Juice from the fresh pomander dripped through her white-knuckled fingers. "Don't make me use a Freeze on you, Ember. You're behaving like a child. Compose yourself."

Grinding her teeth, Ember sat. She hoped those at the table were far too distracted by the bear's appearance to notice that she had stood. She couldn't be sure about others in the great hall. Certainly Fletch had noticed. She kept a demure mask as the bear was prodded to move forward, moaning from weariness, or hunger, or the weight and agony of the chains. She could see cuts on the bear where the spears had prodded too forcefully. Dark blood, dried and matted, some likely festering. Indeed, many of the women had pomanders to their noses while he passed, as though the stench of him was unbearable.

He won't live much longer.

The key that Fletch wore, the one she had found in Arundel's study, more than likely opened the door behind which the bear was kept. She would find the door, and somehow get it open, even if it meant stealing the key.

    She searched the hall for Gregory, and was surprised to see him laughing, surrounded by a flock of ladies looking much finer than she.

CHAPTER ELEVEN

They've all drunk enough that the hall should be spinning, Ember thought as she pushed herself through a narrow hallway leading to a sitting room.

Once the bear had been prodded away, the Zarian dancers had returned with platters of *sumbac*, the orange liquor glistening in their small crystal cups as seductively as the gleam of the Zarian's dark skin, if Ember went by the looks of rapture on the Council member's faces. Only Arundel had seemed removed, from the dancers and from the others in the hall, a quiet drinker beneath a somber frown. Ember knew he had slipped into his darker mood, and that he would probably retire to his study sooner than later. With him being distracted, the others drunk, and Gregory fully involved in dancing with every other woman in the hall, Ember had decided she was safe to leave.

No shifting though. Salena had made her promise not to tonight, although now Ember was beginning to regret that move.

"How am I supposed to get around quietly in this ridiculous dress?" she whispered. She tugged the taffeta through a tight doorway, and swore at the sound of tearing fabric.

She brought the dress up to the light of a torch, careful not to bring it too close to the hungry flame, and examined the small rip. Hardly noticeable, she decided. She might even be able to put some stitches in it later, though as she dropped the dress back down, the thought melted away, already forgotten.

She had searched all four floors of the keep, though she knew it was unlikely she'd find the bear there. More than likely, he was kept below, or in a separate holding entirely.

The only things beneath the great hall were the cellar and the dungeons.

She wiped moist palms on the smooth, red gown, and headed toward the stairway leading to the dungeon. Smooth flames from pillar candles lit the quiet halls. Strands of music and laughter from the great hall whispered through the thick stone walls, barely audible.

It was a good thing, with the dungeons being so close. As far as Ember knew, they were mostly empty now, but for a good part of Ember's childhood they had been full. Shifters, mostly, imprisoned for their disobedience. Others, too, who were accused of helping shifters. Ember had one jolting memory when she had disobeyed Salena and went below as a mouse. She hadn't gotten past the first cell when she decided to unlock it to free a miserable man with no teeth and long, dirty nails who had been moaning and rocking in a corner. She had been swamped by the scents and sounds of despair and pain and death, and hadn't thought about her actions.

The man had run out screaming and tried to stomp her to death.

Salena had been livid, but Ember was shaken enough to never return.

She pushed the memories away as she reached the dungeon stairway. Yellow stone made up the steps and walls, which were stained black from torches lining either side. The warmth from the torches didn't dispel the cold air that stretched its fingers around the seams of an ancient iron door and seeped up the stairs. There was no way to get through the door as an animal or a human, unless one knew how to undue a Binding.

She crept down the steps in her doeskin slippers, her breath causing the torches to spit and waver.

The door was as she remembered. Iron spikes, steeped in a Glamour to make them appear sharp as needles, studded the immense door. A slab of iron as wide as the length of her hand and nearly as long as her arm served as a bolt. The end of the bolt narrowed to a spearhead, which slid through a thick band of iron forged into a snarling lion, so that when the door bolted, the spear drove through the lion's snarling jaws. Faint silvery lines crawled across the bolt.

An old Binding. Someone had either forgotten to re-set the spell upon leaving, or hadn't yet left. The door bolted from the inside as well, making just as an effective barrier at keeping prisoners in as it did at keeping unwanted eyes out. Ember had already considered the possibility of someone being with the bear, and had gone over her plan half a dozen times.

She grabbed the handle of the bolt and pulled. It slid out smoothly, and the heavy door swung silently toward her with a breath of chill, clammy air. Beyond, torchlight flickered in a vast, dark hall.

Ember squeezed through the opening, the mounds of taffeta pulling at her tight bodice, and looked for a guard. A simple wooden chair mantled by cobwebs sat by the door, next to a small table on which was left a forgotten hunk of bread, covered in a green fuzz.

Ember swallowed and walked deeper into the hall. The torches illuminated rows of bars along either side but left the shadows beyond them untouched. Her slippers and dress whispered against the stone floor and echoed back from the dark caverns of the prison cells. The hall ended at a narrow corridor, and as she stepped toward it, the shadows stirred out of the corner of her eye.

Two pale limbs slid through the iron bars.

Handless arms, she realized, attached to a man whose mouth moved silently. *A Silencing spell.* The scarred stubs waved at her, beckoning, and the man's eyes looked feverish and old and lost.

Hand removal was a punishment doled out by the Council for wizards who misused spells. One hand for spells used to steal or harm another person, two for killing or forcing someone against their will. The Council's definition of 'person' hadn't included shifters during the rebellion, however. Shifters had been property, to be dealt with as the owners saw fit. Ten years after the rebellion started, new Council-members had altered the laws, declaring shifters only be punished for injuring or killing another, and only if found guilty by trial. But by then, most of the shifters in Lach had been killed already.

Ember turned away and pressed into the corridor. Small wooden doors presented themselves on either side every twenty paces. All unlocked, each held the same thing behind them: a small room with a chair and a set of iron rings set into a corner of the stone floor with a pile of heavy chains next to it.

As she went silently from room to room, the cold sense of spells crept into her mind. The spells felt further away, but the corridor ahead ended at a stone wall. *Surely there's more to the dungeon than this.* Another door, perhaps, in one of the rooms.

But the rest of the rooms were the same as before, and that left her at the stone wall.

The spells were closer, pulsing in her mind so that she could almost identify them—but it was like trying to pick out a buttercup in a field of wildflowers. Too many spells wound together, some in odd configurations that left her puzzled.

Like that spell around the bear's neck.

But she would need to be close to work them out, which meant finding another door—a door that would also lead to the bear.

"Just beyond here," she whispered as she put her hand on the cold stone wall.

But the stone wasn't cold. She gasped as its warmth spread under her palm.

Surprised, she backed away, and too late noticed the way the torchlight suddenly moved behind her.

She put her arm up as she turned. A spindly hand grabbed her. The edge of the blade in her sleeve stung as it bit into her.

A pair of perceptive eyes loomed above her, and a smell of heady, over-sweet lilies clamped down on her nose.

"Let me go," she demanded. She tugged her arm, but the movement only pressed the blade in deeper.

"Fletch," she gasped, clenching her hands into fists. "Release me."

Suddenly his face was too close to hers. Molten eyes, a smooth jawline, and a slice of white teeth in a smile that made her stomach churn. He inhaled, his thin nostrils flaring as though smelling a fresh-cooked ham.

The hair on Ember's neck stood on end.

"I can smell them," he said in a raspy voice. "I've smelled you in Arundel's study. What's a pretty girl like you doing running around the dungeon floors? Nasty things are down here. Things that might eat you up."

His tongue moved wetly against the back of his teeth. A glimmer below his neck caught her eye. *The key.* She could snatch it and run, but the spells were just as strong as when she had first laid eyes on it. *Binding, Blinding, and Freezing.* Touching it would make her helpless.

The plan, Ember reminded herself. *Stick to the plan.*

"I was looking for my father's pet," she said, sounding far more cool than she felt. "I was interested in seeing other animals he kept."

Nausea roiled up as his warmth breath washed over her face.

"But I see I've found one of them," she rushed on, and gave her arm a final yank, grinding her teeth against the pain of the knife.

He loosened his grip, impossibly strong given his wiry frame, and stepped back as she bolted down the corridor, taffeta bundled in her arms.

His laugh followed her like a snake through sand.

CHAPTER TWELVE

Breathless and sweaty, Ember swept through the corridor toward her bedchamber. She kept a hand along one wall to steady the dizziness threatening to pull her down.

This stupid gown is going to kill me.

She would disrobe and take a hot bath to cleanse her skin of Fletch's filth. His floral stench lingered on her skin, and her arm had begun to itch where he had grabbed her. Or perhaps it was the wound from Gregory's knife that made her want to scratch. She would have to return the knife some other time.

She heard a familiar voice just as she rounded the corner, and her heart lifted for a fleeting moment before her eyes found the source.

Gregory, pressing his lady-friend up against the wall, his face buried against her neck.

The woman's green brocade gown crushed against her and she giggled, her pallor flushed with drunkenness. Her hair was no longer fine-spun wheat, but a tousled mass of gold. Pieces of straw nearly the same shade clung to her tresses and gown.

Whatever remaining breath Ember had fled, and she braced herself against a wall. The pain in her chest darkened the edge of her vision.

The woman noticed her through slit eyes, and a smile curled her painted lips. "Gregory," she said, nudging him back. "We have company."

Gregory turned, looking heated and distracted and equally rumpled.

"Ember," he said, red tinging his tanned cheeks. The top buttons of his red tunic were undone, revealing a bit of smooth, firm chest decorated with red lip marks.

Clutching a hand to the irritating stays of her bodice, Ember straightened. "Please, don't let me interrupt," she said with utmost formality. "I'm heading back to my rooms."

"Ah, well don't let us stop you," he said, jerking open the door closest to him. "We were just heading into ours, too—"

"I'm Arietta," the woman said and stepped forward unsteadily. "You're a friend of Gregory's, are you not?"

"Ember. Ember Thackeray." She gave a false smile, wanting nothing more than to be in her own chamber, alone.

"Of course, Lord Arundel's own daughter. A pleasure to meet you. You'll have to forgive my appearance. Gregory was just introducing me to his fine mare."

It amazed Ember that the woman—Arietta—could keep up her politeness when she was so clearly drunk. Or was she just pretending?

"Pigeon is a fine horse," was all Ember could think to say. Imagining the pair of them rolling around in the hay stacks made her feel ill. She herself had done the same with Gregory only last summer. At least they had been drunk off love rather than drink. Or had it been love after all?

"Perhaps we can all go visit Pigeon tomorrow," Gregory said, his tone edged with unease. He guided Arietta by her waist into his room, his rich clothes and the woman on his arm making him look a stranger. Arietta nodded at Ember and was led away willingly, the unsteadiness gone from her movements.

Gregory went in, and started to close the door.

Suddenly his knife was in her hand, and she let it loose.

It thudded into the door, just next to Gregory's head.

He froze, then loosened and muttered something to Arietta. In a whirlwind he stepped out, yanked the knife from the door, shut it, and strode toward her, furry digging into his brow.

"Are you out of your mind?" He asked in a strained whisper as he held up the knife.

"I wouldn't have hit you," Ember replied, pulling herself up to her tallest height, which was within a hair's breadth of his.

"That's not what I mean. I suspected that it was you at the race, but I didn't know for sure. What were you thinking?"

"I wanted to protect you—"

"Protect *me*? Damn it, Ember, you were nearly sliced in half by that woman. If you knew who she was, you'd know she's legendary at the races. Don't you think it might seem odd that a lone wolf tried to attack her in the final moments of a race?"

"She suspected nothing," Ember lied, heat scorching her face.

Gregory shook his head, exasperated. "You don't understand. You put me at risk, too. If your father finds out a shifter helped me win the race, he'd question me, or worse."

She hadn't considered that. "I'm sorry, Gregory, I didn't realize—"

"But you never realize," he said, and ran a hand through his cropped brown hair, dislodging several pieces of hay that drifted down around him. "This is why I can't be with you, Ember. You do whatever you want, without thinking about consequences to those who love you. Instead of protecting you, I'm always protecting myself from you." A short pause, only enough time for Ember to open her mouth for a retort before Gregory hurried on, "And the race was mine to win, not yours."

Ember stared at him, baffled. "You might have been killed!"

"I don't give a damn," Gregory persisted, his face reddening. "I didn't want your help. I never asked for it. The only thing I've ever wanted was to win that race, and you took that from me."

Ember's heart thudded in her chest. "What are you saying?"

Gregory shook his head, anger and hurt pinching his mouth. "Just forget it, Ember." A hand shot through his hair. "I accepted Arundel's offer to be his messenger."

Ember's throat went dry. "What?"

"I'm to be his new messenger, exchanging letters between members of the Council—"

"But you hate Arundel," Ember interrupted. She dug her nails into the tight stays that ran up the sides of her gown, wishing she could tear them out. "You think he won't make you run those horses into the ground? You're setting yourself up to be used, to be his own abusive hand—"

"I would never abuse a horse, Ember," he said, looking offended. "But doing this is the only thing that makes sense to me."

"How does that make sense? My best friend working for a man who would certainly have me imprisoned if he knew what I am—"

"It makes sense to be close to him and to show him that I'm loyal, just like my father has been for decades. He would dismiss rumors about shifters helping me."

But it wasn't logical, not when she knew how Arundel treated his horses, and how seeing the abuse seemed to make Gregory's blood boil.

Ember pressed her lips together, not trusting herself to speak.

Gregory fingered his knife and sighed, and the smell of sweet orange *sumbac* touched her.

"We're too different, you and I," he said. "I'm a commoner, you're a lord's daughter. You're a shifter and a wizard, and I have no such abilities. You're restless, and I want to settle. I know you can find someone who will suit you better than I."

Ember's throat felt thick. "I can see that you already found someone for yourself." She picked up her gown and turned toward her room.

"I won't reveal you, Ember," he said. "No matter how close I get to the Council."

She glanced back at him, and his gaze reminded her of the distant gray cliffs that trapped Mirror Lake.

She lifted her chin and strode away, ignoring the feeling that she was leaving something unfinished. *I was going to tell him about the bear. I was going to tell him about Fletch.* He might've understood, might've helped her. But it didn't matter now. Nothing did, except getting her damn dress off.

CHAPTER THIRTEEN

A CROWD ROARED and cold metal kissed Ember's neck. Thick, hot air stuck to her skin.

The iron around her neck yanked her forward, and she opened her eyes as she stumbled.

Thousands of blinding candles shone above hundreds of pairs of laughing eyes. Why were they pointing at her? Some laughed so hard they doubled over, and their guffaws echoed around the hall like the caws of feasting crows.

Another yank, and she fell to her knees. Naked, she realized. Is that why they pointed? The chain attached to her iron noose grew taut, and the man at the end of it made her blood freeze. Arundel shouted at her and grinned; he wanted her to shift into a chicken, or no, a rabbit, to give better chase. The crowd roared, and Arundel's eyes looked feverish.

No, turn into a lion. A beautiful lion. I will cut your throat myself and skin you, and lay on that skin while I fuck my wife into submission.

Instead of shifting, she was running. The floor of the hall turned to dirt and the people morphed into towering trees. He hunted her in broad daylight, and there was nowhere to hide, no weapons to protect herself. She could shift but traps lay everywhere—in the air, hanging from the trees, hidden in logs. Arundel would catch her. His rapid tread closed in behind her.

Suddenly she tripped, and he was on her, his hands wrapping around her throat.

But it wasn't Arundel. It was Salena. *Mother, why are you strangling me?* Her mother's nails dug into her.

Don't lie to me, Ember. Arundel is your real father. There was no book. Why would you lie about such a thing? I haven't trained you right. I'll just have to start over...

The world whirled into blackness. She wasn't being strangled. But the scent of lilies permeated the air, heady and suffocating, and the stench of foul breath lingered behind it, close enough to touch.

Fletch.

He had come to take her away, down to the dungeon, to chain her in iron and drag her to Arundel.

He knows. He knows what I am.

Body screaming awake, Ember scrambled to the other side of her bed. Shadows filled her room, but she could make out the glass doors, the moon-tinted balcony and the lake beyond it.

The sheets tangled and tugged against her sweaty limbs. She heard a raspy chuckle as the weight of the bed shifted. Panic consumed her.

She grabbed one of her long knives under the mattress just as a cold hand snatched her ankle.

She used that anchor to roll upward and slash blindly at his vague form. Her knife sliced through something, and Fletch barked with laughter. His hand on her ankle tightened.

Without thinking, she stabbed down toward her foot. Her knife met fleshy resistance. Fletch howled. His fingers loosened, and Ember leapt away to heave open a balcony door.

Frigid wind swept in from the Orion Mountains and over the lake to blanket her breath in mist.

She ran across the balcony, feet slapping the cold stones. *I need to be quick, quick as a blink.* She jumped up to the railing and gripped the thick slab of iron, barely glancing down at the two rows of torches far below. No guards looked up. They shouldn't be able to see her in the dark. She stood and risked a glance behind her.

Fletch limped to the balcony doors. Something shone in his hand—a knife silver with a Freezing spell. Her knife, his spell. His lips curled in a grin, his teeth like rows of sharp bones. He stretched back his arm, and even as he did so she was lunging forward.

The fall curdled her stomach, the length to the ground shortening even before she completely left the railing. She allowed the heaviness to pull at her faster and faster, willed the knife to go sidelong.

It flashed over her left shoulder like lightning.

She melted into dizziness, and in a moment the wind swooped her up and up, past the height of the balcony and far away from the piercing iron spires of Silverglen.

Fletch shouted at the guards below, and they looked up, seeing him point. She knew they couldn't see her. Next to the torches, human eyes were blind to the night air. She rose higher, allowing the silent wing-beats of the owl to calm her heart, and headed for the mountains.

CHAPTER FOURTEEN

ALL NIGHT SHE flew, knowing she must keep going but unsure of where. North, toward the Orion Mountains. The bulky shadows rose in her night vision like hunched ghosts, and the cold breath of them swept around her wings like the arms of death. Thick gray mist curled in ravines and wound between the rounded peaks like linen.

Ember craned her head to the east, willing the sun to awaken. The fog was beginning to creep into her owl-mind, which was distracting her enough with thoughts of hunting the mice and voles below. She was almost hungry enough to let herself do it. *Just this once...*

She pressed on, gliding over the rolling foothills covered in dense forests of spear pine and golden spruce. The knolls and hillocks were all a part of

Merewood Forest, reserved especially for Arundel's hunting parties. To the east, the forest turned to fields of stumps around the smelter, whose dank iron stench seemed to gather high up in the air no matter where she flew. One of Arundel's mines lay not far north of the smelter and dove into the edge of the mountains. A fair trade with the clan peoples, they had said. The primitives of Orion had set aside their weapons and graciously accepted Arundel's benevolent gift of gold and jewels.

Ember had only ever seen drawings of the Orians, looking hard and quiet with their heavy fur coats, grisly hair and unshaven faces. She had always admired the way they held their weapons in those drawings. With pride, she thought, and certainty, as though their weapon was a limb for them, a part who they were. Not with the angry violence that she expected.

She would be safe deep in the mountains, where Arundel had no claim.

Gradually, the sliver of moon dulled as the eastern sky brightened. She found water flowing through a gorge and followed above it, over rocky cliffs and outcrops and cascading waterfalls, into knobby mountain peaks. She would stay by the water, and where there was water, there was food.

The sun peaked over the horizon, deepening the shadows that pooled in the gorge beneath her.

There will be elk here, and bears, and loping, surly

gorrets. And giant ospreys. These miles of mountains, with their cliffs and rivers and deep lakes, were their nesting grounds. The great birds lived here and southwest along the cliffs of Skye Lake. Ember knew of half a dozen places around the Academy where they could be spotted, wheeling along the cliff-sides and diving for fish and squelkin in the deep, frigid water. Skye Lake never froze, and so the ospreys never went hungry.

I might, if I don't eat soon.

She could almost smell the tasty, plump voles that burrowed under the duff below. Without thinking, she dropped altitude. The darkness would be better for owl-hunting, and would be good cover from discovery. It would be best to find something before the sun fully rose—

The sharp tang of smoke filled her nostrils, and she wobbled in the air.

A clan, she thought. She shifted to a hawk form, straining to keep her balance against the wind as her stomach rolled. The urge to hunt receded, but she knew it would return soon. The longer she remained in another form, the stronger the animal's instincts and the weaker her own awareness. A dangerous boundary, but one that had grown familiar, and flexible, during her time as Salena's spy.

Aching from beating her wings, she glided in a large circle to get her bearings. In the weak dawn light, a thick column of black smoke rose above a mountaintop to the northwest.

That's no cook-fire.

She aimed for it, lowering her position in the air so that she would come around the side of the mountain like a hawk naturally hunting.

Those Orion peoples are dumb as snails, Finn had once said. Unfortunately for him, Arundel had been in the same room and had heard. He had come over to where they played cards—Ember and Devondra and Finn—before any of them were old enough to attend the Academy, and looked at them each in turn with dark, angry eyes.

Who told you this?

Nan Cleresta told us, Finn had said, wiping his runny nose on a blue-velvet sleeve.

The peoples of Orion are hunters, Arundel told them. *They keep to themselves and trade furs and food between clans. Lachians believe they are dumb. I do not. Do you know why?*

Finn had looked down, avoiding Arundel's heavy gaze, and Devondra had fiddled with her cards, pretending contemplation.

They aren't dumb, Ember said, *because they've held the Orion Mountains for three thousand years.*

She would never forget the way Arundel looked at her then, with a flash of surprise and something like pride warming his gaze for a moment before sinking back to his cold, solemn expression.

Very good, Ember. Perhaps you can enlighten your

brother on the difficulties of holding the mountains, and how the clans have managed to hold them for so long.

Arundel had walked away. She never had enlightened Finn because she loved him too much the way he was. He didn't care about politics and secrets; he had no use for them in his happy-go-lucky world. She never wished to taint his dream, and avoided what would certainly drive a wedge between them.

Masses of oaks and ash trees stretched their budding arms up to her, taunting her to stay and watch for rabbits that ventured from the warmth of the undergrowth. She skimmed above them, the stench of burned things stinging her nostrils. She came around to the northern slope of the mountain. Black smoke billowed from a crag near the slope's base, where the trees thinned to make way for a meandering gully.

Ember circled above the spot, giving the column of reeking smoke a wide berth.

Old hovels lay half-hidden beneath the trees, their low, mounded thatch roofs scorched and collapsed, falling like fragile black lace into the earthen pits. A cracked wooden bowl lay sideways outside one hovel, and an overturned basket of berries stained a boulder satin red. She passed over the gully, whose water gushed through a narrow channel, wetting the rocks with its turbulence. The skeleton of a sycamore lay like a bridge across it, and on one bony twig hung a tiny leather boot, swaying gently over the force of the river.

Reluctantly, she closed in on the burning pile. Through the smoldering haze the pile first appeared to be blackened furniture—a stool here, a table-top there—but in between the wood were softer things. Furs, cushions stuffed with animal hair, bundles of hide wrapped around—

An arm. Slender and dark like a tree branch. The fingers gave it away.

Ember wheeled upward, her wings trembling with effort. She needed to find a safe refuge, away from any clans. She had no intention of getting involved in their hostile affairs—

A light whistle, and pain ripped into her side. The force of an arrow sent her spinning.

Sky and rocks reeled as she careened toward a great golden spruce. The bristly limbs flexed as she hit them, slowing her fall enough for her to pull her wings in close. The arrow twisted in her side as it caught on branches.

She strained to stay in hawk-form, but when the final, dizzying thud of the ground hit her, she couldn't hold it any longer. Her side screamed with pain as she returned to human form.

Tall and straight like a tree, the arrow rose up out of her, wavering with every breath she took. The fletching was iron-gray against the sky, neat and familiar.

Something rustled nearby, and she tried to sit up.

I have to get out of here—

Her vision darkened with pain.

Rough hands grabbed her. She could shift—if only her body would listen—into a bear, or a cougar, but her body wasn't working. Too tired, too worn.

She opened her mouth to scream but a hand clamped down over it, and they dragged her away, heedless of the blood running down her side.

CHAPTER FIFTEEN

THEY DRAGGED HER to a rocky outcrop and lifted her under a long stone ledge that nearly hugged the ground. Dim light washed through the crevice, and she was sure no one would find them unless she made noise.

She bit the hand that clamped against her mouth.

"Damn it!" A furious whisper, and instead of moving away, the hand grabbed her jaw.

An angry face of stubble filled her vision.

"If you say one word," he whispered, "we're all dead. So shut your mouth."

There was something familiar about the man, a warm, earthy scent that she recognized. But his fingers dug into her, and the residues of hawk and owl inside her made her want to lash out at his big face with a taloned claw.

"Easy Kitt," said another voice, much calmer. "Let's lay her down. Right here."

Ember felt softness beneath her head, but she couldn't relax into it. The man who had grabbed her face released her, and she saw that his chest and legs were bare but for a skirt of leather tied low on his hips. The other man, the calmer one, squatted next to her. He was dressed like a Lachian—cotton shirt, leather jerkin and pants—but strange leather pouches hung all over him.

Ember reached to cover herself, gritting her teeth against the pain as she did so.

The Lachian didn't seem to notice, and gave her a wide, easy grin. "Kitt recognized you were a shifter," he said. "Though it did take some convincing for him to believe you might still be alive after that arrow."

"Just hurry up," the angry man, Kitt, replied, and moved away toward the entrance of the crevice.

The Lachian opened a wood box, and she glimpsed the hilt of a knife.

Quick as a snake.

Her arm flashed out and her fingers curled around the hilt before the man had time to think. She clutched the handle and pointed the long, curved blade at the stunned Lachian, willing her remaining strength to overcome the sudden trembling that hit her. Blood trickled down her side.

"Who are you?" she demanded.

The Lachian held up his hands, his round, hazel

eyes no longer laughing.

"I'm Riggs," he replied. "Riggs Pitkin. And that is Kitt—"

Kitt seemed to realize that Ember held a knife, and swore, moving back toward them. Riggs stopped him with a wave.

"If I don't get that arrow out of you," Riggs continued, "you aren't going to last much longer."

Ember resisted the urge to look at the wound, too aware of the blood seeping down her bare side. "Who shot me?"

"Some bastard wizard," Kitt muttered. "If you both don't shut up, we'll all be target practice." He rubbed a hand over his stubble and crouched to peer through the crevice opening.

The pain was making Ember pant, and she fought off the nausea that swam over her.

Riggs pried the knife from her hand. She closed her eyes and opened them when she heard a metallic *ting*. He moved through his box of tools—knives, scissors, needles, glass jars—touching each one delicately.

"The arrow-puller," he whispered to himself. "I need that, and the ebon tincture, and of course, Norman—"

His ears splayed as wide as honeyed pastries, sticking out from his round face so much that when they twitched, they nearly flapped. He looked up and grinned at something behind her.

"Lady, meet Norman. He's a special friend of mine."

Something soft tickled her ear, and warmth washed over her cheek. She tilted her head, and found a great beak surrounded by plumes of orange and red. A large golden eye met hers.

I'm dreaming. Or I'm dead.

But she could see each feather on his face, each fiber of scarlet and gold and orange that clung and melded together. The bird strutted forward, bending his head to peer at her. His tall scarlet crest rose in curiosity. It was the most beautiful creature she had ever seen.

"A firebird," she whispered, grimacing as Riggs poured a yellow liquid over her wound. "I thought they were all dead."

"In Lach, maybe. Here, bite this." He placed a strip of leather inside her mouth. "I'm going to remove the arrow, and you need to hold still." He glanced toward Kitt. "And try not to make any noise. We want to make it out of here alive, okay?"

Without waiting for a reply, he picked up an odd spoon-like device and pushed it into the wound.

She took full advantage of the strip of leather, biting it so hard her jaw ached. If she slackened her jaw, she knew she wouldn't be able to keep down the sickening onslaught of pain. The arrow stuck deep in her side, though it hadn't come out the other end, and Riggs had a long way to go to reach the tip.

Moments, it had to have been only moments later, yet somehow it seemed like hours, he had the arrow out.

She watched through slit eyes as he doused the hole in her side with more yellow liquid. Even with the arrow out of her, she could feel the damage burning inside her, could see it bubbling up from the opening. *Too much damage.*

The firebird peered at the wound, and Riggs backed away, wiping the blood off his hands with a towel as if it were no more than dirt.

The bird's crest rose to its fullest, a foot high and tapering at the top, and as he stretched his head up, the words of a children's rhyme went through Ember's head.

Silent song
Wishing dust
From the firebird
Life is thrust

Flaming breath
And feathers, too
The fire shifts
Old to new...

He beat his wings once, twice, three times, and the air that rippled over her went from warm to hot as the firebird expanded his chest. His beak crackled open and flames darted out and down into her.

She clamped her fists against her mouth as her wound filled with fire, a horrible heat that tore through her insides and swept up her veins. Amber, ocher, and white gold blinded her, and the scream of cobalt heat deafened her mind.

She wouldn't cry out.

She wouldn't make noise.

She fainted.

CHAPTER SIXTEEN

EMBER AWOKE THIRSTY and ravenous. She bolted upright. Bright midday light flooded through the long narrow crevice that ran beneath the lip of the stone ledge, warming the chill air inside the cave-like nook.

She was alone.

Her side felt sore, and when she pulled away the hide blanket that covered her, she was surprised to see the tender circle of flesh where the wound had been. How long had she slept for? It felt like days, at least.

There was no sign of the two men who had saved her, nor of their firebird, though they had left the bloodied arrow beside her. She studied the gray fletching without touching it.

No spells. The arrow had been shot for fun, then. The wizards likely didn't suspect what she was. She could only hope that they hadn't seen her as a human, and that they wouldn't find her here.

She used the sharp edge of the arrowhead to slice the sheet in half. She wound one half tightly around her upper torso, wedging the ends under the wrappings to make a snug fit. She did the same with the other half, knotting the ends tightly around her hips to form a very short skirt, almost like an undergarment, except that she had nothing to go over it. It reminded her of the hide skirt that the man, Kitt, wore.

Even the Zarian dancers wear more than this, she thought as she studied her pale limbs. But anything was better than being naked.

Gripping the shaft of the arrow like the haft of a knife, Ember stalked to the entrance of the crevice. The air had warmed considerably, thickening the stench of burnt flesh. The forest was well-lit, the breeze singing through tree-boughs and mingling with the endless chatter of songbirds, as if death didn't linger thirty paces away.

She had no intention of going back into the village. She would look for Riggs and Kitt, or find their trails to wherever they were going. They had to have come from somewhere. Perhaps they knew other people in the mountains, people she could stay with.

She turned sideways to face the village as she slid beneath the far side of the ledge, half-squatting to duck under the widest space that the thick milky stone allowed. She could still make out the remains of the hovel roofs and the black smoke that hung like mist between the trees. *The fire will burn for days yet.*

She turned to go, and bumped into a muscled chest covered with fine brown hairs.

Ember leapt back and wielded the arrow. A flush burned up her cheeks.

Kitt lifted a thick brow at her arrow and crossed his arms.

"You are a shifter, correct?" he asked.

"I know that *you* are a shifter," she replied. A wild guess, but it would explain his scent. Different, yet familiar.

"Well that's not too difficult to figure out," he replied.

Ember tried not to scowl.

Riggs came up behind him, sweat pearling on his forehead and upper lip. Small leather-bound bundles hung from his belt and bandolier, and he carried a bulky satchel from where he produced a copper flask.

"Here," he said, proffering it. "You must be thirsty."

She was, desperately so, but she took the flask slowly and drank little.

"How long was I asleep?" Ember asked, handing the flask back.

"A few hours," Riggs said. He stuffed the flask back in the satchel. "Do you feel better?"

"Like I've slept for days." *Firebird magic.* She eyed the canopy, but saw no flash of orange. "Are the wizards gone?"

Kitt's eyes narrowed. "How did you know there was more than one?"

Wizards never travel alone. Always as a patrol or with an Escort.

"A guess. The damage done to the village seems to be the work of more than one."

Riggs nodded. "We didn't find any survivors."

"The wizards headed southeast," Kitt said, nodding his head in that direction. A silver streak of hair along his temple flashed in the sunlight, seeming out-of-place among the rest of his brown hair and so near his youthful face.

"Any idea as to why they would've burned down a clan village?" Ember asked, though she could think of some possibilities. A bad trade, a wrong word said, a threatening move.

Reluctance to give up their claim on valuable land—

"We aren't as concerned about why as much as we are about who," Kitt replied, rubbing a hand over his face. "Though I think we already have an idea."

Ember remembered the gray fletching and said nothing.

"Where were you off to, anyways?" Riggs asked, taking off his satchel and sitting on a small boulder.

"To find you. I'd like to go with you," she said, raising her chin.

Kitt's sharp white teeth bared as he smiled. "Perhaps you should tell us your name first."

"Ember."

"Ember," Kitt repeated, glancing at Riggs. "Ember who?"

"Ember Nobody," she replied. Arundel Thackeray wasn't her real father, which meant his name wasn't hers either. "I'm looking for my father. He was a shifter, and rumors say there are shifters here."

Kitt frowned and his lips became a grim line.

It was only half-true, what she said about the rumors. She had heard just as many rumors about shifters in Ekesia, and even as far south as Zari. Ember had always been careful to give Salena bits and pieces. She might even suggest a different city than the rumors had told her, and by the time they reached Arundel's ears, the rumors would be fairly distorted. Normally, the arrival of the proud, violet-clothed patrols would have been easy to spot, and shifters would have had time to flee if they were smart. The problems arose when Arundel had the patrols travel in disguise, giving them time to search the cities and set their traps without being recognized.

Kitt's gaze flicked around the village. "We should go. Riggs?"

Riggs stood and pulled his satchel over his shoulder. "I say yes."

Kitt nodded. "We're going to our main camp," he told Ember. "If you want to come, you'll have to keep up and watch for wizards. If we run into any and they threaten us, we shift and fight. Got it?"

Ember gripped her arrow shaft and straightened

her back. "Of course."

As soon as the words left her mouth, Kitt's arms burst upward and in half a moment his form whirled dark and his skin prickled to feathers. Wings beat the air rather than arms and a small hawk rose to the canopy.

Ember stared as the hawk swiveled through the trees. Her fingers tingled and her heart beat her chest like a Zarian drum. *So that is what it looks like.* What would it be like to fly with another shifter?

"Sorry about that," Riggs said, startling Ember. She had forgotten he stood there. "He can be rather abrupt sometimes." He bent to pick up the hide skirt that had dropped from Kitt's new form.

"I've never seen someone shift before."

Riggs eyed her. "You've never seen another shifter?"

"There aren't any left where I come from."

"I'm sorry to hear that," Riggs said with a frown.

They began walking the way Kitt had gone, northwest along the river gorge. Ember grimaced whenever her bare feet landed on a pine needle the wrong way, or whenever her toe jammed against a jutting stone.

"So you are a healer?" Ember asked, partly out of curiosity and partly to distract herself from her throbbing feet.

"Yes," Riggs said, pulling himself over a thick fallen tree, carefully minding that the pouches and satchel didn't get caught on the rough bark. "My father taught me. He was a great healer once, in Kingsbury. Do you know of the city?"

"I lived near there," Ember said. *Not entirely a lie.*

"He was a far better healer than I, and a shifter."

"A shifter?" Ember twirled the arrow shaft. "Was he found out?"

"No. He escaped the city during the rebellion, with me in tow. We lived in Orion for a long time."

"So you're a shifter, too?"

He laughed, and it was a warm, comforting sound that danced against the hushed roaring of the river.

"I can do this," he said, and his hand jutted toward her. Coarse black hair sprang up over his tanned, thick arm and spread over the top of his hand, forming patchy thickets of fur. Riggs grinned and twitched his ears at her.

A giggle bubbled up her throat.

"Kitt has tried to teach me to do more," he continued, "but it's useless. I will forever be a half-shifter."

And I forever a half-wizard, she thought.

Riggs stooped to pull a clump of wild onions hidden beneath a cluster of broad-leaved mayapples.

"But you're fully a healer, are you not?" Ember asked as he tapped the dirt off the small bulbs and tucked them in his satchel.

"Through and through," he said with another

grin.

Ember smiled and clambered onto a small boulder, the arrow shaft clamped between her teeth. The skirt and top she wore made the climb relatively easy, though she still felt too exposed and preferred her own canvas shirt and trousers that she wore back at home.

Silverglen.

Thoughts of Gregory flitted back, and Fletch, and the bear she had failed to release.

I won't go back there. She pulled herself up onto the flattened top of the boulder. *I can't go back. Not with Fletch knowing the truth.* She wouldn't see her mother again.

Or Finn.

Even though Finn didn't know who she really was, she missed their late-night talks, his silly jokes and teasing that always made her feel better about her difficult time at the Academy or about being picked on by Devondra. He had made her childhood bearable, and she loved and respected him because of it. The idea of never seeing him again made her heart pinch.

She stood and inhaled the cool, clean air of the mountains. Dense conifers surrounding the boulder. Riggs' head bobbed below her, half a dozen feet down, as he made his way around the base of the rock. On either side of her, the mountain's forests sprawled up to the blue-tinted sky, some slopes steeper and rockier than others. The gorge had shrunk, and was now a shallow stream, perhaps twenty paces wide. Oaks speckled with leaf-buds, alders, maples, and white-barked sycamore trees clung to the banks like ancient sentinels. Their twisted branches gathering above the stream were far prettier than Arundel's arcade of twisted iron.

A perfect spot for spying, Ember observed.

A flash of pale feathers caught her eye. A small hawk, perched in the heavy limb of a sycamore, tore at a tiny bundle of fur grasped in its talons.

Or for hunting.

Disgust and hunger simultaneously churned in her stomach.

"Riggs?" she called down from her rock.

Riggs looked up, his face pink and sweaty, from where he clung to the south side of the boulder. *It must be frustrating to always be in human form,* she thought. "Do you have food with you?"

His sheening brows drew together. "Food?" Perplexed, he fumbled around for his satchel with a free hand.

"On the other side," Ember said, motioning her head toward the north side of the boulder. Without waiting for a response, she scrambled down the northern slope of the boulder, realizing how easy it would be to climb down in the form of a squirrel or a goat, and that it would be easiest of all to fly.

A shadow passed over her as she reached the base of the boulder. The small hawk—Kitt—flew in front of the sun and dove through an opening in the trees ahead. He landed on the ground at the edge of the opening, his pale feathery body disappearing for a moment among fern fronds. The ferns stirred, and the sun fell across Kitt's bare shoulders and back as he stood.

Ember stared at his form, mesmerized by the way the light played along his slender muscles as he moved, curling around the ridges and swaying, dipping into half-hidden curves of darkness. He stalked into the clearing, his step determined, his thick thighs strung with tension.

Coldness kissed Ember's mind. The source of it was buried deep in the grasses that Kitt trudged through.

"Kitt, no!"

Without thinking, she sprinted towards him, like a rabbit diving through undergrowth, like a horse leaping over fallen logs, her mind probing the spell, her eyes tracking Kitt's every move like she was the hunter, only she didn't want him to get caught in the trap she knew awaited him.

He didn't seem to hear her. She would be too late, she realized, and watched in dismay as he bent down, right down into the spell whose metallic chill shivered up her spine.

SNAP!

The unmistakable sound of a jaw-trap biting something solid cracked through her nerves as she emerged into the clearing.

But Kitt stood with his arms intact, and turned toward her, his face hard and his eyes narrowed.

"It's a trap," Ember gasped, half-kneeling and half-falling next to the large iron contraption. In its teeth was a stick, only a stick, and the force of the jaw had caused it to break in half. Ember breathed over it, unable to stop her body from trembling.

"I saw it while I was flying," Kitt said in a tight voice.

"I saw it, too," she said. The spell—a Freeze—was faded, likely from exposure to rain, and weakened enough that she might be able to undo it—

Kitt reached down to pick it up.

"No!" She lashed out, grabbing his wrist before he could touch it, and she found herself too close to his nudity. She met his gaze, her face flaming, but he seemed unaware or uncaring of the effect of his nakedness on her.

His hand curled into a fist, and the tendons in his wrist corded beneath her fingers.

She snatched her hand away and licked her lips. "There is a spell," she whispered, unable to meet his eyes. Her hands felt empty suddenly, and she searched the ground for a sharp stick. Where had she put her arrow?

"You're a wizard," he growled.

Something in his voice made her meet his gaze, and for a fleeting moment she was looking into

Arundel's eyes—the hatred he held while riding a horse into the ground, the anger that pinched his lips as he set a spelled snare, the wild violence as he swung an ax into the head of a struggling boar.

In the next moment her heart beat and she spun away, her mind already forming the image of a wolf, or a rabbit, and her body soaking into the nauseating swirl of—

Someone shouted and a force slammed into Ember's back.

Huge paws smashed her arms into the ground. Their curved, needle-sharp claws pricked her skin, a minute pain compared to the massive strength bearing down on her back, smothering her into the ground. The rumble of the cougar's growl shuddered between her shoulder blades and the heat of his breath twined around her throat. Out of the corner of her eye, long teeth bared in a snarl, inches away.

Vaguely, Ember heard Riggs shouting Kitt's name.

The weight on her shifted, lightened, but the heat and strength stayed steady, like a barely-contained fire.

"Give me one good reason why I shouldn't kill you," Kitt snarled into her ear.

Because I'm a shifter, just like you, she wanted to say. But it wasn't entirely true, and he would know it.

"Not all wizards are the same," she said instead. "You don't know me. I'm not like the others."

"Prove it," he spat, and pushed away from her.

Dazed, she tried to sit up. In a moment, Riggs was at her side, gently grasping her lower arms to help her and wiping the pricks of blood with a cloth.

"You're shaking," he said. "It's alright now. He won't hurt you."

Ember only half-heard him. She rubbed her hands over her neck and watched as Kitt grabbed his skirt from Riggs' pack and tied it back on with quick, steady movements.

Do all shifters hate wizards? Perhaps she should've stayed in Silverglen; she might have been safer. She ran a hand over her cheek, where sticks had dug a pattern into her skin. She didn't know these people, and she certainly had no idea what this Kitt was really capable of.

Murder. I saw murder in his eyes.

"Riggs, you go to main camp," said Kitt, tightening the last knot with a snap of the leather strips. "We can't trust this one. Seabird can decide what to do with her."

Riggs snorted. "You want me to leave her with you, after what you just did? You're mad."

"You'll be safer on your own, without a shifter around. No one will suspect who you are, if you play it off well. You can use your story about collecting rare medicinal plants to bring back to Lach. Even better if you're found with Seabird."

"Unless they recognize him," Riggs said dryly. He proffered a piece of bread to Ember.

Her stomach felt knotted, but she forced herself to take the bread because she couldn't remember the last time she had eaten.

"We'll wait here," Kitt continued. "It's not much further, but I don't want to risk taking her there."

"Alright," Riggs said. "But there's one thing you have to promise me." He stood and pressed his face close to Kitt's, seemingly untroubled by the fact that he stood a full three inches shorter. "No more threats. You don't touch her."

They glared at each other for a moment before Kitt let out a slow breath. Ember took the opportunity to reach into Riggs' pack, quick and careful as a mouse. *No, he won't touch me again.*

"I won't touch her unless she tries to hurt me," Kitt promised. His eyes glided to Ember, scowling in suspicion. "What is she—?"

Slow and steady. She pulled out a piece of dried meat and a couple of small apples, ignoring Kitt's look of shocked confusion. There was plenty of food left at the bottom of the bag to last Riggs days, and she needed more sustenance. She tugged at the strip of meat with her teeth, suddenly too hungry to think about where it came from or what it was. The sweet juice of the apple washed over the meat's saltiness.

"Can she not hunt?" Kitt asked Riggs in a lowered voice.

Ember pretended not to hear, though she couldn't stop a flare of anger heating her cheeks. *Why not just ask me yourself?* And they watched her like she was some strange animal they had never seen before. Ember straightened and took another bite of the apple, making sure no juice spilled.

"I don't know," Riggs replied, watching Ember with equal perplexity. "There are some few like that at camp, you know. Besides myself, of course," he added with a wry smile.

"Sorry, Pitkin. I don't count you among other shifters anymore."

"Ouch," Riggs said, mocking pain as he rubbed a hand over his chest. "Doesn't my scrubby fur count for anything?"

"It might, if it covered more than your arse. You should get going. You'll have a full moon tonight."

"I suppose that means you want me to travel all night without getting a wink of sleep?" Riggs stalked to his satchel and hauled it over his shoulder, tossing Kitt a hide blanket roll. "I'll just have to find some of those wide-eyed berries." He winked at Ember, his ears twitching as he grinned, and set off north.

Ember finished eating and watched him go. The knife she had stolen from his pack pressed against the small of her back as she leaned against an oak tree.

"Who is Seabird?" she asked.

Kitt didn't turn from where he stood, watching as Riggs disappeared into a dense thicket.

"How big is your main camp?" she tried again.

Kitt's back was rigid. His arms didn't hang at his

sides, but seemed poised there, on the verge of movement.

"What's to stop me from trying to find your camp on my own?" she prodded.

"I hope you aren't that stupid," he replied shortly, turning his head so that she could see his profile. A silver streak of hair started at his temple and ended just past his ear, a mark of age that belied the youth of his face.

He doesn't look to be many years older than myself.

"You promised you wouldn't touch me unless I tried to hurt you," said Ember.

"The safety of the camp is a much higher promise. No one would have issue with me attacking a stranger who posed a threat to camp."

"And how am I a threat?" she asked.

He turned his face away.

Ember sighed and leaned her head back against the oak's rough trunk. She wished he would say something, even a lie. She would at least have words to pick through, then.

A vermin hawk landed on a branch above her and glared down with red eyes.

He's quick and quiet.

She scowled back at the hawk until he took off and flew the short distance to the river, no doubt to hunt again. Where Kitt had stood, there was now only a crumpled deerskin skirt and the blanket roll from Riggs.

Ember grabbed the hide blanket and found a spot to rest beneath a soft pine, where the long needles formed a thick, springy bed at the base of the trunk. She stretched the blanket over her and took out Riggs' knife. She pulled at the air along the blade with her fingers, crisscrossing and looping it around in a simple, one-handed Freeze pattern, and as the air recognized her motions and intent, it seemed to condense, forming silvery, thread-like strands wherever her fingers went. She tapped the surface of the blade to bind the Freeze to it.

"Done," she whispered, sinking the blade into the ground next to her. She let loose a sigh and tightened the blanket around her. A vermin hawk called nearby with short, nasal whistles. She kept her eyes toward the sound, watching for movement in the great trees that loomed over the river.

The sun sank in the west.

CHAPTER SEVENTEEN

EMBER JERKED AWAKE, intuitively grabbing the handle of Riggs' knife as she did so. She had slept far too long.

A dense, moon-lit fog hung like a curtain around her, hiding everything but the scaly trunk next to her. She tugged the blanket off, her skin prickling in the chill, damp air.

As she stood, a low growl rumbled through the fog.

Kitt.

She stumbled toward the noise, tripping over sticks and jutting rocks, straining to see movement.

There. As she saw him, in the form of a lithe cougar, his growling turned to screaming, and he thrashed at something that she couldn't make out, his hind foot caught—

A spear materialized out of the fog and jabbed his hind leg.

Without thinking, Ember hefted Riggs' knife like a throwing dagger and loosed it at the dark form, willing it to strike anything solid. But it wasn't a throwing knife and didn't have the balanced weight of one, so it could go sidelong—

The fog muffled a shout. The sound was enough.

Ember leapt to the snare around Kitt's foot.

Blood seeped over his fur as he slumped against the ground, growling at the form Ember couldn't quite make out. When she bent over the snare, he flinched and snapped toward her hand.

"Kitt!" she said, looking into two large golden eyes. She loosened the snare loop over his hind paw. "We need to go."

A low chuckle slithered past her ears. The hair on her neck stood on end.

It can't be him. She peered through the dense fog at the wizard's form. Tall and skinny. Spindly hands grasped the haft of his spear, unmoving and locked into her knife's Freeze. Oddly, both the spear and the snare were unspelled. Had he simply been hunting for food? *There's no such thing as simple with a wizard. Especially with a wizard traveling through Orion.* He wouldn't be alone.

She could see the hilt of Riggs' knife sticking out from the wizard's calf, but she couldn't make out the detail of his face, where the fog seemed to thicken.

"Kill him," Kitt said through gritted teeth, in human form now. He was trying to stand, but he couldn't lean on his wounded leg.

Ember pretended not to hear and rushed to tuck herself under his arm like a crutch.

"No, I'm fine," he continued. "You still have a chance. Kill him, or he'll come after us."

Killing might be an option for someone like Kitt. Like Arundel. It wasn't an option for her. Couldn't be. Still, something tugged against her. The yearning to stop the wizard, to control the situation. Knowing she could kill him, and that she would be stronger because of it. Ember shoved the feeling away. "We need to go. The spell won't last much longer." Ember strained against Kitt's weight as she helped him up. "We need to move as quickly as you can." She forced her feet one in front of the other, willing her strength to lend speed to Kitt's movements.

Another chuckle rose behind her and ascended into a short, raspy laugh. She could never mistake that sound.

Fletch.

She pushed Kitt forward and squinted through the fog. They wouldn't be able to get very far away before he broke the spell. Her magic wasn't strong enough, and Fletch was persistent.

"We need to find a place to hide," she said, looking around.

"Up there," Kitt replied, pointing upslope. "An

old tree."

She tugged him in that direction, listening for any footfalls behind them. She heard nothing, and sensed no cold beyond that of the fog.

"Wait," Kitt panted. He reached down and pulled a clump of reddish moss from a rock. "Blood-moss. For the wound."

Sweat shone on his forehead, and his face was paler than the moonlight. She helped him stand straight, wishing she could see better in the fog.

A dozen more steps and they arrived at the foot of an elm tree. The trunk spread nearly as wide around as the hovels in the burned village, and the roots looked to be trunks of their own, hunched and twisted over the sunken ground. Beneath the roots lay darkness.

Kitt slumped to the ground and pulled himself through a gap in the roots. Ember smoothed the leaves he had disturbed on his way down, and lowered herself after him, being sure she left not even a twig standing out of place.

No moonlight came into the hole. What light the fog hadn't obscured, the roots took the rest of. A few feet down from the roots, the cool ground formed a bowl framed by soil and the rough, furrowed wood of the semi-hollowed trunk.

She touched hot skin and withdrew her hand.

"You're shivering," Ember whispered. Her stomach tightened.

"Shock." Kitt pressed the blood-moss into her hand. "I need you to bind the wound. Tightly."

He guided her hand to his wound, and winced as she pressed the moss there. Quickly, she pulled at the knot of her upper garment and unwound it. She bound the fabric firmly over the moss, and Kitt's blood stuck to her fingers like syrup.

"Thank you," Kitt said when she was done.

Ember peered out of the roots. The fog had thickened. She could see nothing beyond the great elm roots. She thought of casting a Glamour over the roots so that only ground would appear beneath the roots rather than their hiding place, but dismissed the idea. All wizards had some sense of spells, not the way that she did, but Fletch's senses seemed eerily amplified compared to other wizards. She couldn't risk drawing his attention.

He must've followed me here, but how? She had flown away from Silverglen; no tracks had been left behind. Perhaps he was on some other mission for Arundel, then.

Her heart banged.

Looking for me? Arundel would've eventually noticed her absence. And Salena, of course. They might have sent out patrols to bring her home. Had Fletch been with the patrol at the burned village? Had he suspected it was her they shot down? Most likely, the burning village had nothing to do with her.

She listened to Kitt's ragged breathing and

rubbed the goose-pimples from her arms.

What would Kitt do if he knew who she was? What would other shifters do? A daughter of Lord Arundel, the man who suffocated the rebellion and murdered thousands of shifters. *The man who saved Lach by killing a piece of its soul.* A sick man. A monster.

Even some commoners of Merewood held a deep hatred toward him. Ember could only imagine the hatred other shifters had for him. If they were anything like Kitt...

Ember shook her head to dislodge the thought.

I am not Arundel's daughter. I'm nothing like him. Hadn't she proven that by not killing Fletch?

Her real father might be out there somewhere. She would focus on finding him, and on finding other shifters.

Resolute, she formed the image of a cougar and shifted, filling most of the empty space with her fur. Gingerly, she lay with her side along Kitt's, her feline warmth permeating the small space.

Sounds outside the hideout amplified. A mouse burrowed through the duff, an owl hooted in a three-beat rhythm, a snake slid out of a log nearby.

She listened and watched for the wizard.

Kitt's breathing steadied.

CHAPTER EIGHTEEN

EMBER AWOKE TO the touch of the sun on her bare-skinned shoulder. She stretched the stiffness from her human limbs and rubbed the warmth back into them as she peeked through the tree roots above.

No sign of a human. No spells that she could sense.

She breathed relief.

"Why didn't you kill him?"

Ember twisted in the small space. Kitt sagged against the decaying wall of the tree hollow, his head resting against the wood as though he was too tired to hold it up. His leg wrappings were soaked a rusty red. The wound would need to be cleaned, Ember figured, though she had no water to clean it with. She would have to go to the river.

And he needs to drink. Kitt's green eyes shone

against sallow skin pricked with sweat. He covered himself with his hands, casually, waiting for her answer.

She kept her eyes carefully trained on his face, just as he was doing to her, and pulled her knees up to her chest.

The idea of killing Fletch made her insides pinch. Would she enjoy killing a man she hated? Would she grin, like Arundel always did after a hunt, because she would be the one in control? Arundel had always said *power through knowledge,* but he lived his life gaining power through killing. He had enjoyed killing, but it was more than that. She had felt the tug of it before, and had resisted. The idea of gaining control, of feeling strong by inflicting harm on others made her sick. "I don't believe in killing," she said.

"He would've killed you. For being a shifter."

"You don't know that."

Kitt smirked, though it looked more like a weak grimace. "I've seen enough to know. He smelled of madness. And blood."

Ember repressed a shiver. "I'm going to fetch water," she said. "And then we should head out for your camp."

"No."

"You won't last much longer out here, not without water. Maybe Riggs could take care of your wound, but without care it will get infected. Who knows when he'll be back? With the fog last night, he might not have traveled. And you look feverish."

"I'm not taking you to camp. You aren't to be trusted."

Anger flamed through her.

"Why? Because I didn't kill someone? How exactly would me being a murderer make me more trustworthy?"

Kitt clenched his jaw and closed his eyes. A drop of sweat rolled past the silver streak of hair along his temple.

"Fine," Ember said. "I'm going to get water and scout. Don't move."

She shifted to a cougar, ignoring the wash of biliousness and the uncomfortable shifting of senses, muscle, and bones, and leapt out of the hole.

The sun rose to a late-morning poise. No deep shadows, but warm air and bright, dancing flashes of light played in the trees and along the forest floor. Hundreds of twigs snapped above as the elm boughs swayed in a breeze. She counted two robins, five chick-sparrows, a dozen or so tree-peckers, and at least six fat brown squirrels scrabbling to find what remained of their winter caches.

The forest floor revealed smaller noises. Mice. Voles. Perhaps even a ground-chuck. A game of cat-and-mouse might be a welcome pleasure—

No. She had gone her entire life without hunting, and she had no intentions of engaging in Arundel's sport, even if her stomach was a bit hollow. *I need to find water.*

The river they had followed the day before was back where she had left Fletch. And Riggs' knife. There was a good chance Fletch was there with other wizards, or perhaps even patrolling the river for the escaped shifters. But how far up the river would they go?

She decided to head northeast along a steep, west-facing slope until she had traveled a fair amount of distance north, then cut directly west to meet the river.

A rocky outcrop protruded over the river below, creating a high bank on either side. *Too much exposure.* If Fletch or other wizards were waiting along the river, the small ravine would be a perfect trap for any animal. She crept north, padding around large trees and winding through clumps of saplings that struggled to fill gaps in the canopy. Up ahead, the river split into two shallower streams, one heading up-river northwest, the other northeast.

She was panting by the time she reached the edge of the river just south of the split. Ember slid along the wet, cool ground on her belly, burrowing through thick emerald-green ferns and bobbing mayapples until she reached the river's edge. The river's width was half again as long as her cat-body, deep enough that she couldn't see the bottom, and fast enough that the noise of rushing water prevented her from hearing as well as she wished to. She crouched and drank the icy water.

Now, she would just need to figure out a way to

get water to Kitt—

A metallic scent trickled downstream.

Not Arundel's metal, but the metallic whiff of a spell. Ember darted away from the river, low in the ferns and her paws sinking into the forest floor. Feline instinct brought her to an old ash tree that had fallen on a great oak, a perfect ladder into the canopy.

She would be safer shifting to a bird and flying back to Kitt. She could avoid being seen, possibly captured, or even killed—

Her claws dug into the slippery trunk of the ash tree. Driven more by the cougar's curiosity than her human fear, she lay in the crotch where the trees met, and waited.

Four wizards. One heavier than the others. All men.

A more distinct tread reached her ears. Her spine grew as rigid as the trunk beneath her. *Riggs.*

The patrol came into view along the opposite bank of the river, just north of the split. Three wizards, then. Two fair-skinned and one—the biggest—as dark as a shadow. Riggs trudged behind them.

No rope or ties. Perhaps they weren't afraid of him running away. But what would they want from a non-shifter, unless they believed he knew where to find shifters?

They crossed the two smaller streams and headed south along the bank, stepping with care to avoid crushing vegetation.

Ember flicked her tail in amusement. *There's no*

hiding your trail from shifters. Even if they didn't leave a visible trace, the pungent smell of them would linger in the forest for days. *Sweat and fear.* And a female. Ember looked more closely at them as they approached beneath her. *A Glamour. Of course.* The faint silvery threads of the woman's Glamour shimmered when she tilted her head to the sun. Beneath it, she was finer-boned, lighter-skinned, her hair bound in tight braids rather than the loose, cropped hair of the illusion. Ember wondered if the other patrol members knew the wizard was a woman, as wizards couldn't see the spells the way she had always been able to.

"How much further?" the dark-skinned man asked.

"Not much," said Riggs. His voice was steeped in weariness, and he sank onto a fallen log as the dark man paused to swig water from his canteen.

The two light-skinned wizards stepped away from them and scanned the surroundings. Each carried an arm-length sword, and Ember sensed a Freeze bound along the blades.

The tall dark wizard wore a sword strapped to his back, over a leather jerkin. Along the hem of the jerkin hung bits of gray fox fur that seemed to dance as he moved. He was Zarian, then, though he spoke like a Lachian.

"You said you found the girl at the burned village," the Zarian said now. "Do you have reason to trust her?"

Riggs frowned and his hand glided protectively over his satchel. *He noticed the missing knife.*

"She warned Kitt of a trap. The patrol at the village shot her down. I don't think she is working with them."

"But you said she threatened you?"

Riggs sighed. "She was injured and didn't know who we were. It's only natural to be defensive—"

"Seabird! Up above!" A shout from one of the wizards.

In one liquid motion the Zarian whirled toward Ember, his sword slithering from scabbard to hand. The tip gleamed in the sun as he pointed it at her.

Steady as stone.

She gazed down at Seabird's broad face, smooth but for the thick scar that ran from temple to chin. *A fighter, then. And a leader.* He was older than Arundel, his bristly hair shaded like salt and Ekesian pepper.

An oddity of a wizard, if only because he wasn't working for Arundel.

Riggs jumped up, and his satchel thudded to the ground. "That must be her. She's bigger than Kitt. As a cougar, I mean," he added sheepishly, half-stumbling to reach Seabird's side.

Seabird lowered his sword. "You are Ember?"

Ember flicked her tail in response.

Seabird turned toward the other two wizards and made a motion for them to lower their swords. He tucked his own back into its scabbard.

"Where is Kitt?" Riggs asked her.

As much as Ember enjoyed watching them safely from above, she forced herself to climb down. If the man was truly Seabird, the leader of the camp that Kitt had mentioned, she would need to gain his trust.

She pawed her way down the fallen ash and leapt to the ground, landing only feet from where the woman wizard stood. Her sword pointed down at an angle in front of her, her arm tense and ready to sweep up in a defensive blow.

Ember twitched her tail and turned away, retracing her steps to the old elm.

The wizards pulled Kitt out of the hollow. Ember sat at a distance, watching as Riggs bent over Kitt's limpid form.

"I need a litter," Riggs told the wizards. He opened his wood box and he fingered a small row of tiny flasks. He pulled one out and tipped the clear liquid into Kitt's mouth. "It's an ellium tincture," Riggs explained as Kitt sputtered and pushed his hand away. "Just drink the damn stuff. You'll feel better for it."

Seabird dropped a bundle of cloth in front of Ember.

"We need to talk," he said, and walked away to help with the litter.

Ember grabbed the musty bundle and went behind a tree. She shifted back to human form, her skin at once pimpling at its sudden bareness. She would miss the better hearing and smell of the cat, but she could think clearer as a human. She could smell her own ripeness, and had the urge to lick herself clean.

I am human. Rational thinking. Logic. And hot baths.

Not to mention food. Her stomach twinged.

The bundle turned out to be a worn, scratchy commoner's tunic, sized a bit large in the waist.

"Ember, help me, will you?" Riggs asked when he saw her. "His leg can't move while I do this."

Even with the ellium tincture, Kitt twitched in a feverish sleep. Ignoring the heat that fanned up her face, Ember placed her hands on either side of Kitt's wound. The bandage had been removed and the gaping hole flushed clean—or as clean as it could get. Riggs sewed the skin shut with deft fingers and rinsed the spot again.

"Where is Norman?" Ember asked. Surely the bird could heal his wound quickly.

Riggs shook his head. "I don't know. He's not at my command. And anyways," he added, throwing a clump of blood-moss into a small mortar and grinding it efficiently, "Norman only gifts a person once. Kitt was given his a long time ago."

He spread the poultice over the wound.

Ember couldn't stop a jolt of curiosity about Kitt's previous injury, nor the way the curiosity twisted with inexplicable guilt. "I didn't do it," she said.

Without taking his eyes off the wound, Riggs gave a weak smile.

"I imagine that if you did, he deserved it."

"A snare caught him while I slept. The fog made it hard for me to find him, and by the time I did..."

Ember left the rest unsaid. No reason for them to question her about the wizard. And why she hadn't killed him.

"A patrol?" Seabird asked, lowering himself in a crouch across from her. "Did you see any of them?"

He had steel eyes, she noted, black as a raven's feather.

Ember shook her head. "There was too much fog. We were able to hide until morning."

Riggs frowned and tightened his jaw, but didn't look at her as he finished securing the bandage around Kitt's leg. He didn't believe her, no doubt because she hadn't produced his missing knife. Seabird, too, looked too perceptive to be deceived so easily.

"I hear you are a wizard," Seabird said casually. His deep voice was one of command, but it held a rolling softness that reminded her of velvet. "It's been a long time since I've met a wizard-shifter. They were never so common, in Lach, and never highly regarded by the people."

Ember rubbed her hands over her tunic-covered thighs as Riggs finished wrapping Kitt's wound. "Are you the leader of the camp?" she asked.

"I am."

"Are more shifters there?"

"The camp has many people," he said, emphasizing the last word.

Riggs packed up his wooden box and wrapped it in deer-hide.

"I'm looking for my father," Ember said. "He was a shifter."

Seabird gave a slight nod, and a tiny red jewel hanging from his left earlobe flashed in the morning sun. "Does he have a name?"

Ember stood. "Of course he has a name. But my mother never told me what it was."

"What was your mother's name?"

"It doesn't matter. They never married. She's dead now." Ember was getting tired of lying. But then again, she had been lying her entire life, hadn't she? "I would like to join your camp."

Seabird raised his dark brows and stood, crossing his arms one over the other in a comfortable stance. His steady gaze held her still, though her heart hammered her chest.

"Where are you from?" he asked.

"Near Kingsbury," Ember replied.

Seabird's face remained motionless. "What street did you live on?"

Ember hesitated, trying to recall the street names from the few times she had been around Kingsbury. Would Seabird know every one? "We moved around a few times. The last was Licking Lane."

Seabird's mouth twitched. "How did you get by?"

Easy. "We washed linens, for those who could afford it."

Seabird took a long breath, and his nostrils pinched.

Ember lifted her head a notch, trying to calm her quickening pulse.

"You're a decent liar," Seabird finally said. Before Ember could open her mouth, he went on. "I've worked with a lot of spies in my days. Who do you work for?"

Heat flushed up Ember's neck. *Far too perceptive.* Ember might not be a spy now, but Salena had raised her to be one. "I work for no one. I told you, I'm here to find my father."

"A convenient excuse," Seabird rumbled. "Now, tell me the truth about what happened with Kitt."

Ember swallowed, glancing down at Kitt's prostrate form. "I did see the wizard who attacked him."

"And?" Seabird prodded.

"I threw a knife at the wizard. Spelled with a Freeze." Ember met Riggs' annoyed glance. "I took the knife from Riggs' pack for protection before he left."

Heavy silence fell between them, broken only by Kitt's deep breathing.

I sound ludicrous, Ember thought wildly. *They'll never let me join them, now.*

"And after you stabbed the wizard?"

Ember let out a huff. "I didn't kill him. Is that what you wish to hear? I left the wizard behind and hid until this morning. We don't kill people where I come from."

"Even if they wish to kill you?"

Ember shot a glare at Seabird. Why did these people assume the worst about wizards? "I don't know that the wizard would've killed either of us."

"But the wizard stabbed Kitt. It could prove a lethal wound, could it not?"

Ember sought Riggs' reassurance, but he was busy checking Kitt's wrappings.

"It's not my place to decide who dies," Ember muttered. She was no patrol member or Escort.

"No?" Seabird said. "One day, that may be the only decision you have left to make."

Ember crossed her arms and jutted her chin forward. She wouldn't sit there and argue with the man. Either he would accept her or he wouldn't.

Seabird acknowledged her stony silence with a brief nod. "Our group only accepts those who have something to offer in abilities. Each of us has a role to fulfill. What can you give us?"

Ember let out a breath, straightening her back against the urge to sag in relief. "I can start a fire," she stated.

Riggs gave an audible snort as he tucked his box into his satchel.

"I can wash linens and cook," she added.

From the look Seabird gave her, he wasn't impressed.

Ember scrambled to think of something else. She had spent so much time eavesdropping in the kitchens;

surely she could make something nice. Something spectacular.

"I can make stuffed lamb chops," she said. "Sweet-meat pies, bread pudding—"

Seabird's deep, rolling laughter cut her off. She stared at him, unsure of what to say.

"If you can cook like that," he said, "we'll be eating like a lord."

Ember smiled with a confidence she didn't feel, and helped hoist sleeping Kitt onto the newly formed litter.

CHAPTER NINETEEN

Ember discovered the camp when she realized it was hidden. To others, even wizards, there was no sign of life beyond that of the trees and plants, the rocks and the meandering stream.

To Ember, the camp appeared as a web of spells.

She sensed them with her mind at first, a vast ring of coldness, a thousand or more spells strung between trees in complex, two-handed formations. As they neared, Ember saw that a translucent curtain of Glamour and Silencing spells formed a type of perimeter whose ends met at the base of an escarpment. The fine spell strands only appeared at certain angles, gilded by the dusk light in a way that only Ember could see. Walking through them felt like walking through cobwebs.

"There's an entrance, over here," Riggs said, too

late.

Inside the perimeter now, Ember watched as Riggs stepped between two great stones. No spells there, she sensed, wiping the tickling sensation off her arms. She had created somewhat of an open patch, and did what she could to fill it. The problem with the longer strands of spells was that they were weak. Shorter strands held up better to physical pressure— either by bending with it or moving around it. The longer strands, like those she had walked through, simply broke apart.

Inside the camp lay more spells. Glamours on the ground, hanging from tree boughs, and even stretched across the entrance to a cave that was tucked beneath a crag. Were they traps, like so many of the Glamours at Silverglen, but meant for patrols rather than shifters?

The river they had followed to the camp widened and grew more shallow, forming a stream that wandered under the trees and past the cave, its banks smoothed by flat stones and moss. Children played in the water along with shifters in otter and fox forms, and their shrieks of laughter bounced off the crags.

Others, wearing the scarce covering of deer hides similar to the Zarian fashion, could be seen carrying firewood, hanging washed blankets, skinning rabbits, and planting seeds along mounds that looked oddly familiar. They used hovels, Ember realized, just as the Orion clans did. Only the entrances to these hovels, and some of the roofs mounded with dirt for planting, were sewn with a Glamour.

Hidden. Everything is hidden.

It was a wonder the shifters could find anything.

Ember flinched when she felt a cold, wet nose against her hand. A wolf-like dog pushed its muzzle against her. Ember sunk her fingers into his coat and laughed when the dog wriggled against her.

"He's not a shifter," Ember stated. She knew it somehow from his simple gaze, and from the way he snorted and wagged with pure joy. A dog's greeting, not a human greeting.

"That's Jasper," Riggs explained. "My father found him as a pup abandoned in a den and took him in."

"He's cute." Dogs were a rarity at Silverglen. Arundel kept only five for hunting, which he left in Fletch's care when they weren't being used.

Riggs reached down into a low-growing clump of sapphire-weed and lifted the wide piece of wood on which they grew. "Welcome to camp," he said, giving her a wink and a twitch of the ears before heading down the steps into the hovel. The wizards followed with Kitt's litter.

Satisfied with Ember's scratches, Jasper bounded away to play with the children in the water, and a fresh wave of laughter and screams erupted as he shook water from his coat.

"The camp is small," said Seabird, coming to stand beside her. "About a hundred people. Most are shifters. Survivors of the rebellion."

"I never could have imagined so many shifters in one place," Ember said. They had begun to notice her presence in the camp. Some stared blatantly, while others looked over their shoulders, and still others pretended not to be curious at all, going about their chores and slipping like ghosts in and out of visibility as they walked through the hanging Glamour spells. "How many wizards are here?"

"Five." A frown creased Seabird's forehead. "It's a challenge to keep the spells in good condition. Especially after a heavy rain."

Ember nodded. "Where shall I stay?"

"Wherever you like. There are no empty homes left, so you will have to share. I will introduce you to the kitchen staff."

Ember swallowed a sudden wave of panic.

The kitchen, it turned out, was in the cave. They crossed the stream where a thick slab of wood ran from one smooth bank to the other and walked into its rounded mouth.

Smoke from a great fire streamed up into a hole of the cavernous ceiling. The echoes of a handful of voices came from the few who stood at wooden trestle tables, standing in the light of the cave opening. They chopped and stirred and tossed diligently, and the scents of onion, garlic, and meat washed over her. They barely glanced up when she came in, except for an especially tall woman who wore a full-length leather dress trimmed in feathers and fur. She looked to be Ekesian, or perhaps Zarian and Ekesian, with her wide, dark eyes and skin the shade of a silk-nut.

"Sea," she breathed, and she glided up to Seabird, brushing her cheek against his in greeting.

Seabird gave a white-toothed grin.

"Ember, this is Asenath. She's a great wizard, and a good cook, too."

"Good?" The woman waived a hand dismissively. "I care only about the aesthetics. I have no skill when it comes to taste. That's mostly Etty's work."

"Ember expressed interest in working in the kitchens," Seabird told her. "She has some nice dishes in mind.

Asenath's face lit up. "Well, that's perfect! Etty could use some help now."

Etty, looking sweaty and stern, stood at a table near the fire in the back of the small cave. She looked Ember up and down while she cleaned out a turkey.

"Ember, you said?" she asked in a husky voice. "Stuffed a turkey before?"

Ember shook her head, trying not to look too closely at the red parts Etty dragged out from the turkey's body cavity.

"Lord's cook, is what Seabird made me think you were. By the looks of you, I'd say scullion. Come here now, don't be scared. It's dead."

Precisely. Perhaps she should've told Seabird she could sew, or chop wood, or—

"You know how to tear? With your hands? Don't look so puzzled. There," Etty said, motioning to a bowl and a loaf of hard bread. "Tear that into bits. You a shifter?"

"Yes," Ember said, taking up the dense, nutty-smelling bread.

Etty, a bit heavy-set, finished cleaning the inside of the turkey and started chopping onions. The sharp spray of them stung Ember's eyes.

"You're new, so I'll give you some advice," said Etty while she chopped. "This camp isn't anything you've seen before. You're young, so you wouldn't remember the old days. Back in Lach." Etty sniffed, though Ember was certain it was only from the onions. "Don't be surprised if you see shifters eating in animal form. Most like it better that way. And mating. It's hard to keep up with all the breeding. As far as the bare skin, you'll get more than enough of it. You look us in the eyes or don't look at us at all. It's what's proper."

She tossed the onions in with the bread.

"Stuff as much breading and onion in as you can. We don't have butter, but the bird juice does just fine. And it's rude to look on if a couple is mating," she continued seamlessly. "You'll get used to it soon enough, and then you won't hardly notice."

Ember doubted that very much.

"Wizard rules don't apply much here. Even Seabird doesn't have a stick up his arse like other wizards. Now we tie up the flaps of skin using these sharpened twigs and sinew. Make room for the spit-stick to go through."

"How did you all come to be settled in a clan village?"

"It was Seabird's doing. Used to be that we made our own camp. That was before a patrol found us out. A shifter gave us away."

"A shifter?"

"He was offered a reward, a place back in Lach. Very tempting for many of us. Twelve people were killed for it. That's when our healer disappeared — killed him too, no doubt." Etty speared the turkey with the spit-stick, pushing through the flesh and bone like butter. "We moved camp. Seabird bought this one from a clan who wanted to move north of here. Clans close to the border are restless nowadays."

Ember helped Etty set the spit over the fire. The turkey gleamed in the orange light, the skin sweating until pink juice rolled down its side and fell, sizzling, into the hands of the fire.

"Now, we turn it like this while it cooks," Etty said, gripping the handle of the spit and rotating it steadily. She eyed Ember. "You planning on wearing that rag for good?"

Ember looked down at the over-sized garment and shrugged. "I hadn't thought about it."

"You look out of place. I know someone who can make you something better."

Hopefully not like yours, Ember thought. Etty's

outfit was unfortunately tight-looking, accentuating the bulges along her sides and causing them to spill out like dough between the top and bottom pieces of hide.

Ember opened her mouth to politely decline.

"Why are you here, anyways?" Etty asked before she could speak. Ember hid her surprise with a frown and began cleaning off the table with a soapy rag.

"I'm looking for my father. He disappeared before I was born. I don't know anything about him, but he might look like me..."

Ember glanced hopefully at Etty, who studied her face while she turned the spit.

"Dark hair like a raven," Etty muttered. She looked away. "I knew someone with that hair once. Gone now. Come here and give this a turn. Don't burn it now, keep it moving."

Etty grabbed the bucket of turkey parts and left the cave, calling Jasper with a shout as she did so.

The heat of the fire burned Ember's skin, and soon she was panting and sweating in an effort to keep the turkey turning. *I mustn't burn it,* she thought desperately, thinking of the shifters who had looked at her when she arrived, and the ones who hadn't.

She tried not to think of the man with hair like a raven.

CHAPTER TWENTY

RIGGS LOOKED UP when Ember came down the steps to his hovel. A fire crackled in the center of the space, shedding yellow light on the ground where Riggs had spread out his healing implements. In the darkest spot of the hovel, Kitt slept on a low cot beneath the watchful gaze of Norman, who perched above him.

"I have just given him a tincture," Riggs said, waving for her to enter.

Ember closed the door to the hovel and stepped into the warm breath that exuded from the fire. She set down the bucket she carried, full of water. The rain from her sodden dress pooled on the packed dirt floor and steamed in the heat.

"A bit late for a swim, isn't it?" Riggs asked, amused.

"It's pouring out. Do you mind if I stay here tonight?"

Riggs grinned. "Stay as long as you wish, but be forewarned. People will talk."

"But you're a healer," Ember said, smiling. "Surely women sleep here when they're ill."

"Are you ill?"

Ember grinned and lifted a foot. Two days without shoes left her feet muddy, scraped, and bloody. She wished they would callus so she could walk like a wolf or a cougar through the mountains.

Riggs made a *tisking* noise with his tongue. "Too ill to walk, I suppose?"

"Most definitely."

Ember settled next to Riggs, relishing the fire's heat as it dried her soaked dress. Riggs' hovel, it had turned out, was farther from the kitchens than she had thought, and she hadn't been able to avoid the sudden rainstorm. After that muddy sprint and a long day in the kitchens—where she had discovered the kitchen staff here to be just as chatty as the kitchen staff at Silverglen—the quiet, embracing warmth of Riggs' hovel was a welcome solace.

"Does he still have a fever?" Ember asked as she began washing her tender feet in the bucket of water.

"Not anymore. He needs to sleep though. He'll have to rest longer than he'll like."

"Perhaps you can slip some ellium tincture into his soup," Ember suggested.

Riggs laughed, though Ember could sense the slight tension in his voice and the way he leaned over his tools, not quite looking near her.

"I'm sorry about your knife," she said abruptly.

Riggs' smile died, and the crackling of the fire filled the momentary void of silence.

"It belonged to my father."

Your dead father. Ember hunched over the bucket.

"I would've taken it back if I could, only the Freeze would've been broken."

"You've no need to apologize. You did what you had to do."

"But you need it, don't you?" Ember motioned to the couple of knives that remained in his collection.

He fingered one, which was long and toothed. "We could always use more knives. We have no access to metal here, and no smithies."

Ember, who had been born to the ringing of smithies in Silverglen, stared at Riggs. "No smithies? But how do you...?"

"We use what we have. What we brought when we fled Lach."

Ember winced as she washed the last of the mud from her wounded feet. She could go back to Silverglen, steal a bundle of knives, return here—

No, that would be far too risky. If Fletch had told Arundel what he knew—that Ember was a shifter and had fled—Arundel might well have a trap waiting for her at Silverglen. And no one ever escaped Arundel's traps.

Ember pulled her feet close to the fire. "What about the clans?"

"The mountain clans? They mostly keep to themselves and aren't exactly friendly."

"But you've traded with them before, haven't you?"

"Me? No. Seabird, yes." Riggs shrugged. "But it's Seabird." As if that explained everything.

Ember sighed. "Why were you and Kitt at that burned village then, if not to trade?"

Riggs adjusted a glass vile. "We were looking for survivors. We saw the smoke from camp."

A risky move. Kitt must have guessed that it was either a clan burning out a clan, or a patrol burning out a clan. Either way, exposing themselves for the benefit of a couple clan members seemed like too big of a risk to take, especially for someone like Kitt.

Ember took a leap. "Were you spying?"

Riggs' brows raised. "I am not a spy. I'm a healer," he said, waving a hand over his box and tools.

"Kitt, then," Ember pressed. It fit, somehow. "He's a spy for the faction."

Riggs gave a half-smile of amusement, but said nothing further.

There was more, Ember knew. She watched as Riggs placed his tools back into his box, muttering each name as he set it in its proper place.

A thought struck her.

"You *were* looking for survivors," she stated. "From the raid." Had his father been one of the ones taken?

Riggs' hand paused over a pair of scissors. Then he gave a reluctant nod. "Six of our people went missing during the raid. We assumed the patrol captured them, maybe even killed them. Kitt and the others have been looking, but..."

Ember's throat cinched. She hated thinking how they had likely died by Arundel's hand. "When did it happen?"

Riggs studied a blade of the scissors. "Near the end of winter." He tucked the scissors into the box. "Sixty-five days ago."

Ember could tell that it upset Riggs to speak of it, but she swallowed her words of comfort. She would be surprised if anyone lasted more than a few days in captivity of one of Arundel's patrols. She wouldn't give him false hope.

Riggs packed the rest of his box with tender hands. She wished she had something of her own father, her real one, to touch and hold and cherish.

But that was assuming he was dead.

"Do you know anyone older with hair the color of a raven?"

Startled, Riggs looked up at her and frowned. "Sure, there are several people. There's Nolene, Verena, and Peter—"

"Peter?"

Riggs gave a sheepish grin. "If you mean people with dark hair who might be your father, well, Peter is only ten..."

"That's it then? Three people?"

Riggs frowned. "There's Deon, but he's about our age. There have been others, in the past. Even my father had dark hair."

Ember smiled. "Was he a very good shifter?"

"As good a shifter as he was a healer. By the time he took Kitt in, my father had given up on teaching me about shifting."

"He raised Kitt?"

"As his own, once we found him. Or rather, once Kitt found us." Riggs pulled out a small wide-mouthed jar with a green substance and handed it to her. "An ointment for your feet," he explained.

The cream cooled and soothed her raw skin, and she dabbed it on liberally as Riggs continued his story.

"It was Norman's doing, really. Kitt was fifteen at the time, and though he was older than me by a couple years, he had the silly notion that he could shift into a firebird."

"Was it that silly of a notion?" Ember asked, feeling her face burn. She remembered all the times she had tried herself, only to be drastically disappointed.

Riggs smiled. "It is if you've grown up watching other shifters try again and again only to fail. Firebirds aren't normal animals. They have a bit of Ineoc in their blood."

"Is that what your father taught you?" Her parents made a point of never mentioning any other god beyond Yathe. Arundel, because he laughed at the idea of Ineoc as a god. Salena, because she preferred not to believe there were any gods at all, or at least that they never held sway over her life.

Riggs nodded. "Him and others. So my father found Kitt, trying desperately to become this magical animal, so worn and frustrated with the shifting that he appeared to be a parrot with gray, tattered wings and a croak like a toad. Not even a hint of fire in him. And Norman, all the while, sat perched in a tree up above, looking down at him as if he was the strangest, most hopeless creature he had ever had to deal with."

Ember burst out laughing, and the fire popped and sizzled along with her. On his perch, Norman fluffed his wings and bobbed his head in agreement, his crest fanning open in a brilliant ray of scarlet.

"He shifted back to human form when he noticed my father watching him," Riggs continued. "'You cannot take the form of a firebird,' my father told him. 'They have something that you do not.' Rather than asking my father what that was, Kitt refused to listen and spent the next week trying even harder to turn into a firebird. Once he gave up, he came to my father to ask what exactly it was that the firebird had that he did not.

"My father always had more patience than I. He knew Kitt would come around, and he knew Kitt would learn to listen better, over time."

Ember couldn't imagine anyone more patient than Riggs. "What was his name?"

"Neal. Neal Pitkin."

A soft, kind name. Ember smiled and lay back, wishing she had fresh linens to wrap her feet in. Linens, it seemed, were another rare commodity in the camp. She would have to do without.

The door to the hovel creaked open, and Ember sat up at the unsteady patter of feet on the steps. A young boy with springy brown hair tugged at the hand of a woman not much older than herself, who wore an elegant full-length dress of softened deer-hide and rabbit-lined boots.

Her wide eyes stared unsmiling at Ember as she came to the base of the stairs, and when the boy released her, her hands flew to rest on the bulge of her belly.

"Lexy," Riggs greeted the woman. "You look dry. It must've stopped raining outside."

"It did!" the boy said, the many gaps in his teeth showing in his grin as he rushed to Kitt's side. "Kitt! Wake up, Kitt," he commanded. The boy took hold of Kitt's hand, then his arm, then either side of his face.

"He's sleeping, Vinn. He needs to rest," Riggs said, standing.

Vinn's hands dropped to his side and he looked from Kitt to the bird to Riggs. In a blink, the boy's face collapsed and he was rushing headlong into the pregnant woman's arms.

"He won't wake up, Lexy," the boy sputtered into her leg. "Why won't he wake up?"

The woman said nothing but smoothed a hand over his head.

"He's not feeling well, Vinn," Riggs explained, walking to Kitt's bedside to adjust the blanket.

A shiny eye peeked out from behind the woman's dress. "Is he going to die?"

Riggs shook his head and came to kneel in front of the boy. "He won't die, as long as I can help him. He will be awake tomorrow, and you can come see him then. Okay?"

The boy sniffed and nodded and the woman took his hand to lead him back up the stairs. Ember ignored the feeling that the woman watched her as she closed the door to the hovel.

"Does she speak?" Ember inquired, watching as Riggs laid out a bedroll.

"About as much as Norman does," Riggs said. The firebird cocked his head at the sound of his name.

"And the child, is he Kitt's?"

"Not in blood, no. But in all else, Kitt is like a father to the orphans. You'll see."

Wood cracked and sizzled as the logs in the fire shifted. Embers shimmered between black and orange.

CHAPTER TWENTY-ONE

THE FOLLOWING NIGHT, Ember earned herself guard duty along the perimeter of the camp. Well, at least 'earned' was the word Seabird used, but Ember had the feeling he said it for the benefit of the children nearby while she passed out sweetbread.

A harrowing day of cooking, cleaning, and endless gossip in the kitchens had left Ember too exhausted to shift, so she walked the perimeter on foot, stepping lightly so as not to open the wounds that had begun to heal from Riggs' ointment.

She could make herself some shoes to speed up the healing, but she didn't have any hide, and the idea of hunting...

She shivered.

Besides, she didn't have any weapons, and even if she could find some, she wouldn't use them to hunt.

Arundel's dark, brooding eyes loomed up in her memory, watching her over a strong nose and a wine-filled iron chalice. Oiled leather in her hands, warm and musky, and the sharp cold of the new dagger as she slid it out of the sheath.

The best thing a woman can do is arm herself. She must be prepared for any danger, be able to defeat any enemy.

She had kept Arundel's words as close as the dagger he had given her, though not for the reasons he intended. Far more frightening to Ember than the cruelty of men was the cruelty of those who hated shifters. Torture, death, enslavement. Shifters were animals, beneath normal humans and certainly beneath wizards. The mindset had been pervasive, and had caused the rebellion.

So many had died, Salena had told her. *Your father...*

She had thought Salena would say he was a murderer, that he had been the one to kill them, to lead others to do the same. Now she wondered if her mother had meant Arundel at all.

Ember clenched her hand. She missed her dagger. Missed the security it provided, the strength it gave her. The hilt sturdy and reassuring against her palm.

Weak moonlight streamed through the canopy and tossed shadows along the forest floor.

Fletch was out there, somewhere. She could

imagine him, tall and pale, lurking in the shadow of that great white pine, watching her. Watching the camp.

Ember turned toward the camp, and was surprised to see a distant fire. A gap had formed in the perimeter's Glamours. The rain from the day before had disintegrated a spell, leaving only a couple strands that hung like limpid thread between two sycamore trees.

"The wizards must have missed it this morning," Ember muttered to herself. They had re-worked the perimeter as soon as the rain had stopped, though she had been too busy in the kitchens to help out. Not that they had asked her to.

Using two hands, Ember mended the Glamour as best she could, and walked down the perimeter only to find more inconsistencies in casting. The Glamours spread out patchily, as though a blind man had strung them up, forming a loose, jilting pattern.

She wondered, while she worked, how long it would be before a wizard came close enough to sense the circle of spells, and what would happen when the wizard grew curious enough to venture inside. They needed more weapons. More swords, and archers. They needed a place to retreat to, with solid walls. Ember thought of Silverglen, which burgeoned with traps and Glamours to keep strangers out or to capture them. Even before the rebellion, Silverglen had been impenetrable.

How could the shifters feel safe, out here in the

forest, with only mountains and trees to keep them hidden from patrols? How long did they trust the safety to last?

A twig snapped behind her.

Ember grabbed a stick from the ground and swung around, jagged end pointed up. A pale figure emerged into the moonlight.

"Lexy," Ember breathed. She lowered the point of her stick.

The woman, wearing the same deer-hide dress as before, clutched a bundle to her chest. Her shoes barely made a noise against the twigs and leaves of the forest floor.

"You should go back to camp," Ember said gently, remembering Seabird's instructions to be sure no one went outside the perimeter. "You can't shift."

"I can," Lexy whispered, her eyes dark against milky skin.

"But it would kill the baby," Ember said. When Lexy remained silent, she clenched her jaw. "You wouldn't do it."

"I would," Lexy replied. "If I had to."

Her face looked gaunt in the light of the moon, and the bulge of her stomach was nearly invisible against the shadows. Still, Ember saw strength in the steadiness of her gaze, in the firm set of her mouth.

She offered the bundle to Ember, her two naked arms like slender sycamore branches. "It's not like what I sewed back in Lach, but it's sturdy. I hope you like it."

Ember took the bundle, and soft, velvety deerhide caressed her fingers. Clothes. Garments like the others wore. Warmth blossomed in her chest.

"I don't know how to thank you."

"You don't need to. You are one of us," she said, backing away.

You don't know me. You don't know what I am.

"Is there something I can do? Something you need or want?"

"You are already doing me a favor." Lexy motioned to the gap where Ember had been mending the Glamour, and turned away.

So she did see me. She knows.

Ember hugged the bundle, the scent of hide tickling her nose, and smiled.

CHAPTER TWENTY-TWO

"OH NO! NO, no..." Ember muttered as she squinted into the small opening of the stone-lined oven. The stench of burnt bread stung her nose. The lump of dough she had carefully placed in there earlier had transformed into a lump of coal.

Cursing, she grabbed the metal prongs and slid the blackened bread off its stone shelf and carried it, smoking, to the counter.

It didn't look edible, not at all, but Ember used a knife to test it anyways. The lump was rock-solid, but she found that with excessive prying, she could reach a bit of softer bread in the very middle. Dry and crumbly, but maybe edible. Soaked in broth.

"What are you doing?" a shrill voice asked from behind.

Wymer.

Ember whirled with her knife in hand.

"I'm making sure the bread is cooked," Ember said through gritted teeth. Wymer always had to be snooping around her in the kitchen. He waited for her to make a mistake, as though gathering evidence to prove she never worked in the kitchens back in Lach.

Wymer, bony and already balding at his young age, ignored the knife in her hand. He held a wooden tray with a bowl of steaming stew, no doubt confident enough that she would never actually use the knife and risk spilling the stew. He looked around her at the bread and snorted. "More food wasted, I see. That loaf was worth more than one of your fingers."

"I didn't mean to burn it," Ember put in, raising her chin a notch and hoping he couldn't see the heat burning up her face.

"Of course you didn't. A broom is more mindful than you. You even managed to overcook the squirrel," Wymer added, scowling to where the squirrel sat motionless on the spit. The squirrel looked shriveled and dry. "Stringy by now, I'll bet." He shoved the tray at her. "Etty wants you to take this to Seabird. Quickly."

She took the tray, trying not to slop the stew out of the bowl, and walked to the mouth of the cave. Etty was dressing a small boar that had been brought in by one of the shifters, to be cooked over the fire the rest of the afternoon for supper. It would be a lean meal, as they usually were, with the stores from the past winter gone and spring barely beginning to slip into summer.

A few others helped Etty, and one other churned milk into butter.

But where had the milk come from?

Ember opened her mouth to ask, but just then Etty noticed her.

"Leave it at his door. Before it gets cold," Etty snapped, shooing her away with a wave of her hand.

Sternness in her voice, but a sort of kindness in her eyes. She was giving Ember an easy task, one she knew Ember was capable of. One a five-year-old child would be capable of. *She knows I never worked in a kitchen.* Ember swallowed and walked out of the cave, expertly balancing the tray as she crossed the stream.

The heat from the fire gone, her bare legs felt cool in the breeze. Well, not entirely bare legs, but they might as well be. Lexy's garment, though different from Etty's in that it was one piece rather than two, was a bit too short for comfort and left her shoulders and arms exposed to the wind and sun, not to mention eyes. But the hide was soft and pliable, giving way easily to any movement. The dress allowed her skin to breath, as it hugged her loosely, and was held up by a small knot gathered above her left shoulder. Overall, a clever design for someone who had to shift quickly. She would have to find a way to thank Lexy.

The sound of children's laughter arose like a chorus from a small clearing in the forest. Careful of the tray, Ember peered through the trees. Twenty children, of all ages, gathered around a log. Were they all orphans?

"Can anyone tell me why the tree owl is brown? Why is it important for them to be brown?"

Kitt's voice, in a tone that made him almost unrecognizable. She moved forward a few steps and saw him sitting on a log, his wounded leg propped straight out, and a cane resting beside him.

"So he can be like a tree!" one child said, raising his arms to mimic branches.

One of the older girls scoffed. "Owls are colored like the bark so their prey won't see them."

"That's exactly right, Loria," said Kitt. "And how can you and I use that ability to hide, besides for hunting?"

A breath of silence, and then Loria muttered, "To hide from patrols."

"Exactly. If you see any stranger, or group of strangers, you shift to an owl and fly up to the highest tree. That's how we stay safe."

With a scowl, Loria spun away and strode off into the main camp. Kitt watched her for a moment, and Ember longed to see his expression. The girl was clearly upset with him, but why?

"Now, I want you all to practice hiding," Kitt continued, waving his cane up toward the canopy. "I won't be able to find you today, but you can choose a partner to do that. Away with you!"

He playfully poked his cane at them, and the group of children exploded into a storm of feathers and claws. They dispersed into the trees, and in a blink had all but disappeared.

Ember couldn't stop a smile from tugging her lips.

Until Kitt stood and saw her.

She moved her eyes to the ground and continued along her course to Seabird's hovel.

"Ember."

Suspicion in his voice, still, and weariness.

Ember slowed, and came to a stop as the unsteady sound of his limp grew close.

"I'm going to Seabird's," Ember said before he could speak. She wondered if he would try to taste the soup for poison.

He came up to her, his face drawn and pale. He glanced at the soup, a frown balanced above green eyes the shade of moss, and looked away toward the kitchen.

"I can't hunt in this state," he stated. Anger, not directed at her, pinched his face. "Do you think there's enough extra food for a meal?"

If it hadn't been for his serious wound, she'd have given him a tart reply. And if it hadn't been for the fact that she'd burned the bread. Ember dipped her head. "Of course. Etty always makes plenty for the children." The children, Etty had informed her, who weren't yet allowed to hunt. Once they reached the age of ten, they were given a guide to teach them. By age thirteen, they could hunt alone. After that, most of them fed themselves, just as the adults did. Hence why Kitt and Riggs had given her such funny looks when she dug around in Riggs' pack for food, before they came to camp. Hence why Kitt's question made her feel just a little bit smug.

"Good," he said, and turned to go.

She should let him go, leave him and his suspicions alone. Curiosity snagged her.

"That girl, Loria."

Kitt stopped and leaned on his cane, a part of his profile visible to her. The part with the flash of silver hair that didn't belong.

The question that had been burning in her heart was stuck there, and suddenly she couldn't put it in words.

Kitt poised there, waiting in silence, or perhaps giving silence in his answer for the question he knew she asked. Ember had a feeling it was the latter. She sighed. She could figure it out on her own, later, if she really wanted to.

"I'm glad to see that you're doing better," she heard herself say. Was she glad? She looked back at where the children played hide-and-go-seek in the clearing.

Yes, she was glad.

Kitt twitched his head. A nod? His mouth remained unsmiling, his expression tight.

She clutched the tray and continued her trek to Seabird's hovel, only relaxing when she heard Kitt's limping walk trailing away from her.

Seabird's hovel was the second largest after the children's hovel—or the orphan's hovel, as some called it—and was situated next to a giant slab of stone. Each hovel had some significant marker recognized by those living in the camp, marking where the hovels and doors were. It was necessary, given the abundance of Glamours. Seabird's door lay to the right of the stone, smothered in strong Glamours that made the door appear to be a thicket of brambles.

And smothered in a Silencing spell.

Ember's pulse quickened.

The spells could be for privacy, Ember reasoned, remembering how Asenath had kissed his cheek that first day. But it could be for something else.

She set the tray down at the base of the stone, just outside the hatch door, and glanced around the woods.

A few milled by the river, bathing or washing clothes and dishes. Others gathered by the kitchen to eat, or to take a nap in the sun. Kitt was nowhere to be seen.

Ember tiptoed around the hovel's roof, which she could just make out beneath dense layers of Glamours. The smoke-hole showed evidence of being long-forgotten, as dense ferns and grasses clustered around it and the space entirely lacked spells. Ember bent close and closed her eyes against the stinging smoke that puffed from the opening.

"...lost contact with her after the last attack on the camp..."

Seabird's voice, low and soft. Perhaps she would be able to hear better as a mouse—

"...linked with the burned village?"

Asenath. Was this some sort of meeting, or idle talk?

"...very possible... Kitt and Riggs saw patrols searching the remains."

"...too dangerous..."

Frustrated, Ember held her breath and shoved her ear over the hole, knees digging into the vegetation. The smoke curled over her face like the dry, hot breath of an old man puffing a pipe.

"It might be a good idea. We would have to negotiate with the clans again, and we don't have much left after the last time. We will be safer further away. I will ask the others what they think." A pause, and the sound of shoes being tossed to the ground. Seabird's voice took on a velvety tone. "In the meantime, let's you and I do some thinking. Both of us should be able to come up with something, don't you think?"

"Ryscford," Asenath sighed with pleasure, "I believe we can come up with something marvelous..."

Ember withdrew, trying to stifle her sputtering cough as smoke worked its way into her lungs.

Ryscford. Seabird. It all made sense now. Seabird was just a nickname, or perhaps a cover, for who he really was. Ryscford Seago was his real name. Ember never knew him, but she knew of him from history classes at the Academy. He had been a rare gem among the Council, a wizard who respected shifters as equals, and who had led the shifters in their rebellion after he was removed from the Council. The commoners at Silverglen who still secretly cared about shifters spoke of him as a hero. A true leader. But it was said he was killed during the rebellion, that his head had been delivered to Lord Arundel's great hall and was seen by the rest of the Council. Proof of his death.

He faked his own death. And now he leads a shifter faction in Orion. Did the shifters know his true identity? Would it matter to them?

A gasp arose from the smoke-hole, and Ember moved away, a blush creeping up her cheeks. She stood, assessed that her surroundings were the same as before—well, except for the crushed fern beneath her—and brushed off her dress.

What she really wished to know was why Ryscford had chosen to lead a faction of shifters. Did he do it to protect them, or did he have a plan in mind? There weren't enough shifters to lead another rebellion, so what then? To hide, perhaps, to grow their numbers.

Whatever the reason, Ember thought as she headed back to the kitchen, *I will find it.*

CHAPTER TWENTY-THREE

AFTER DAYS OF solemnly noticing how most of the shifters bathed in the river at camp—or in their hovels using buckets—Ember could hardly believe her luck upon discovering a hidden waterfall northwest of the camp.

Here, the river twisted between rock outcrops and spilled over the crest of a smoothed boulder, forming a curtain of mirrors and crystals. At its base, the water gathered in a knee-deep pool lined with flat rocks before gushing out the other side to return to a calmer river.

Everything transforms, Ember thought as she soaked in the pool. Even a simple thing like water could alter entire landscapes. *There is power in being able to change things*, her wizard professors had always said. Well, shifters could change things, too, and the change wasn't some silly Glamour formed out of air. She could change the very bones in her body. Surely there was power in that?

Even more odd, Riggs had told her that Ineoc, the god worshiped by many shifters, represented transformations. The firebird was his token symbol. Or *her* symbol, depending on how you saw the deity. Didn't wizards see the significance of that? Ineoc was change, Yathe was everything boring in the world — order, silence, restraint. Anything that wasn't life.

"They see what they want to see," Ember muttered, remembering Lady Dell's reverence for Yathe. Odd that his symbol was the sun, something beautiful and essential to life. It seemed to her that the sun and the firebird should exist together, that order wouldn't exist without the chaos of change. One might balance the other.

Is that what Ryscford had created here? A balance of shifter and wizard? Society had never been that way, as far as Ember knew. They had lived apart, and once together, shifters were deemed inferior and denied rights that wizards were given. They had been treated as servants, pets, and slaves.

The rebellion had begun with Arundel's father, Doune. Salena had told her the story dozens of times, as though afraid the knowledge would be lost if she didn't.

Not lost, but twisted.

Ember ran her fingers through her hair,

untangling the strands in the water.

Over the years, people blamed Arundel for starting the rebellion, but really it had started with Doune's abusiveness. Violent and temperamental, Salena had told her. His shifters were slaves. Once, he hunted one who had escaped. When he found his shifter, Doune killed him, causing the shifters' mate—a raging hawk—to attack and blind him.

This spurred Arundel to action. He sought out the shifter who had blinded his father, and while he was away from home, the mate found her way to Arundel's mother. A servant later found his mother's body, gutted and faceless.

Shifters were dangerous. Arundel had never used those words exactly; it would have shown he was afraid. But to Ember, wizards were just as treacherous. Who knew what had happened in Arundel's dungeons?

Ember shivered and made her way out of the pool, letting the air clear her mind.

She was growing fond of the sun touching her skin. Exhilarating. Wholesome. The breeze, warm now that it was midday, found every curve and crevice. An intimate touch she used to cringe at in human form.

Thanks to Lexy's dress, she felt more comfortable with the exposure. Preferred it, even. Her arms and legs had tanned, her feet had formed calluses. She had come to appreciate the soft looseness of the deer-hide dress, which gave her more freedom for shifting than her trousers and cotton shirt at Silverglen.

Silverglen.

She tried not to think of it as she bent to pick up her make-shift spear. She had formed it from a stick, and had whittled the end to a sharp point using one of Riggs' knives. Just below the tip and at the blunt end, she had bound two stones for weight and balance.

She missed the food, and not having to prepare it. She missed Finn, too, and Gregory. Most of all, she missed her weapons.

She didn't miss Arundel. She didn't miss her suffocating room, or her sister's dreadful antics. Silverglen and the Academy were a dungeon compared to this...

Trees and ribbons of blue sky. Mountains. Sparkling rivers, the scent of moss, and children's laughter.

She could be happy here. Free. If only the patrols weren't there, somewhere. If only she knew there wasn't someone looking for her, that they weren't all hiding.

Kneeling on the ground, she bent over the spear and concentrated on creating a one-handed Freezing spell. It was simple, something she had been doing for years. Why not try a two-handed spell? A combination of Freezing and Blinding.

She took a deep breath and began, wracking her memory for each twist and pinch of the fingers, every flick of the fourth or fifth fingers that commanded the air. Casting the spell was like trying to play Finn's harpsichord, with different hand positions producing entirely different sounds. To her chagrin, she had discovered that she had as much trouble playing the harpsichord as she had casting spells. At least until Finn's lessons.

She finished the spell with a quick weave of her hands, and bound it to the spear point.

There.

She held up the spear, hardly seeing the spell in the sunlight, and sensed that she had cast it decently well.

Nothing that would impress Professor Nels. She certainly did not miss her churlish, often volatile spells-master.

"He can take his pig-nose and shove it into a pile of dung for all I care," Ember declared. Finn's words, not her own. She had been trying to keep her silly, childish tears at bay while he strode up and down her room at the Academy, his mop of hair beating his head with each step.

"It's not right that he should treat you this way," Finn fumed. "He wouldn't dare give me such a low score, even on a bad day."

"But I'm terrible at it, Finn," Ember croaked. A tear squeezed out, and she flicked it away. "I'll never come close to your abilities. I'll never graduate—"

Finn halted and kneeled in front of her. "Of course you'll graduate. Don't be silly. I'll help you, if it would make you feel better. But no matter how poorly you do on these stupid examinations, you'll always be a wizard."

And a shapeshifter. Her throat ached to tell him. Instead, she sniffed and gave him a half-smile. "Unless I get my hands cut off."

A little joke, but Finn shook his head and grasped her hands. "Only the worst criminals deserve that punishment. You are far too kind and gentle, Ember."

And you are far too good a brother to deserve my lies. She swallowed against the burning in her throat. "Want to go Glamour the bathroom stalls with Professor Nel's pig-nose?"

Finn grinned. "Maybe not as kind as I thought. Of course I want to."

Ember smiled at the memory. She only wished Salena had reacted as Finn did, with comfort and confidence in her.

A shadow flitted over her shoulders.

With arm raised, she turned to see a pair of wings flashing open against the sky. An immense hawk swung from a head-first dive into open-taloned attack, as if catching a mouse, only—

The hawk latched to her raised arm like bait, its pointed talons knifing into her flesh. The hawk beat its wings once, twice, and Ember thrust her spear between them with a cry, aiming for a non-lethal blow. Her arm was released, and the hawk disappeared into the canopy above.

Ember crouched, spear pointed above her head, unable to stop herself from trembling. Not because she fought another animal; she had done that before, in the forests of Merewood, never killing anything but always escaping in the end. But she couldn't run from the shifters.

She had nowhere else to go.

Ember watched from every side, her eyes sharpening on any leaf that shivered.

The hawk loomed in one of the openings above, its bulk nearly black against the sky. Wings snapped closed and it dove at her.

Ember shifted her stance. If she tilted the spear to the side, she could hit the hawk and knock it out, or at least Freeze and Blind it with the tip—

A falcon streaked in from above and pummeled into the hawk. Feathers exploded, and the hawk spun off-kilter. The falcon whipped around Ember, its wings beating as fast as her heart, and thrust itself into the hawk again, this time swirling into a hawk and pulling them both to the ground.

More feathers flew as they rolled. In a blink, they were a pair of cougars, beige fur rippling in the sunlight and lips pulled back from bone-white fangs reaching for the throat. One found the other's neck.

ROAR!

They whirled into bears, standing nearly twice as high as Ember on their hind feet.

Ember crept behind a thick tree, intent on staying

out of the way. Her spear felt slick in her hands.

A moment later they were at each other's throats, clinging to whatever they could grab as they pushed against one another, and the sound of their breathing rumbled like thunder over the quiet hush of the river.

In a blink, they were wolves, snarling and baring sharp canines. Ember was sure she saw a glint of red among the gray coats. One pounced on the other, jaws clamping hard enough on the neck to cause the other to yip.

The sound sent shivers down Ember's spine.

The weaker wolf was forced to the ground, belly exposed. The other gave a vicious shake before backing off.

The defeated wolf snapped into human form, kneeling and gasping on the ground. Ember recognized her as the shifter who lived in the hovel next to Riggs. She wiped the smear of blood from her throat with a trembling hand and stood. Straight as a stick, she had narrow hips and skin the color of sandstone. Ekesian. Her hair, a slightly darker shade, fell to her bloodied nape, and piercings covered her brows and ears. A single gem of black, like a moonless night, glinted just beneath her lower lip.

The other wolf shifted, and Ember's heart banged against her chest.

Kitt. He had a few scrapes, but what drew her attention was the swollen wound on his leg. He bent over and gasped for breath, looking as pale and exhausted as the woman. He had ripped his stitches.

Glowering, Ember stalked out from behind the tree and grabbed her deer-hide dress, turning away from the two as she tugged it over her wet body.

"You're a wizard," the Ekesian woman accused, and Ember turned to see her spit blood to the ground. "I saw you doing a spell."

"I'm a shifter," Ember stated, tightening the loose garment with a quick knot over her shoulder. "And I'm capable of protecting myself," she added to Kitt, picking up her short spear.

The Ekesian woman scoffed. "I could've easily killed you if I wanted—"

"Enough, Jinni." Kitt glared at the Ekesian woman, who scowled back. "She's part of the camp now, for better or worse."

"So you're on the wizard's side, now?" The woman sneered. "Fancy a fuck with her, do you?"

Kitt made a move to lunge at her, but the woman only grinned. Heat burned up Ember's cheeks. She scowled at the both of them, her nails digging into the wood of her spear.

"You knew she was a wizard, then," Jinni continued. "She's kept it secret, but why not from you?"

Kitt gave her a grim look, but said nothing.

"The others in the camp won't like it. You know that. It'll make them wonder...what else is she keeping secret?"

Two brown eyes, of a shade that competed with

black, confronted hers.

Ember straightened her back and raised her chin, angling the spear tip toward her just enough to suggest a threat. She poised her face to hard stone.

Before Kitt could reply, Jinni swirled into a crow and flew off, her raucous caws sounding like bitter laughter.

"I think she hates wizards more than you," Ember said, eying Kitt's wound. "She was forced to watch as they killed her mother."

Kitt frowned. "It's rude to eavesdrop."

That is what I do. "I was not raised to think so."

"The rules are different here." He met her gaze, and, remembering the etiquette Etty taught her, Ember averted her eyes.

"I wasn't keeping it a secret. Being a wizard, I mean. You knew, and Riggs, and Rys—Seabird," she corrected. Did Kitt know who their leader really was? What was it Riggs had said once, when she first met them, that the patrols might recognize Seabird? "And I've done other spells out in the open. I know at least one other has seen it."

"The shifters appreciate transparency. Many, like Jinni, are suspicious."

Like you.

"If you insist on being a wizard," said Kitt, "the only way you'll survive here is by learning to fight as an animal."

"I know how to fight. I can defend myself." She

raised her spear. "This is tipped with a Freeze and a Blinding spell. It should stop a bear in its tracks."

"Should," Kitt repeated skeptically. "But what if a shifter changes from a bear to a snake in the last instant? Quickly enough to strike you with a lethal dose of venom?"

Ember remembered the speed with which Jinni and Kitt had shifted, how they had matched each other in pace and nearly in strength. Doubt flickered through her.

"You underestimate my abilities with a weapon," Ember retorted. He underestimated all the wizard's abilities. How did he think the wizards had stopped the rebellion?

"I can see that you need more practice," Kitt said, lifting a thick brow and motioning to Ember's bloodied arm. "You wizards have your tricks and tools, but shifters have their strengths, too. How do you think we are all still here, after the rebellion?" he asked, his words mirroring her own thoughts.

Perhaps because the wizards have been hiding you, she wanted to say. But that was unfair, and beyond the point. She was a shifter, and to belong here as a shifter, she needed to do what other shifters did. And, she thought with a shudder, she didn't want to be caught without a weapon again. Like when Kitt had pounced on her. He was too fast, by far.

"How do I learn to fight like an animal?"

"You learn by doing. I will help."

Ember flushed and shook her head. "But you're injured—"

Kitt waved the worry away like an annoying fly. "I'll heal soon. We can start with the basics, tomorrow."

He began to walk away.

"Why are you helping me?" she asked in an emotionless tone. Too soon for him to trust her, and an impossibility that he no longer hated her.

For a moment she thought he wouldn't answer, but then he paused in his limping gait.

"I'm tired of shifters dying," he said.

He left, the sun and leaves playing hide and seek along his back and shoulders and the breeze lifting clumps of his ruffled hair. His hands were fists at his sides.

Ember watched him go, barely able to catch her breath. She had expected the truth from him; hadn't he been honest with her from the first? She just hadn't expected that particular truth.

A truth that made her wonder what he had seen during the rebellion, and what he had gone through afterwards.

And it meant he no longer wanted to kill her. That was progress, wasn't it?

CHAPTER TWENTY-FOUR

Metallic clanging beat the air with its rhythm. An inhuman heartbeat.

But he wasn't inhuman. He was her father. Tall, broad-shouldered, and strong. The summer sun warmed her shoulders where she sat watching him hammer a bar of iron. Would he make her a toy? Or something pretty for Mother?

She loved the way the sparks glowed as they danced before fizzling out. Loved the way her father would sometimes stop, and smile at her, or give her cheek a playful nudge with a blackened knuckle. She giggled and asked when she would learn how to make things out of iron.

It takes strength and endurance, he said.

I am strong, she replied, unsure what endurance meant.

And you will be stronger when you're older, he said, then raised a great hand to tousle her hair.

Mother called and she ducked away, glancing behind to see her father lifting his hammer over the red iron again, a look in his eyes she didn't recognize then. A pinched sort of anger that made her chest heavy.

But Mother's cool hand wrapping around hers made her forget, and the clanging grew distant as they left the smithy.

CHAPTER TWENTY-FIVE

*S*URPRISE IS ESSENTIAL, Kitt had said, *and quickness. Always go by your gut feeling. Not all dangerous creatures are big and strong. Sometimes you surprise yourself.*

Well, she certainly had.

Ember lumbered toward Kitt, her back heavy from the weight of a tortoise's shell, her limbs curled and strong. Perhaps a tortoise wasn't the most ferocious of animals to start with, but she felt better having a shell to retreat to if the fight started to get out of hand. She was fairly certain Kitt wouldn't attack her as he had before. Would he?

The tortoise's natural instincts took over, and she raised her neck, beak open, poised like a snake ready to strike.

Be sure about your attacker's intentions, she heard

Kitt say again. *You must trust your senses.*

He waited as a smaller tortoise, his head high and tilted so as to watch her movements.

She lunged at his exposed neck, only to miss as he suddenly reared up. Using his shell as leverage, she clawed her way up to meet him, certain that she could tip the balance with her heavier weight. His beak found her throat and she pushed him back with her front claws, digging her rear claws deep into the humus of the forest floor. The balance tipped, and she was winning, her powerful limbs causing him to topple—

The resistance disappeared. A fierce raccoon rushed at her face, his black mask wrinkled in a snarl.

Ember squeezed into her shell, heart hammering. The raccoon couldn't get to her in there, she knew, but that wasn't the purpose of the lesson.

With regret, Ember shifted to a raccoon, vulnerable for the half-second it took for her to catch her bearings.

Sharp hearing, sensitive nose, lithe movement.

Before she knew what was happening, Kitt pounced on her, his teeth like pins on her neck. She screamed in frustration and clawed at him, trying not to do real damage.

Until his teeth sank deeper. Enough to draw blood.

Twisting, outraged, she shifted to a squirrel.

A dart squirrel, smaller and quicker than a raccoon. With a rattling chatter, she gave the raccoon's arm a snappy bite and leapt away, then scaled the rough trunk of a chestnut tree up into the canopy.

She needed a moment alone, a few seconds to settle her—

A sharp tug on her tail, and she whirled, chattering ferociously at the chick-sparrow that had crept up behind her. He chirped back, puffing up so that he was nearly the same size as her, and scowled out of one beady black eye.

Ember shifted yet again, nearly falling off the chestnut limb in her haste to re-orient.

A dulled sense of smell was drowned by an incredible scheme of colors, brilliant shades that held no human name.

Light and quick, she had no trouble darting away when Kitt dove at her. She landed on a sycamore here, a tag alder there, unable to help a nervous titter each time Kitt caught up with her. He was fast, and seemed to know where she would land almost as soon as she did.

She settled with an infuriated squawk on a fallen silk tree.

Another sparrow answered. SQUAWK!

She fluttered around to find Kitt behind her.

And a hoard of other chick-sparrows, watching her as they might watch an unwanted jay-bird. Ember fluffed her feathers, dread washing over her.

Did he expect her to withstand being mobbed? Chick-sparrows were relatively small, but terribly vicious if they felt they were being threatened. Like they did now. By her.

In a blink, Kitt flew toward her, and a great noise of chirping and beating wings burgeoned into the air.

Ember shifted, forcing her body to change with so much haste that vertigo gripped her, and she doubled over, clenching her throat against her rising breakfast.

She panted, reciting her mantra with every breath: *Reasoning, intellect, planning...*

"It gets better, you know."

Ember tried, and failed, not to twitch like a bird at the sudden voice. The man who had spoken to her appeared a bit older than Kitt, with fine black hair that covered stomach and chest before creeping up to hide half his face in a thick beard. Even with the beard and his face turned away from her, she could still see his smile.

"Deon," Kitt exclaimed from behind her. "Glad to see you're back."

Kitt, his deer-hide skirt back on, strode to meet his friend, and gripped his shoulder with a grin.

Saying nothing, Ember reached for her dress and pulled it on.

"And I'm glad to see you walking about again. If it weren't for the stitches, I'd think nothing had ever happened," Deon said, his teeth stark against the black of his beard.

Deon was right; Kitt was far more energetic

today than he had been the day before, which had only made Ember feel more tired than she already was from staying up half the night guarding camp.

"Did you find anything?" Kitt asked in a lowered voice.

Weariness forgotten, Ember reached for her spear and stood, watching as Deon's smile slid into a frown.

"No. The trail was days old, as you told us. We lost it on the river. They're being careful, probably hiding under spells."

"They know we're still alive," Kitt said, his face grim. "They'll likely keep searching, if they don't get lost in the mountains. We'll have to be extra careful. Only leave camp in groups of three. Someone will always have to scout."

Deon nodded, then glanced warily at Ember before continuing. "I've another message. Seabird wants to see you. He looked troubled."

Kitt's mouth twisted, and he snapped, "When does he not?" He looked away with a quick release of breath. "Alright," he said apologetically, with a look that Deon didn't meet. "I'll come, once I'm finished here."

Deon raised a brow and gave Ember a curious look before dipping his head in acknowledgment. "I will let Seabird know," he said to Kitt, and then, to her, "You're lucky to have the best teacher in camp." He winked.

Heat rushed up Ember's neck.

"My thanks," Kitt said with a small smile.

Without so much as an introduction, Kitt let Deon walk away.

Ember tried to smooth her bristling feathers before remembering she didn't have any. *Planning and intellect,* she continued her mantra sternly, as she had done hundreds of times before. *Reasoning and problem-solving.* Human. *Introducing strangers when they meet. Civility.* Ember took a calming breath and forced her scowl to disappear.

"Are you part of a council, then?" she asked Kitt. Satisfied, she watched as he turned, the surprise in his face quickly hidden by suspicion and a scornful twitch of his lip.

"No." He walked toward her, hardly a limp in his step. "You need to learn how to suppress the nausea," he said, as though continuing with a conversation they had had earlier.

Ember quirked an eyebrow. *Easier said than done.* "Of course," she replied tartly. Then, as casually as possible, "Did you know Ryscford is thinking of moving camp further north?"

Kitt halted, his face tight and bloodless, gaze sharpened on her.

"Who told you? Or is it something you learned by eavesdropping again?" Another twitch of contempt, and a new gleam of anger as carmine pricked his cheeks.

"The latter," Ember admitted. "He grows worried

of the camp's safety."

"Hiding deeper in the mountains will not be safer for the camp. Clans are scattered everywhere, moving with the seasons—" he stopped, realizing who he was arguing with.

"But the camp isn't safe here," Ember pressed. "You have no walls, hardly any weapons. The spells won't keep the patrols out forever—"

Kitt scowled and took a step toward her. "We would have no problem with patrols if *you*," he jabbed a finger toward her chest, "had killed that wizard. But you left him out there, so he could search for us and bring other wizards to help."

She couldn't keep the anger from her tone. "Killing wizards won't stop them from coming, and it certainly won't make wizards think any better of shifters."

Fire lit the moss of Kitt's eyes, and his lips pulled back in a snarl. "I don't give a damn what the wizards think."

Murder in his eyes again. Arundel's look.

"Is that why you wish for us to stay here, then? So you can find and kill wizards? We should go deeper into the mountains, find a place with solid walls, or build—"

"Enough!" Livid, red-faced, Kitt ran a hand over his stubbly face before bringing his arms down to his sides. Methodical. Controlled. His shoulders and torso were tense, as still as the face of the mountain. A cougar ready to pounce.

Ember crossed her arms, barely holding back a tongue-full of scathing words.

"Don't presume to know me, wizard-shifter," he said in a low voice. "We all have reasons for our actions. Even you." His eyes bored into her. "You always push for the truth. You dig and dig, but you run from what you find."

Her first instinct was to deny it. Her pulse throbbed in her throat as she forced herself to hold Kitt's gaze, to see his dislike and distrust. To see that he held something away from her, like most people did, and to feel a curiosity, more than she ever had before, of what it was he protected so fiercely.

So she would stay. And she wouldn't run.

The tension in his shoulders eased minutely. "I'm going to meet with our wizard leader. You need to practice shifting quickly. As quickly as you can. Suppress the nausea," he reminded her. The anger was already pulling away from his face, though she could still see it in the way he moved, his limbs rigid as he stomped away.

Likely to cause a fight with Seabird. She longed to watch, but made herself think of a shape instead. And another, and another.

Swirling, whirling with each shape, she swayed against the ground as a snake, hopped as a rabbit, dug into the humus as a badger, before giving up all activities. Otter, deer, cougar, wolf, bear—

Going from small to big stretched her body to the point of exhaustion. She dropped back in human form, on all fours and heaving up what remained of breakfast.

Reasoning and intellect, she reminded herself through the dizzy haze of her mind. She wiped her mouth and crawled away from the smelly, wet heap of vomit. *Planning...*

She would do it again, only this time there wouldn't be any breakfast left to lose.

CHAPTER TWENTY-SIX

Even here, riding high on the rays of the setting sun, she could make out smoke from the shifter camp. She should be glad that wizards couldn't fly and see for themselves. From the ground, the smoke would be less visible because of the dense vegetation and the immense slopes that hid them.

Ember pressed her tail feathers down, sinking into the forested gap between mountains where the camp sprawled, half-hidden in glamours, along the river.

She was weary, not only from the morning she had spent tending the small vegetable garden, or from taking on ten different animal forms in half a minute—which had resulted in vomiting, but only once, and briefly—but from the constant searching she had done with any spare time. Deon and others had searched already, yes, but she had searched for days longer, and in all directions of both the burned village and the old tree where she and Kitt had hid. She searched to spy, in hopes that at some point the wizards would have to speak to each other about their plans. Patrols didn't just wander around looking for shifters. They had missions, given to them by Arundel or another member of the Council.

She wanted answers to her questions. Were they looking for her? Had Arundel and Salena sent out more patrols upon discovering that their daughter was missing?

A thought struck her. Arundel might believe she was stolen by shifters. Revenge by those whom he hurt.

Ember shuddered after landing on a thick branch, her feathers quivering and fluffing before smoothing down again.

She shouldn't assume the worst. Besides, she hadn't found sign of Fletch, or any other wizard, and that was good, wasn't it?

She peered at the undergrowth beneath the canopy, which had darkened considerably once the sun had sunk behind the western mountain. She spotted her dress where she had left it, a bundle tucked beneath a thick root of a hickory tree, her spear nestled inside it.

With a quick flap and a skillful swoop, she landed next to it and shifted, forcing herself to begin re-orienting to her human form before the transformation completed, a method Kitt had taught her. She would solidify faster that way, and her senses would stabilize quicker because of it. It was a different way of shifting, a deeper exercise of her mental control than what she was used to. Less reactionary. More focused intent.

And it was becoming habitual, she thought with a grim smile as she pulled on her dress and knotted it above her left shoulder. With patrols potentially after her, and hateful shifters, she may have need of speedier shifting.

Darkness seeped into the camp, signaling the beginning of her guard duty. The spells glinted silver at night, and she made out several holes in the glamour along the perimeter of camp. She tried a one-handed spell first before digging into the more difficult two-handed spells, trying to remember the details from her spells-class that she had failed to remember for her practicum.

Ember smiled. Dev, no doubt, would have no issue with the glamours. She'd want to make the glamour into some sensual fortress, complete with fountain and rose-covered arcades.

Her smile faltered. Dev would never believe what Ember did now, hiding a camp with glamours. She wouldn't believe Ember was capable of it. She could just imagine Dev giving a half-smile as though Ember told a joke, and tilting her head at Ember like she did at Professor Nel's scrawny, three-legged lapdog.

Ember shuddered and shook her head to clear the webs of memory from her mind. She shouldn't care what Dev would say. It didn't matter anymore, now that she was part of the shifter camp. What did matter was that she was doing what she could to help, even if it was as silly as Glamour spells. The spells were one of the only defenses they had.

She squinted at her current Glamour, two silvery strands looped like an elegant necklace from a chestnut branch to that of a dogwood laden with white flowers, effulgent against the dark. She pressed her nose into the blossoms, pulling the sweet scent down into her belly. A warm, comforting scent that reminded her of Gregory. She plucked a flower off and tucked it behind her ear, humming as she searched along the perimeter for more holes.

Leaves rustled ahead.

Ember squatted behind a sunberry shrub and watched for movement. At first she saw nothing beyond the pale gleam of the perimeter's Glamour, but then she caught a glimpse of movement low to the ground.

A wolf. Or rather, many wolves, trotting silently away from camp. South. She watched, hardly daring to breath, as she made out one pair of ears after another. One of those pairs glinted along the edges, as though lined with earrings.

Jinni?

She led a group of seven, moving as naturally as

a true-born wolf. They moved like shadows through the ferns and mayflowers, liquid dark against pale-limbed sycamores and fallen ash trees. In a few moments, they were gone.

Ember stood, longing to follow them.

A tall figure appeared where the wolves had come from and stopped just outside the perimeter, watching in the direction the wolves had gone.

"They go to hunt," said Seabird in an unhappy tone. He wore his leather jerkin decorated with strips of fox fur above baggy pants.

"You don't want them to hunt?"

"It's not the hunting, but where they go after the hunt," he said.

"Why don't you stop them? You're our leader." She turned back to her spell-work so as not to appear too interested.

"I cannot control them," Seabird said with a smile in his voice. He walked to where she stood, assessing the Glamour with black eyes. "As a leader, I'm here to protect the camp, not force people against their will."

Ember's eyebrows rose. "That's surprising to hear from someone who used to be on the Council."

Seabird hid his own surprise well. "So you know who I am. Good. But as I've told others, you should continue calling me by my false name."

"People still speak of you, back in Lach," she said as though she hadn't heard him. "They call you a martyr."

He lifted his hands to help her patch the Glamour. He couldn't see the strands as she could, so his spells overlapped other spells and sometimes left large gaps. "The Council had to believe me dead. Otherwise, they would've kept looking. They knew they would succeed in stopping the rebellion if they killed me."

"The man whose head you sent," Ember said, no longer hiding her curiosity. "Did you kill him?"

Seabird froze mid-spell, his face hard. Ember wondered, fleetingly, if she had gone too far. "He died on the battlefield like a true soldier. He fought bravely for what he believed in, as foolish as those beliefs were."

The tightness in his voice was familiar. She had heard so many others like him, and she knew the tone whether she was a mouse or a bird or a human. A heavy knot of shame, pride, and above all, love.

"He was your brother," she heard herself say. She held her breath when he looked at her, his gaze a reflection of the night sky.

"Sometimes we must make painful choices for the good of others. Sometimes," he added, "it is a matter of killing rather than being killed. Neither are easy."

Her throat cinched, and she went back to methodically casting Glamours. Her limbs trembled with the urge to shift into a bird and fly far away from this man who killed his own brother. But she remembered, all too clearly, Kitt's accusation. She wouldn't run away. She couldn't.

"How are you getting along in camp?" Seabird asked, the deep toll of his voice carrying the grief away. He turned back to his own meandering spell-work.

How could he move away from his grief so easily?

"Well," Ember lied. Truthfully, not a day went by that she didn't get reprimanded in the kitchen. Out of everyone there, Asenath was the only one who hadn't scolded her for a mistake.

Did Asenath know about Seabird's brother?

"And have you found your father?"

The question took her by surprise. She hadn't spared a thought about her real father in the last two days.

"No," she said, her tone edged in frustration. "No one seems to know anything about him."

Seabird nodded, grim. "We've lost so many over the years. And more during the attack on camp."

"Like the healer?" Ember put in, remembering Riggs speaking highly of his father. Had the man been killed, or had Arundel taken him to his dungeon? Ember repressed a shudder.

"He was a good man," Seabird said with a nod. "He did well raising Riggs and Kitt." He eyed her with sudden concern. "I hear Kitt is giving you lessons. Are they going well?"

Was anything going well? "I've just had one so

far." She hesitated before saying, as casually as possible, "He told me you are considering moving camp further from Lach." She squinted at her current spell, simple and short, as though she didn't strain to hear his answer.

"And he informed me that you stabbed a wizard without killing him," he said in a tone as casual as her own.

In the darkness, she thought she saw a smile. She didn't bother hiding her scowl. This again. Kitt must have guessed she would lie, but he underestimated Seabird's ability to see through falsities. Was Kitt's open suspicion his way of sowing distrust of her in the camp? "Do I have to kill wizards to be accepted here?"

Seabird chuckled. "Kitt is reasonable in all else except matters of wizards and wizardry. Perhaps now that he is taking on a wizard as a student, he will change his attitude."

Ember repressed a snort of disbelief.

Seabird continued, solemn. "I don't like that all shifters have so much hate for wizards. But I can't blame them, not after seeing some of what they've been through."

But if the shifters hated the wizards, and the wizards hated the shifters, how was everyone supposed to get along?

"I should be off now," Seabird said. "It grows late."

A question pressed at her. "How did you get

them to accept you?"

This time Ember could see the smile and the white teeth beneath. "Accept? I would say 'tolerate,'" he chuckled but his eyes were serious, and he looked at her as if he knew what she really asked. "It took patience, Ember. I had to convince them to see beyond differences. I showed my strengths. Acknowledged my weaknesses and used them to my advantage." He paused as a warm breath of air stirred the vegetation around them. "Know who you are, who you want to be. Strive to be that person, and they will come to see you with admiration and respect."

He left her alone in the woods, surrounded by shadows scented with dogwood blossoms and a gauzy curtain of spells that curved away in an endless maze of silver threads.

Who was she?

More importantly, who did she want to be?

CHAPTER TWENTY-SEVEN

SHE CERTAINLY WASN'T a cook.

She had failed to make a day tart, the simplest of dishes that she had witnessed Arundel's cooks make dozens of times. Eggs, which she had gathered from bird nests near camp, herbs from the small kitchen garden, sunberries, a pat of butter (she had found an entire log of it in the kitchen cupboard), onion, and a bit of cheese. Where the butter and cheese had come from, she still hadn't a clue. She only knew that they were a commodity in the camp and that she had taken some.

Only to waste it.

Ember pushed herself to shift faster in the darkness of the hovel. The day had barely been born, Riggs and Norman slept, and here she stood shifting in the dark, bone-weary, sickened, and furious.

She hated the oven's fire. Unpredictable. Inconsistent. She had no idea how the cooks kept it steady and calm. First the fire was too weak, and after she added more tinder and a flat piece of wood, it sparked and crackled to life. Exactly where she wanted it. But then it consumed the wood and the tarts with it. By then it had grown too hot for her to even try saving them.

So she had watched her hours of hard work get eaten by the fire and tried not to be disappointed.

And now she had to go back to the kitchens, as if nothing had happened. As if she had not wasted a thing.

She stopped shifting and leaned over, gasping for air and pushing down the bile that burgeoned up. Riggs stirred where he slept on the cot, and Ember held her breath, hoping he would stay asleep.

His deep breathing ensued.

She released hers and stood, then pulled on her deer-hide dress, silent as a mouse. She was glad she only had to worry about waking Riggs; Kitt had gone back to his own hovel days ago, as soon as he was able to walk.

She crept up the rough stone steps to the door, which she squeezed out of and carefully set back against the ground.

Spring touched the air, cool enough to prickle the skin, heavy with the prospect of rain. Mountains to the east blocked the rising sun, leaving the camp in shadows until late morning. Above the mountain slopes, the sky reminded her of Mirror Lake, a murky black washing into purple to the east. Bulky clouds gathered to the north, half-hidden by the tail of night. A storm.

Sighing, she pinched her cheeks and stuck her nose against the nearest dogwood blossoms before plucking one and sticking it behind her ear. She hoped to look a little less tired than she felt, in case someone realized certain ingredients were missing from the kitchen and that that meant someone had either cooked or stolen from the place overnight.

Stopping at the river, she sluiced crisp mountain water over her face and rinsed the bile from her mouth. She drank, and the coldness sank down, settling her stomach. No one else in the camp stirred. Beyond the gurgle of the stream, robins sang random, whimsical notes while thrushes played their lilting flutes and wrens carried on their endless chatter. No doubt some of them noticed their missing eggs.

Not wanting to linger too long at the river, Ember brushed back her hair with hasty fingers and crossed over to the cave opening. She would need to clean out the oven first, now that the fire had died, before others arrived and witnessed the burnt remains of day tarts.

"...they gave more this time than last," Ember heard Asenath say as she walked in. Etty stood next to her at the chopping table, both with backs turned on the cave entrance. Disheartened, Ember glanced toward the brick oven, and saw with dismay that someone had already cleaned it out and started a new fire.

"It's still not enough," Etty said in her stern voice. "The children are weak as it is. It's only a matter of time before the next injury."

"I agree they need more, but it's dangerous going out there. Every time, they risk discovery—"

Etty seemed to sense that Ember stood in the cave entrance and turned with squinted eyes.

"You," she said to Ember. "Early today, I see. Come churn this cream."

Without a word, Ember went to the table, waiting for Etty's vocal lashing for foolishly wasting food the night before, and grabbed the handle of the small butter-churn. There was little cream inside, a small portion of what was left in a jug beside it. Beside the jug lay a large hunk of yellow cheese, a pot of honey the width of Ember's hand, and a sack of flour, which Asenath used to make dough.

She caught Asenath giving her a meaningful glance as Etty poured cream into a small pot, and she ducked her head, keeping her eyes intent on the churn.

Thunder rumbled in the distance.

"You keep churning that slow and steady. Careful not to slosh it out," Etty reminded her.

There was hardly enough cream in the container to risk it sloshing out, but Ember nodded obediently.

Etty took her pot of cream to the oven fire,

pulling out the hook set in the top so that she could hang the pot at a safe distance from the extreme heat of the flame.

Ember turned toward Asenath, about to ask whether she had cleaned out the oven, when someone stomped into the cave behind her.

"Storm's coming," Wymer pronounced.

"Of course there is," Etty snapped from where she stood stirring the cream. "Did you get what I asked for?"

"With the help of these fine ladies," Wymer said, unaffected by Etty's impatience as he motioned a bony arm at the cave entrance. Two of the kitchen girls came in carrying baskets loaded with wild leeks, chives, berries, and mushrooms. They both rolled their eyes at Wymer before joining Asenath and Ember at the table.

"Good," said Etty, turning her concentration back to the cream. "Now chop them." Wymer's smug smile fell, and Etty added, "We'll be making tarts for supper today."

Ember paled and focused on churning the cream, ignoring her tired limbs and the uneasiness that lingered in her stomach.

"Easy peas," Wymer said airily as he came to the table to half-heartedly chop leeks. He grunted when he saw the honey, cream, and cheese. "That's all they got? I bet if I'd gone, we'd have twice as much."

Ember repressed the urge to ask who 'they' were and where they had gone. Did the appearance of the food have to do with the wolves she had seen the night before? *It's not the hunting,* Seabird had said, *but where they go after the hunt.*

"Why don't they try threats?" Wymer continued over the sound of chopping and churning cream. "Maybe an old snarl at the throat, teeth exposed—"

"You'd be better off keeping your thoughts to yourself." Asenath's tone was cool but clipped. The bits of fur on her dress danced as she kneaded the dough.

He snorted and opened his mouth, only to close it again with a shrug when he caught Asenath's warning glance.

Thunder growled overhead.

Wymer turned toward Ember instead. "Why so quiet today, Em? You look like you've seen a burnt loaf of bread."

Ember pretended she didn't hear him. He reminded her of the stable-boys in Silverglen who made fun of her for dressing like a boy. They had stopped making fun of her when they found out she carried a dagger, not that she had ever had to use it on them. But even if she had her dagger now, she doubted Wymer would care.

The noise of pattering rain filled the cave.

"Wymer," said Asenath, "Why don't you bring this loaf to the oven and see if Etty needs anything?"

Seeming glad for an excuse to leave the chopping, Wymer hastily set down the worn knife and took up the mound of dough. Ember shot Asenath a grateful look. An exchange that Wymer didn't miss. Ember couldn't help but notice his frown, the ugly curl of his lip, and the way his balding scalp tinged pink.

She willed the cream to turn to butter faster. A cool, wet wind swept into the cave and stirred the chopped leaks on the table. The girls began to tell Asenath where the leeks and mushrooms came from, and how they had only picked a small amount of what grew there. Ember feigned interest, certain that Asenath was the one who had cleaned out the oven and that Etty didn't know. But even if the tarts had been entirely eaten by the fire last night, surely Etty would notice that there was now less cheese, butter, and onion than the day before.

Unless the new food distracted her too much.

"Ember!" Etty called, causing Ember to flinch. "Fetch me that pot o' honey."

Ember grabbed the roughly made honey-pot, noticing its uneven bottom and the opening in the top that didn't quite match the shape of the lid. Her fingers found coarse grooves that looked to be claw marks, as though an animal had picked it up.

A hawk, perhaps.

Cold blossomed in her chest as she walked toward Etty. The pot had been made by a villager, Ember guessed, which meant that Jinni and the others—if it was indeed them who had brought back food—had crossed from Orion into Lach. Ember held the pot up to see the minute potter's mark etched into the bottom.

Her foot met resistance and she reeled off-balance, crying out as the pot slipped from her grasp.

CRACK!

Ember found herself flat on the ground. The honey-pot lay just out of reach, the honey seeping from three shards of pot and gathering dust from the cave floor.

"You clumsy fool!" Etty rushed to save the honey with a bowl and spoon. "This is the only honey we have until fall."

"I'm sorry," Ember said, dazed. Sitting up, she glanced back to see what had tripped her.

Wymer. He towered behind her, his arms crossed, looking on with a smugness that made her long to brandish a dagger.

"I have no patience for clumsiness," Etty said, huffing as she stood, the bowl of rescued honey gripped in two hands. Red-faced, she went to her pot of cream, her plump jaw set in a way that contradicted the slow, careful stirring of the cream. "Nor do I have patience for waste. You've used up all of my patience, Ember."

"But—"

"No. You'd be of better use elsewhere."

Ember stood, watching hopelessly at Etty stirred. "Is there nothing I can do to—"

A sharp, fired glance from Etty and Ember snapped her mouth closed.

"Go," Etty commanded. "You, Wymer, clean up that mess."

Ember ignored Wymer's look of contempt as she spun away and strode toward the cave entrance.

How dare he trip her? *Incorrigible man. Boy, rather. Repulsive. Impudent.* A host of other names only Dev might have used ran through her head. He wouldn't have dared do such a thing if he knew who she was. The daughter of the most powerful lord of the Council—

She shook her head. No. Not his daughter. She would not associate with that hated man.

A gentle touch to her elbow made her jump away, palms out as if to grapple.

Asenath, looking as startled as she felt, spread her fingers in peace.

"I'm sorry you've had a hard time here. It's not so easy for some of us. That's why I prefer decorating the dishes with silly Glamours rather than cooking." Asenath smiled. "I am better at it, and it suits me."

"The children like it," Ember admitted. Even something as simple as a decoration made life at camp better. Why couldn't she be good at something? "But what else can I do?"

Asenath rested a reassuring hand on Ember's shoulder. "We could always use more meat."

Thunder clapped. The vibrations rattled through the cave and into her bones.

"Are you suggesting I hunt?" Ember couldn't

keep her voice steady.

A slight frown wrinkled Asenath's silky forehead, and her hand dropped away. "We all must work for the good of the camp. All of us have responsibilities, whether we like them or not."

Ember straightened her back, not trusting herself to speak. She gave a brief nod and stepped out of the cave, into the lashing breath of the storm.

Torrents of rain drenched her as she crossed the river. The wind howled through the trees and whistled past sunberry shrubs. The forest shuddered around her, though she couldn't see much beyond curtains of cold rain.

She had been a fool to think herself free here. Foolish to believe she could have a place in the kitchens. Foolish to believe she could ever be accepted in this camp of shifters.

She had tried to be one of them, and failed. And now this, now they asked her to—

Lightning arched overhead, blinding her with a flash. Thunder snapped and rolled. Ember ran.

A short, slippery distance, and she threw open the hovel door, sliding on wet feet down the steps, and jerked the door closed behind her.

Quiet shadows bathed the space below. Riggs stood near the fire, a stick in hand, prodding the small flames to life.

He looked up as she slid down the steps. "Ember?"

"Riggs. I can't work there anymore."

Shivering, she came toward the fire. Her skin thirsted for warmth.

"What happened?"

She held trembling hands over the meager flames, feeling the dread curl through her.

"I burnt the tarts. Wasted. I wasted food, Riggs. All those children, starving because of me. And Wymer." She said his name with as much hatred as she could muster. "He tripped me and I dropped the honey. The last of the honey, until fall."

The fire blurred before her, but she couldn't stop, wouldn't stop the words from leaving her tongue.

"I have to do something. They are starving and I have to play a part, it's my responsibility. It's my fault."

Her body shook like a leaf in a gust of wind. The withered dogwood blossom tumbled from her hair and landed on a coal, curling and blackening before a flame devoured it. She felt cold. Unbearably cold.

"I must do something," she continued, looking at Riggs to be sure he understood. He didn't. He was riffling through his medicine box, pulling out a flask, worry and confusion etched over his kind, wide face. She longed to tell him everything—the words thrust against her lips—but she couldn't. She mustn't. Ember shook her head before he could offer the flask and gazed back into the fire. Why was she so cold?

Riggs shuffled away and came back, and a woolen blanket came across her shoulders. She clutched it with both hands.

"You're alright now." Riggs soothed a hand over her back. "You don't need to do anything except calm down. The fire will warm you."

As if remembering his task, he leapt to get more wood from one shadowed side of the hovel.

"I must do something," she repeated in a whisper. If she said it enough to herself, she would think of something, anything besides what she knew she had to do.

Kill. Hunting was killing, and she didn't like to kill. The word brought up Arundel's face, his hands, strong and lean and capable of so much. She remembered the scent of metal, tangy like blood, hard and controlling. His grin, the pleasure and hatred shining in his eyes like madness, like sickness. He never minded the blood, the way it dyed his clothes carmine and stained his skin brick-red. When she was little, he had touched her with those bloodied hands, touched her tenderly, like a father, to hug her or bring her to see his conquest.

But he wasn't right and Salena knew it. Her mother understood and tried to bring her away. He was angry but never hurt Salena. He hurt the horses instead, and cows, and the pigs, and the dogs.

How could she, Ember, cause harm like he did? How could she hunt and kill for anything, for anyone? The idea of getting pleasure from such a thing sickened her.

But she must, she must do it, whether she liked it or not. The children needed to eat, they needed to be strong. They needed to survive, to hide or defend themselves from the patrols.

The patrols that might be looking for her.

"Ember. Are you alright?" Riggs kneeled across the fire from her, patient as ever.

"Yes." Her throat felt thick, her voice husky. "I must learn to hunt." With the words said aloud, a strange numbness fell over her. Cold calm seeped into her limbs with certainty, and she let the blanket fall away. "I need to find Kitt."

The shadows in the hovel stirred. "I'm here."

Before she could speak, Kitt walked into the light of the fire.

CHAPTER TWENTY-EIGHT

IF IT WASN'T for the icy calm wrapping around her, Ember might have shifted into a bird and flew off, beating her wings against the stormy air in a fit of anger and shame. But her frozen heart wouldn't, couldn't let her feel anything beyond mild surprise...and something else.

The firelight warmed Kitt's skin to an amber hue. It dipped into the pink scar of his thigh, coursed along his torso and arms, and wound up around his throat like a snake seeking heat. She would like to be that snake.

If Kitt were anyone else.

Ignoring the warmth that tingled up her wet spine, she lifted her chin.

"Kitt, eavesdropping?" she said in mocking disbelief. "Impossible."

Kitt lowered his head, and the silver along his temple flared. "I was here before you arrived. It was unintentional."

Something in his tone had changed. Softened.

"And you decided not to announce yourself," Ember prodded, fighting to see his eyes beneath the shadows. He poised as though waiting, a frown creasing his forehead.

"I didn't want to upset you further."

She smiled and would have laughed—hadn't Kitt rather enjoyed upsetting her, the wizard-shifter?—had he not suddenly lifted his gaze and rested it on her, dark and serious.

The frozen coil of fear in her heart cracked. She looked away, into the fire. "Will you teach me to hunt?"

Kitt moved to kneel next to her. His eyes shifted from shadows to their usual mossy green, and he leaned toward the flames, thoughtful. "I will try. After the storm."

She could smell his familiar, wild scent, nearly hidden by sweat and the sweet, earthy poultice Riggs used to heal Kitt's wound. Remembering the healer, she glanced up and caught Riggs' ridiculous, ear-flapping grin and a look that held far too much interest.

She glared at him, effectively wiping the grin off his face. He cleared his throat and pretended to rummage in his medicine box, looking happy and even happier when he pulled out a leather flask.

"Will you share this with me?" Riggs offered the

flask, and Kitt took it with a small smile.

"To celebrate what, exactly?" Kitt asked, tugging out the small cork and sniffing the contents skeptically.

"A truce," Riggs announced. "Between wizard and shifter."

Kitt's eyebrows rose. "You're the only one who isn't a shifter here, Pitkin." He took a swig from the flask and handed it to Ember.

"Isn't it a bit early for..." She sniffed the flask. "*Sumbac?*"

"Never," replied Riggs with another grin and a wink. "Paired with biscuits, it makes a perfect breakfast." He dug into his satchel and offered dry, crumbly biscuits. Ember, mouth watering, reached to accept.

Kitt's hand closed around her wrist, stopping her. "Hunting will be easier if you're hungry." His fingers were warm and firm, insistent but not demanding.

She nodded, and he released her. Her wrist felt bare suddenly, and to distract herself, she took a pull from the flask. Orange liquor streamed molten down her throat, summoning memories of the great hall, the murals, the *sumbac* she drank with that man who wanted her. The dancing, twirling, and Gregory. Gregory's reflection in the window panes. Gregory and that woman, the straw in her golden hair, he at her neck.

She had failed to win Gregory, and she had failed

to save the bear. Was the bear still alive?

Silence brought her back to the hovel, and she restrained a flinch when she met Kitt's narrowed gaze.

Skeptical, again. "Is something the matter?"

"You've had *sumbac* before."

Too late, she remembered *sumbac* was a luxury of the rich. A favorite liquor in Ekesia, but difficult to find in Lach unless one lived near the border or knew a traveling trader. The cost of a small bottle would be a fortune to the lowly woman she claimed to be.

"I worked for a rich family back in Lach," she said, quickly forming a scenario in her mind. "They bred horses for a lord of the Council. I mostly washed linens," she said, remembering what she had told Seabird upon their first meeting. "But I sometimes worked as a scullion in the kitchens." She thanked Etty for that last lie, and shoved the cork back into the flask, closing the door to her real memories. "We were allowed a sip during the Festival of Yathe." She offered it back to Riggs, willing her arm not to tremble.

Riggs accepted, took a swig for himself and tried, but failed, to repress a grimace as he swallowed the stuff down. He shook himself and grinned. "Lethal."

Ember smiled, ignoring the feel of Kitt's eyes on her. She hated lying, hated that the lies came so easily to her, with hardly a thought. She was tired of pretending to be someone else. But the illusion was a little thing compared to what Kitt might do if he found out who she really was. What any of the shifters might do.

"How did you get it?" Ember asked Riggs.

"A dead wizard," Kitt replied, his voice quick and flat.

Guilt? Frustration?

Ember shifted as the liquor curled into her stomach. The coldness from earlier touched her again, and she was unable to keep the chill from her voice. "Did you kill him?"

The fire crackled. Kitt made no move to respond. He stared into the flames, as still and quiet as if he had been carved from stone.

Riggs became intent on adding more wood to the fire. "Can you help me with this wood, Ember? If you aren't too affected by the *sumbac*, that is," he said with forced cheerfulness.

Kitt didn't move.

Should she take his silence as guilty affirmation, or a stubborn withholding of a different truth? She supposed she might have an answer had she not been so direct. But she was used to eavesdropping, not interrogating, and she hadn't had much practice with being tactful, beyond what Salena had taught her was proper—and even that she hadn't bothered practicing much.

Repressing her impatience, she stood to help Riggs stack the extra wood, placing each piece with exaggerated care to form a neat, square pile.

"Looks like we got ourselves an expert wood-stacker," Riggs pronounced loudly when she was finished.

"Is that to be my new job, then?" Ember asked, amused. Seeing that Kitt still hadn't moved, she wandered to the door of the hovel to check on the storm. The rain fell softly as a mist now, obscuring the forest in a gauzy veil that glinted as though jeweled by the morning sun. The sight did a little to warm the cold numbness from before.

"Something odd happened in the kitchen today," she said, lowering the door back down. Perhaps she could ease Kitt out of his silence. "A pot of honey, a block of cheese, and cream were left on the table."

Neither of them replied, and she spun around to catch Riggs giving Kitt a questioning look before flashing a smile at Ember.

"Food in a kitchen?" he said in mock confusion. "I've never heard of anything so odd as that."

"It wasn't there the night before," Ember insisted. "Which means someone from the camp either traded for it or stole it."

Kitt broke out of his silence, and anger edged his tone. "We aren't thieves."

"We? So you are part of the group, too?" Ember asked, almost to herself. Is that where the *sumbac* had come from?

Silence, again.

"What's the purpose of hiding it?" she persisted. "Surely others know. Seabird certainly does."

Kitt flinched. "He's more honest with you, then."

The bitterness in his tone surprised her. "Perhaps because I do not hate him," she suggested. Although in truth, Seabird's honesty probably had more to do with the fact that she had already witnessed the wolves leaving camp. "But isn't it you who is keeping a secret from him?" When Kitt held his stubborn silence, she tried again. "Riggs. Did you know about the group?"

Riggs jerked his head up, cheeks flushed. "I—"

"Of course he does," Kitt snapped. "He's the healer. He knows how weak the children get, especially during the winter months. Two we've lost to fever, one to an infected wound."

A chill shivered up Ember's spine. "Then why would Seabird disagree with the trading?"

"Because it's dangerous." Kitt stirred the fire with a stick. "He doesn't believe we should risk the entire camp for the sake of a few children. He spouts about only wanting us to live, but more of us die every year."

Seabird only wanted the shifters to live, which meant he wasn't planning another rebellion. That was good, but surely his protection wouldn't last forever.

"Then what do *you* want?"

Kitt stood, tossing the stick into the hungry flames. "I want what other shifters want. To go back to Lach, and to take what's ours by right."

Another rebellion? Ember gaped at him.

"The storm is gone," he stated. "Let's go."

"You can't be serious," said Ember, refusing to

move from the foot of the steps. "You'd risk everyone's lives for—"

"A place back in society. Land. Homes. Food and medicine. Work," Kitt snapped them off one by one, his arms tense at his sides. "We're tired of sitting here, hiding in the woods, waiting for Seabird to do something. He hasn't done anything since the attack. What we're doing isn't living. It's barely surviving."

Ember couldn't help but remember Lexy, thin and pregnant, ready to kill her child in order to escape danger. She swallowed, unsure of what to say.

Kitt brushed past her and up the stairs. Ember threw an apologetic glance at Riggs, who watched them with hunched shoulders and a pained expression, then followed Kitt out of the hovel.

Kitt stalked ahead of her into the sodden, sun-soaked forest, intent on getting to wherever they were going.

Why was he so angry? For the first time, Ember found herself wondering who Kitt was before he came to Orion. Had he lived in a village in Lach? What kind of life had he had before coming here to live in isolation from society? Perhaps the loss of his past life explained his heedless anger.

"Did Seabird decide whether we're moving camp?" Ember asked, half-running to keep up with his long strides.

"Seabird doesn't decide for the camp. Most of us must agree on it."

"And you didn't agree to move?"

"We haven't decided yet." His voice was short and clipped.

She wished she could slow him down, convince him that it would be okay. She wished, more than ever, that he didn't hate wizards so passionately. So blindly.

"Kitt." She grabbed his wrist and held on, to be yanked a few steps before he jerked to a stop and turned, scowling at her hand. She didn't miss the surprise that flashed through his anger. "Please."

She released his wrist as he folded his arms over his chest, his jaw setting in forced patience.

"What the shifters do, trading for food, is a good idea. Not just for the children." She chose her words carefully. "In Lach, there are rumors about shifter factions who help the commoners. Shifters who bring them food and find lost children."

His expression froze, and it seemed to her that he had stopped breathing.

"If your group is one of them, you're giving the commoners hope. You're letting the people see who shifters really are." *Beyond the differences*, she heard Seabird say. "If the commoners learn to accept shifters, perhaps others will, too." She didn't mention the Council's growing fear, nor that the Council-members had called the commoners mad.

The tension in Kitt's face loosened. "You think the Council would allow us back?"

As long as Arundel is part of the Council... Not only

did he long to kill shifters, but he excelled at convincing other Council-members to support his passionate hatred, though they didn't see it that way. They were too easily convinced that shifters were a threat, to their own families and to Lach as a whole.

Ember straightened her shoulders, which had begun to droop far too much. "I think that given enough time—"

"We're running out of it, Ember."

"If you stay patient—"

"We've no patience left," he said, echoing Etty's own words. "How many years has it been since the rebellion began?"

"Twenty-two." *But it's people like my father—no, Arundel—who believe the rebellion still exists.* He would never cease his tirade against the shifters.

"Aren't you tired of hiding?"

The question made her heart kick.

"I've been hiding for as long as I can remember," she stated, as though it was a sufficient answer. "It's the only thing that has kept me alive."

"Are you alive?"

Of course I'm alive, she wanted to say, but the challenge in Kitt's eyes planted a sudden heaviness in her stomach.

"I'm hungry," she said instead.

The challenge traveled to his lips and transformed them into a smile. "Then let us hunt."

His face blurred and in the beat of a moment he

lifted his arms, feathers sprouting from skin and bone that whirled into inhuman motion. His arms came down as wings, and his hide skirt fell away from his red-tailed hawk form as he lifted to a branch above. He glared down at her for a moment before turning away to preen ruffled feathers into submission.

Ember couldn't repress a grin. His change of pace was dizzying.

Skin tingling, she let herself melt into spinning queasiness before lifting her arms as Kitt had done. She could do it, too. She just had to wait for...

There. Bone solidified beneath her skin. She pulled her arms down, now wings, and reveled in the resistance of the wind against her feathers, rising, rising—

Her talon snagged a corner of her dress. Flapping madly in the air, she struggled to open her talon as wide as it would go, but the dress won. Dropping to the ground, she dislodged the fabric from a sharp claw using her beak.

Kitt keened softly behind her. Was he laughing?

Ignoring him, Ember gathered her strength and lifted into the air, struggling to rise high to minimize her chance of impact with a tree limb. As she emerged over the forest canopy, she caught sight of Kitt, already far ahead of her and flying northwest, deeper into the mountains.

Being the larger hawk, she caught up with him and stayed close. They rounded a mountain peak and rose with the updraft to gain altitude. Kitt adjusted to the change, grabbing the wind with ease and agility, no longer flapping but soaring faster the higher he went.

Ember struggled to keep up with him. A sudden gust lifted her wings, and the abrupt change made her waver in the air. A mere twitch of her wings would send her spiraling. She pushed the distracting thought aside and realized Kitt had disappeared.

She called out in a shrill scream and searched the horizon, the clouds above, the elms in the distance, and the forest that moved like water beneath her.

She found him as she passed another mountain peak, lazily tracing a circle above the northern slope as he rode a thermal draft. She joined him, shrieking her annoyance as they soared higher.

He veered north, out of the warm air and over the silver streak of river that delved between the toes of the mountains.

Kitt lowered himself so that he glided above the river, and his shadow swam on the surface like a fish. He gave a sharp keen and dropped down to a dead chestnut tree, turning his wings outward and thrusting his talons forward at the last minute to grab a bare limb.

Ember landed next to him with less finesse, feathers fluttering and pieces of bark tumbling below as she grappled with the branch. Finally, she gained balance and composure.

Kitt perched like a stone beside her. His hungry

eyes were on the riverbank below, watching for movement.

Reluctantly, Ember followed his gaze. For a moment she saw only leafy shadows dancing along the rocks, except for one shadow that seemed longer than the others, slithering like a—

Kitt dropped from the branch and aimed for the snake with deadly accuracy. The snake seemed to sense him and dove into a crevice as quick as a mouse. Defeated, Kitt landed on the rocky bank and peered at the hole. Ember shook the tension from her feathers, her human side relieved that the snake had escaped, and tried to ignore her own hawk's frustration.

And hunger.

Kitt flew back up to the branch, seeming not in the least discouraged as he steadied himself once more to watch.

They waited as the sun grew big and heavy in the sky, until the snake sidled out of the crevice and into a pool of light to bask. With her hawk-eyes, Ember could see every detail of the snake. The dusky, checkered back, the wide black eyes, the gleaming scales along its spine, and the thick flesh that squeezed into a spiral. Her hawk side yearned to strike.

She looked to Kitt, who glared at her with his own hawk-eyes, waiting.

Damn.

Heart racing, she bunched her wings and clung to the last of her control as if it were the only thing she had left.

She leapt from the branch to where the snake waited. Her hawk-mind pressed her to lean slightly to the left, and she did, and to open her talons, to lean back with the tail spread full—

Just as she whipped her talons out, the snake reared up and snapped at her.

Ember flapped her wings in a panic. Her hawk-mind, sensing the snake's musk, screamed at her to grab it, but she ignored the urge and lifted away. She landed on an oak branch and didn't bother looking back. Trembling, she opened her beak to gasp air, unable to stop her human fear from clashing with her hawk's excitement. She was unsure of what terrified her more: getting bitten by the snake or having to kill it. Neither of the scenes ended well in her human mind.

A rustle of feathers and a gust of air as Kitt landed beside her. She preened herself to hide her shivering feathers and savored the warmth of his presence. Gradually, the trembling subsided. Ember closed her eyes.

A slight touch from Kitt's wing.

He hunched, on the verge of dropping. Ember's hawk senses sharpened on the ground. Soft movement, half-hidden beneath a berry bramble, the dusky gray that could only be a rabbit. Her hawk mind pushed her, clawing at the wall her human mind had created.

Kitt launched, ducking around branches and flying toward the rabbit's backside. Somehow, it sensed his approach and began running, scurrying for the thickest brush. Without hesitation, Kitt plummeted down, racing to where the rabbit would be in just a few heartbeats. He grabbed the rabbit with precision, landing on its back and reaching at the same moment for its neck.

A quick twist with his beak, and the kicking rabbit died.

The familiar sensation of hunger and disgust rolled in Ember's stomach.

Kitt secured the rabbit in his talons and flew up out of the canopy, heading back toward camp. Ember followed, relieved that they were finished for the day. Would Kitt chastise her for not catching anything?

She followed him to the spot where they had shifted earlier, just outside of camp. They glided down to their respective clothes. Ember swirled back to her human form, tugged on her dress, and waited, re-orienting herself to her human senses and breathing in the warmth of the sun on her shoulders until Kitt finished dressing.

"Are you ready?" he asked.

She wasn't ready, not at all, but she turned and made herself walk up to the rabbit lying in front of Kitt. Ribbons of blood curled around the rabbit's neck, and one glassy black eye stared up at her in terror.

"A healthy rabbit, considering this past winter," Kitt remarked. "Normally they are scrawny this time of year. We can give the fur to Lexy. She might make a good pair of shoes for one of the children."

He ran a hand over the rabbit's side, smoothing the fur where it had tangled during the hunt.

Ember knelt and touched the rabbit's shoulder. Still warm. Not wanting to, but driven by curiosity, she stole a glance at Kitt.

Ruddiness tinged his cheeks and his eyes shone the color of rain-washed moss. Rather than the pleasure she expected, his unsmiling expression looked focused.

"Have you skinned an animal before?" he asked.

Ember nearly shook her head until she remembered who she was supposed to be. Ember with no name, a former scullion. She couldn't recall whether she'd ever seen a scullion clean an animal, so she went with a safe answer. "I've seen others do it before."

Kitt didn't seem to care about her answer as he furrowed his brows and concentrated on the rabbit between them. "Rabbits are easy. If you have a good knife, it makes the job quick." He pulled out a knife from the leather sheath tied to his skirt. "First we skin it to save the fur. Notch the hide here," he explained, cutting the hide and slipping his fingers inside. The skin pulled off easily, rolling inside-out to expose the pink flesh underneath. He set the skin to the side. "Then remove the tail, cut the feet, and sever the head." He moved as he spoke, handling the rabbit with careful efficiency. Ember tried to ignore the sound of splintering bone and focused on the steadiness of Kitt's hands. "Now we gut it." He slid the knife just under the skin of the belly, cutting a slit all the way to the end. "Be careful not to cut the organs. They'll spoil the meat if you do. Move them out of the way so you can break through the bone, and then we can take everything out."

Holding the carcass up with one bloodied hand, Kitt pulled the organs down and out with the other, his face grim as he tossed them into the woods. He turned back and held open the empty cavity. "You can see the fat here," he pointed, "left over from the winter. Looks like he's been eating better than we have. We got lucky catching such a healthy rabbit. If you're still hungry, we should rinse this and get it to Etty."

The hunger had soured in her stomach, but Ember nodded.

Kitt noticed her discomfort. "The worst part's over. You'll get used to it. Maybe next time we can surprise Etty with two animals rather than one."

Let's hope so. She regarded Kitt as he tossed the rabbit's head and feet deeper into the forest. "Aren't you afraid of losing yourself when you hunt like that?"

He held the wet, bloody carcass and waited for her to stand. "When I hunt as an animal? Never. Why?"

A twinge of envy. She rose, trying to keep her voice light. "Because the animal always wants what it wants. Which isn't always what I want."

They started walking into camp. Compared to flying in hawk-form, walking in human form made her feel like a slug crawling through the dense shrubs and brambles that sprawled across the forest floor. She made herself slow to Kitt's pace.

"I find that I perform better when I follow the instincts and trust that I can regain control when it's done."

Yes, you do have a tendency of letting go. She still felt the memory of his cougar's breath wrapping around her throat, and the puncture of sharp claws in her arm.

She swallowed. "I think I'll check the perimeter." She waved a hand at Kitt. "You go without me, it was yours anyway. Thanks for the lesson."

Kitt glanced at her before looking down at the rabbit. His frown slipped into a scowl. Did the man never smile? Of course he did, Ember thought, reminding herself of when he taught the orphans. *Just not around me.*

"The wizard took a newborn. During the last attack."

Ember halted, straining to hear his low voice. The carcass in his hands seemed forgotten, and the leaves overhead painted his face with shadows.

"He killed the babe before defiling and killing the mother. I caught him as he drove a spear through her throat." He looked at Ember, and the shadows were nothing against the darkness in his eyes. "I cut off his hands and castrated him. Then we ate him."

Bile rose in Ember's mouth, and she saw her own disgust reflected in his expression. She glimpsed something else there, too, something she longed—no, needed—to see, but her own anger chased it away.

"Why are you telling me this?"

"You wanted to know the truth. Do you feel better for knowing now?"

Heat pounded in her veins. "Do I feel better knowing you're a cannibal?" she asked in a strained voice. "That you're more beastly than—" Arundel. My father. But Arundel wasn't her father and he had eaten animals he had killed—why not shifters, too? "No."

She wanted to scream at him; she wanted to understand. She could only walk away, and that's what she did.

Revulsion churned in her stomach. How had she not known? She had spied, yes, and heard stories before, but she'd never seen the real war of the rebellion. She'd seen Arundel abuse and kill animals, but had never ventured in the dungeons in animal-form—except for the one time as a mouse—for fear of discovery. She never saw first-hand the cruelty that took place beneath Silverglen, and she had never seen the horror other shifters experienced. Nor the horrible things the shifters did in response. So many terrible things had happened, and not just inside the walls of Silverglen's dungeon.

I will never understand and I should be glad.

Why wasn't she?

CHAPTER TWENTY-NINE

THAT NIGHT, EMBER stalked the camp's perimeter like a caged cougar. Her disgusted anger had fizzled away with a meager portion of the rabbit stew, somehow more savory than she remembered it being, and had left her feeling unbearably hollow.

Her reaction to Kitt had been foolish. Who was she to get angry with him? She had no right to judge what she hadn't been through herself. Whatever he had done, he clearly didn't enjoy the memory. And it hadn't helped that she had walked away, running from the truth just as she always did. Just as Kitt accused her of doing.

Ember tried to focus on the worn Glamour web sprawling between two oak saplings. She had helped the wizards re-cast the perimeter that afternoon, patching up the holes the rain had washed away, and still she found sections where the camp fires shone through like a beacon. With impatient flicks of her hand, she tied up the space with an illusion of leaves and twigs, even going so far as to add a thick vine of poison-birch.

Maybe the vine will be enough to keep them away. She should search for Fletch's patrol again, perhaps this very night. Finding no sign of them worried her. Patrols usually didn't give up their mission—they wouldn't want to risk Arundel's wrath—but Ember still didn't know what exactly their mission was. She wouldn't try to kill them. She would find a way to listen and watch for—

"Yip!" The distinct wolf-like noise skittered along the forest floor.

Ember crouched, spells and patrols forgotten, and peered in the direction of the sound.

She glimpsed the wolf pack through scrawny sunberry branches. White canines, lagging tongues, ears erect and tails pointed like the prow of a boat. She looked for Jinni at the lead but made out nothing beyond fallen logs and spreading dogwoods.

The spells on the perimeter would have to wait.

With hardly another thought, Ember stepped out of her dress and whirled onto all fours, trotting downwind from the pack as she followed them southwest. She caught scent of Jinni and many others whom she recognized but didn't know. Seven in total.

The group traveled west around the base of a

mountain. They climbed over jagged outcrops, splashed through a shallow stream, and skirted the edge of a blackened clearing smelling of lightening and ash.

The wind stilled and shifted.

In one jagged inhale, the pack ahead turned their black eyes on Ember, their lips curling back into snarls. Jinni turned and spotted Ember, and suddenly the leggy wolf sprinted like mad toward her.

There would be no polite discussion. No reasonable explanations or excuses. The light from the fading sun burned orange in Jinni's eyes and dyed her tongue a brilliant red. Her paws stained black from the ground, and the dust churned up behind her like a shroud.

RUN! Ember's muscles screamed to move, yearned to work under the tension of her own wild pulse.

Instead, she pulled her lips back and gripped the ground, flattening her ears and raising a tail in defense.

Jinni lunged.

Piercing canines constricted Ember's throat and forced her down, threatening to crunch. The sting of drawn blood and the wheeze of her own breath made Ember struggle harder. Jinni pinned her to the ground. Perhaps she wanted Ember to fight back, to satiate her need for hateful bloodshed. Ember rolled instead, her muzzle grinding into the charred earth, and exposed her belly.

Submission.

Panting, Jinni released her and snarled. *I am the leader,* her eyes said. *Defy me and I will kill you.*

As quickly as Jinni had come, she trotted away. Ember leapt up to see the rest of the pack follow their leader beyond the clearing and deeper to the south.

Feeling somehow more confident, Ember shook herself and followed, keeping behind the last of the pack.

Two wolves veered east, splitting up so that one went north while the other curved to the south. The others in the pack continued to follow Jinni.

Ember lowered her nose close to the ground. A faint, musky scent warmed the sedges. A doe. And another subtle smell that sent a shiver down her spine. But she wouldn't think about that now. The others had already picked up the doe's trail, and now Jinni guided them southwest, shifting downwind of the potential prey.

Ember followed, watching the pack for signs of what to do. They edged around a clump of alders, and the smell of deer excrements hung heavy in the evening air.

The trotting wolves burst into a run.

Ember joined them, panting to keep up. Through the oaks, she saw the doe approach at a sprint, chased by the lone wolf who had veered north.

The doe jerked left of the pack, her tail a white flag through the trees and her muscled legs leaping unbelievable strides.

She is made for this.

The pack turned sharply, their shortened strides keeping them just behind their prey. The doe smelled fearful but strong, which worried Ember. Kitt had told her during their lesson that wolves usually took down the weak, the old, and the young. To try for a healthy adult was risky, if not foolish. Ember had a feeling that neither of those things mattered to Jinni.

The doe spun around, halting Ember's human thoughts. The pack circled the doe, lunging at neck and rump, but she kicked out with pummeling hooves and wound in tight circles to prevent any one wolf from grabbing her.

She stood her ground as night's face darkened the woods. One of the wolves latched onto her rump and yipped when she kicked him. The sound of his cry pulled Ember closer, and her wolf's instincts yearned to attack. Another wolf lunged to bite the doe's rump, and the doe spun with such force that she tossed the wolf aside. A flap of hide dangled from her open wound, but the doe fought on.

A third wolf grabbed the doe's throat and earned a sharp kick to her ribs. That wolf fell back, limping, but continued hovering close by, offering her support to the others with snarls and snaps. Jinni, Ember realized. They followed her lead, even though their leader had chosen a dangerous prey, and they trusted her with their lives.

Ember felt the pull, too. She was part of the pack now, if only temporarily. The pack meant survival. And family.

As though sensing her wolf-thoughts, Jinni turned and gave her a challenging, direct look. *Why aren't you helping,* her look said.

Ember's human mind struggled to find an answer, and in that space of a moment, her wolf's senses picked up a subtle shift in the doe's stance. Only three wolves toward her front including Jinni, while the others gathered at her back and sides. Her tattered rump and front limbs bunched. Her head lowered.

Jinni turned back to the doe, not realizing the doe moved on the verge of jumping, or that she stood directly in the doe's path.

Ember's wolf instincts caught fire in her limbs. She shot toward the doe, watching as the prey began moving into the leap.

Within half a second, Jinni and the others realized what was going on, but by then the doe was arcing through the air, strips of hide dangling after, her muzzle bloody from a bite and frothing with exhaustion.

The doe landed heavily, her grace gone and panic riding every inch of her like a hoard of stinging ants. One leap ending began the start of another; a few more and she'd be safe.

That sliver of freedom slipped away as Ember lunged and clamped down on the doe's neck.

Terror filled her nose. Sweat and blood and hide filled her mouth. Ember swung in the air as the doe jerked back, but then Jinni and the others swarmed the deer, pulling with determination.

Trembling, the doe tried to leap again, but the weight of the pack forced her down. She kneeled, hot breath gusting through wide nostrils, and her eyes, like black pools, seemed already empty as she succumbed to shock. Ember released her grip.

Jinni sliced the doe's throat with an un-wolf-like deftness of a claw. The doe shuddered violently as the blood streamed from her.

They waited while night dimmed the sky, until the doe's gaze turned flat and dull. Ember's wolf-side wanted to eat with the others, but her human-side wished to retreat into solidarity.

She shook herself. *It is for the children.*

Another smell that she had caught earlier trailed into her senses.

Ember bent her face to the ground and followed the scent away from the doe, tracing back to where they first found the prey. Her human-mind felt numb, empty, but her wolf senses drove her forward.

She traced through a clump of sunberry shrubs and over a small hill, around three huge oak trees, and into a thicket of brambles. She squeezed past the piercing thorns, hidden by darkness but unable to keep silent.

A faint scent of milk, hide, and hunger. Curled

tightly among the short sedges, leaf litter, and brambles, the fawn formed a small speckled swirl of brown that nearly made him disappear into his surroundings. He waited for his mother to return, Ember knew. But she wouldn't come back, and he would wander for days calling out until falling dead from starvation, if some predator didn't get him first.

He didn't move as she approached, and he remained silent until her teeth clamped on his neck.

She cut off his desperate bleat with a quick, twisting yank.

His skin was soft against her teeth, would easily tear to expose the succulent meat beneath—

Spinning, tilting, whirling.

Ember gasped back into human form, stomach roiling, mind a foggy blur. She clutched the ground, brambles stabbing her fingers. Her sense of smell seemed almost gone. A cool edge to the air, dirt, the faint scent of animal.

The fawn's fur ran like silk beneath her palms.

She dug her hands beneath his body and pulled him against her chest. Light, like a child. Fragile. Soft. Warm.

She carried him back to the others while his warmth faded away. Laid him, still and silent, at Jinni's paws.

Ember whirled back to wolf form.

Jinni gave a low growl followed by a sharp bark.

A sort of gathering call, Ember realized as the

others swarmed around them. They had neatly set aside the meatiest parts of the deer—the legs and rump—presumably for trading, and had been gnawing on organs and bones. They seemed content and relaxed, tails wagging as they nudged against one another. Jinni stood, received a few licks to the face, and grabbed a hefty deer leg. The rest of the pack followed suit.

By the time they neared the small village sitting at the Lachian border, the fawn had grown stiff in Ember's mouth. They trotted down through the last of the mountains and into the wooded hills of Lach. A cluster of mud and daub homes sat near a river, quiet in the lull of night. Smells of human activity cooled in the air—sweet burning maple, ox dung, baked bread, and smoked meat. Ember made out the scents of cows, pigs, and chickens, smells strange to her after so long away from Silverglen, or any civilization.

Jinni guided them to the house on the outermost edge, dark but for a nub of candle burning in front of the wooden door. The meager light fluttered over two honey-pots, a metal canister, and a small cloth sack placed on the stone step at the foot of the door.

The pack edged close, hovering just beyond the touch of the candlelight, and sniffed the air. Jinni lay the first leg of meat beside the offering, carefully nudging it into a secure place against the door, her breath causing the flame's shadows to dance against the wall of the house. She turned, meeting Ember's gaze.

Nudging past the darkness, Ember took the stiffened fawn and laid it gently against the stone step. She licked her lips so her mouth wouldn't feel so empty, and sniffed the contents of the offering. Honey, as before, cream, and chicken eggs. *No cheese this time.*

She moved away as another wolf came bearing a second leg of meat. With the fawn gone, her mind began to clear, and in the clarity emerged a prick of cold.

Cold and metal. A spell.

She muttered a low growl and sank back, cloaking herself in darkness as she shifted to a crow. The others noticed her unease and stepped deeper into shadows, ears and noses working to make out a scent.

Ember flew up over the roof of the house and glided over one after another, tracing the feel of the spell as she would trace a scent.

She landed on the edge of a roof, where the road turned and twisted alongside the river, water churning to one side and mud houses squeezed together on the other. Ember looked down, hopping along the edge until she stood just above the spell. She cocked her head to see below and peered into the darkness.

Peeking around the side of a house, in dirt— stained trousers and a homespun canvas shirt, stood a leggy boy with a mop of black hair. Ember couldn't see the spell but sensed its cold vapor reaching out to her like the fingers of winter. She sensed the spell near his hip.

A spy with a dagger? He watched the wolves, or what he could see of them, but beyond that he did nothing suspicious. He looked too young to be a wizard, but how then did he come by the spelled dagger? Perhaps a wizard had stopped by the village. Perhaps the wizard still stayed, and was here now... The wizard could have been Fletch, and the dagger might be the knife she had used on him.

Ember shivered.

She didn't sense any other spells nearby, and hadn't caught the metallic, proud scent of a wizard since arriving at the village. Either way, it wasn't safe for them to stay. The boy made her uneasy.

Ember flew back to the pack, who had retreated with the goods and made quick progress through the forest. She glided over Jinni, wary that the wolf might think it amusing to snatch her out of the air like a plaything, and landed several feet ahead. She snapped back to her human form, ignoring the customary biliousness and the cool touch of night.

"A boy," Ember said. The pack slowed in their walk, ears flipping back in irritation. Jinni exposed a canine. "He had a spelled dagger. There may have been wizards there..."

Jinni brushed past her.

"The food might be poisoned," Ember insisted. Why not? Ember had heard of much worse ways of wizards killing shifters. If wizards knew about the trading, poisoning would be an efficient way to finish off any shifter factions hiding in the Orion Mountains.

"If we smelled wizards," Jinni said, and Ember turned to see her standing straight as an arrow in human form, "we would have found and killed them." The black gem below her bottom lip shone iridescent as she spoke.

"They could've come and gone. Do you never test the food before you bring it back?"

With a smirk, Jinni waved at the wolves who carried the food. "Test it yourself."

Warily, the wolves set down their food. Ember approached and lifted a lid of the honey-pot. She lifted one and sniffed. Not that her human senses were of much use, and if the food carried a smell of poison she would have caught it with her wolf's senses.

But there were scentless poisons, and tasteless poisons, too.

She dipped a finger in and brought it to her lips. Her finger shook once as the honey touched her tongue, and a moment later the honey delved down her throat, as smooth as the cream that followed it.

She put the lids back on and kneeled, closing her eyes and thinking of the orphan children, Vinn, Loria, and pregnant Lexy.

"Let's go," said Jinni. "We'll make better time flying."

Ember opened her eyes as the burst of seven pairs of wings buffeted her face. Beige and buff feathers lifted around her, some grasping pots and a canister, another clutching the sack of eggs. The small flock of owls rose into the night sky, and their wings beat without a whisper of sound.

Ember looked back toward the village, but sensed neither spells nor boy within the murky dark.

CHAPTER THIRTY

The scent of lilies did not belong on winter's freezing, biting breath. But it was there now, and she didn't need to be a mouse or a dog to sense it reaching over the frozen lake and up to the walking bridge where she now stood.

She peered over the iron balustrade to the snow-covered lake below. Little wooden shanties dotted the white, and splitting down the middle was her father's snow-sled. She recognized him at once. Tall where he sat at the front, with a dark hat and boots, and next to him that pale man who smelled of lilies.

Six of father's dogs raced before the snow-sled, and behind the sled lay a track of pink.

Mama? she said, squinting through the shroud of mist from her own breath. She spotted a dark form in the back of the sled, a second form next to it.

Her mother didn't respond, but stood quiet beside her.

Father must have seen them from below. He lifted a hand in greeting, just like he always did when returning from a hunting trip, and Ember longed to wave back. But her mittens seemed stuck to the iron balustrade and her cold fingers wouldn't move. A moment later the sled flew beneath them in a flurry of blood-tinted snow.

She looked up at her mother, whose face seemed pale. *That was a man in the back,* Ember stated, heart pattering because she knew her father hurt certain people called shifters, and that man might be a shifter.

Like her.

Her mother turned sharp blue eyes on her. *You mustn't—*

Ember ran, already knowing what her mother would say. She mustn't appear interested. Mustn't give any hint of what she was. Father wouldn't love her anymore. Mother would get hurt. She must keep it secret.

The bridge was slippery under her boots, and the tower steps going down to the gardens were slick with ice. She ran past the kitchen and through the gardens, down the torch-lined path to the lake until she reached the rounded steps where her father stood with the man who smelled of lilies. A few of the Escorts stood with them, dark-cloaked and strong as they lifted the great boar out of the sled.

Take it to the kitchens, her father ordered. He stood so dark against the snow, like a great shadow, and his throwing ax and long knife shone silver where they were bound to his belt.

Ember almost forgot he was her father, until he saw her and grinned. He bent to one knee and held out his hands.

My little flame, come give me a kiss, he said.

She ran to him and planted one on his cold, bearded cheek. She was too old to sit on his knee now, so she leaned against it and held one of his hands, wishing she could tell him how she spent her day as a squirrel, and then as a fox, playing in the snow with the puppies from the kennels. But she couldn't forget her mother's warnings.

Causing any trouble today? he asked.

She shook her head and gave a small smile.

Do you know what I've brought home for us?

She nodded. *A boar*, she said. She studied the red that lined her father's nails. *To eat*, she added tentatively.

That's exactly right. Do you know how I killed him?

Four of the Escorts carried the boar to the kitchen. Thick red matted the boar's chest.

Ember shook her head, not wanting to look more.

A spear to the heart. One thrust. He had an odd look on his face as he watched the Escort carry the boar away. He looked happy and angry at once, with a strange light in his eyes that she had seen before.

My lord, the man who smelled like lilies said as he gave a half-bow at them.

Her father nodded. *Bring him.*

The lily man bowed again, looking pleased.

Two more Escorts lifted the second form out of the sled—a man—and her father stood, grabbing a spear. *Take him down below, Fletch, for questioning,* he commanded.

The man's front was bloodied, and he appeared to be sleeping.

Cold shivered through her. *Is he dead, Papa?*

Her father turned to her, startled, as though he had forgotten she was there. The strange light in his eyes had brightened.

He's alive, her father said. *He's a beast, Ember. A shifter. He takes the form of any animal, and he's dangerous. I'm going to lock him up so he can't hurt anyone else.*

Did he hurt you, Papa?

Her father stared at the unconscious man, his lip curling and his brows drawing together. *He did. And others of his kind. You watch out for them, Ember. When you're older I'll teach you—*

Mother's voice cracked the frozen air. *What is the meaning of this? Who is this man?*

Her father winced, but then his face smoothed and warmed into a smile. He walked toward Ember's mother, who had come up just behind Ember. *Salena—*

Ember, come with me, her mother said, gripping her arm. *This is nothing a child should be seeing.*

Her father halted. *She's my child, Salena. I will decide what she can see. She needs to learn what's out there. What can harm her.*

She's barely ten. Her mother's voice sounded strained, as though she was on the verge of crying. *What are you doing with that man, Arundel? Did you hurt him?*

Her father jerked a hand for the Escort to carry the sleeping man away. The man who smelled of lilies followed them, winking at Ember and giving a nod to her mother as he walked by.

Her mother's hand tightened around her arm. Ember swallowed a gasp of pain. The look her mother gave the lily man was the same look she had given Ember's nursemaid once. Strange, that her nursemaid had left suddenly, without a farewell.

I found him hunting in my woods, her father said, coming near. His distant, angry look was pinched. Why did he always look at Mother that way?

And you tried to kill him for it?

I'm only trying to protect you. You know what they did to my family—

I've heard enough. Her mother tugged Ember away.

Her father lunged forward, grabbing her mother by the arms. *Salena!*

Ember was sure he would strike her, or shake her, but he only held her, and Salena stood like a stone in his grasp, her face hard as iron.

Let me go, she commanded.

Father's face seemed to move like a river, until it settled on stern sadness lit by a heat that made Ember feel invisible. He released her, and Salena grabbed Ember's hand, dragging her down the torch-lit path to the great hall.

You're hurting me, Ember said to her mother once they were inside.

Her mother bent down and kissed both her cheeks. *I'm sorry sweetie. I'm sorry you had to see that. You're father isn't...isn't feeling well.*

He's sick?

Yes, sweetie. Come on, let's get you a nice warm bath. Would you like that?

CHAPTER THIRTY-ONE

"She hasn't woken yet?"

Kitt's voice, watery and translucent, shimmered on the edge of Ember's dreams. Or was he in her dream?

"No." Riggs. "She's like a hibernating bear. I haven't seen her move in hours."

"Have you checked to see if she's still alive?"

Riggs guffawed, sweeping Ember's dreams aside as though they were nothing more than feathers.

Delicious, soft feathers like the ones in her bed back home. She sorely missed those. Her body felt immobile, each limb too heavy to lift. She had come back very late last night only to find Riggs up tending to a feverish Loria. The poor girl had been white as a dead fish and shivering under her sweat, only able to sleep restfully with Riggs' tincture and a cool wet cloth against her face.

"I don't need to," Riggs was saying. "I can hear her heavy breathing from here."

"Perhaps it's your own loud breath you hear, Pitkin."

Riggs grunted. "Is she the only reason why you came here?"

"Mostly. I'm not sure she'll come with me, though."

A slight pause. "You told her about the attack?"

"I did."

Coals hissed as someone shoved a stick into the fire.

"You think she'll forgive you?"

"I have no hope of that. I can't expect others to be honest with me if I'm not honest with them. I've a feeling she'd have found out eventually on her own, anyways."

Riggs *hmphed*. "Most likely. She seems a better spy than even you. Personally, I like to keep my secrets to myself. Everyone is better off that way."

Kitt snorted. "You didn't seem to have issue with revealing your patch of hair to the girl."

"Who? Ember? She's a woman, not a girl," Riggs corrected. "And I don't believe my inability to shift is a secret to anyone in this camp."

"No, but perhaps it should be, Pitkin," Kitt teased. "I would think your patchy hair would be an embarrassment to you—"

"As a young woman," Ember broke in, her voice husky with sleep as she rose on one elbow and looked at the two men across the glowing fire, "I find that I'm rather fond of patchy fur in a man."

She meant it as a joke, but they stared at her, one in shock and the other turning red. Her lips tugged into a smile, and Riggs wilted in relief, only to break into raucous laughter when he noticed Kitt's look.

"She's joking, Kitt," Riggs choked. "It's just a joke."

"Was it?" Kitt murmured.

Why did he look at her as though seeing her for the first time? Suddenly self-conscious, Ember adjusted her crooked dress and sat up, brushing her bangs out of her eyes and smoothing her hair. The warmth of the fire curled through her. "You've never heard a woman joke before?"

Kitt flashed a grin with white, pointed teeth. "Of course. Mostly the lewd ones from Jinni. But I'm glad you weren't serious about Pitkin. Women aren't his type."

"All for the better, then," Ember said easily. "I'm growing rather fond of shifters. They display their love so...publicly."

Riggs chuckled and tossed a stick into the fire. "Too publicly, you mean?"

Too publicly for a wizard's society, Ember might have said, but she didn't wish to spoil the mood.

Kitt's grin widened. "I think what the lady means

is that it's easier to choose a shifter if you can see how they love."

A giggle bubbled up her throat, so childish that she wanted to force it back down but it emerged and transformed into a laugh that bent her toward the fire. The others laughed, too, and her face burned but laughing felt so good, like a cool drink on a hot summer day, or like standing beneath her favorite waterfall, or like the thought of touching Kitt.

The last took her by surprise, and the laughter quieted to a warm hush that spread from cheeks to neck.

"Will you be teaching the orphans today?" she asked Kitt.

"No," Kitt replied, leaning back. "The weather is too nice for it. I'm letting them free. But it is good weather for flying...if you're up to it."

Did he mean flying or hunting? "Me? You're the one with the leg injury."

Everyone eyed his muscled leg, propped casually away from him so that it could lay flat on the ground. The wound healed quickly with Riggs' ointment, and the scar tissue now gathered and hardened where once there had been raw flesh.

"It's well enough to fly," Kitt said.

"I'll be the judge of that." Riggs sidled over to his leg and inspected it. "Your wound is still delicate, Kitt. You'll have to be careful not to strain yourself. None of your self-competition today," Riggs ordered, winking at Ember.

"I don't know what you mean, Pitkin," Kitt said with false naivety as he stood.

Ember stood, too, and stretched.

"She'll see for herself, most likely," Riggs said. "Ember, you watch out for him. You'll think he's racing with you but in reality he's racing with himself. Let his ego win," he suggested.

"How can one race with himself?" Ember inquired.

"Exactly," said Kitt before Riggs could answer. "And anyways, Pitkin has never raced me so I'm not sure he knows what he speaks of."

Riggs eyed him in amusement. "Shifters talk, Shearwater. And about more than just the size of your ego."

Ember repressed a short laugh. Kitt gave a shake of his head and hopped up the steps, throwing open the hovel door with a bang before leaping out.

Ember, more awake now, noticed the empty cot. "Is Loria feeling better?"

"Well enough to eat five biscuits for breakfast and play in the river." Riggs adjusted the cleaned blanket that draped over the cot to dry.

Ember recalled when Loria got upset with Kitt during their lesson. She hadn't seen any of that anger last night. "Do you think she's happy?"

Riggs looked up, surprised. "Happy? Perhaps she is today. But...Loria, like others, has a lot of hatred for wizards. She wants to learn to fight, but Kitt thinks she is too young."

"Yes, it would be better for them to hide," Ember agreed. Wizards had too many traps and spells, not to mention the cunning of an adult.

"And that's usually what Kitt teaches them to do." Riggs sat down with his healer's box and started unpacking it. "Either hide or flee. But Loria is different. During the attack, her elder sister hid and made Loria do the same. Her sister didn't make it."

"I'm sorry to hear that—"

"Are you coming?" Kitt called from outside.

"Go," Riggs said with a wave, "before he comes after you as an angry boar."

Ember ducked out of the hovel and into the brilliant rays of the midday sun.

"I didn't realize I'd slept so long," Ember commented as she lengthened her strides to catch up with Kitt.

Kitt slowed. "Rest is to be expected after a night of activity."

Ember peered at him, wondering what he knew. "Did Jinni tell you?"

Kitt frowned as sunlight streamed over his face, and a light breeze flipped his hair as he walked. "She told me about the hunt. That you helped bring down a doe."

Ember supposed Jinni had told him out of annoyance. Either that or sneering surprise. "There was a fawn, too," she said, not caring whether he already knew. A part of her longed to force the memory away, to erase it from her mind and never speak of it again. "He hid in the brambles, waiting for her return, but I found him out. I—"

"You did what you had to do," Kitt said. "You gave him a better death than the one he might have had. You took responsibility for his mother's death. It was the right thing to do."

"It doesn't feel right."

He gave her a sidelong look. "Killing never feels right. Not completely."

Ember trudged through the short sedges, her stomach in a queasy knot. "Then why do we do it?"

Kitt sighed. "We do it to survive. We do it because we need to do it. Food. Clothing. Riggs' father, Neal, taught me that hunting is a way to honor life. The fight to death challenges us and the prey to prove who we are. It is a chance for the prey to show their agility and speed, to use those abilities to their fullest potential. We all carry these strengths, and we all die if those strengths fail us."

"It seems cruel."

Kitt nodded. "But each fight we win, we grow stronger. Each fight we lose, if we don't die, we grow wiser. Sometimes pain and cruelty teach us the hardest lessons."

"Did Neal tell you that, too?"

"No," Kitt replied, examining the trees ahead.

"Not in the way you think."

A raindrop smacked against Ember's face. Startled, she checked the clear skies. Not a cloud in sight.

"It's rain—"

As she spoke, Kitt whirled out of his skirt and into the form of a red-tailed hawk. Without waiting for her, he rose up into the air.

Ember did the same, more careful of her dress this time, and followed him up above camp and to the north. Going deeper into the mountains was safer than heading south toward Lach, but still Ember checked the forest below.

No smoke, no sign of human movement. And no spells that she could sense.

Kitt zoomed ahead of her, riding an updraft along the slope of a mountain. His shadow swam over the trees and rocks below, a smudge of black against the green and beige.

The air warmed the undersides of her wings as she found the updraft. Rain fell from an empty sky, shimmering like dust in the midday sun and misting her face.

Kitt found a thermal current and swooped around toward her, floating over her as she, too, emerged into the current.

Ember gave in to trusting the air. Her feathers were like fingers, feeling the breeze for the opportune moment, for the perfect shift that would lift her just so.

The stream of warmth pulled her around and around until she felt as safe as a cradled babe.

Movement flashed overhead. She looked up in time to see Kitt careening toward her, talons flashing, ready to strike—

Her hawk's intuition kicked in, and Ember rolled at the last minute, exposing her own talons. He grabbed them without hesitation and folded his wings, locking her into a fall.

Her human side barely had time to panic. The hawk seemed to know this, that it wasn't death or even a fight, but the air raced over her wildly as they plummeted down. One second, two seconds. The forest rushed toward them and her heart hammered as Kitt gripped her. This wasn't a fight, and she wouldn't die, and it was really—

He released her, and in the same moment they fanned their wings out, arching away from each other like two leaves breaking off the same twig.

Exhilarating. That was the word.

Unable to stop her hawk-side, she called out, and her heart warmed when he called back. They continued north, weaving between mountains and dipping down into the canopy. Ember shifted between hawk and falcon and vulture, or whatever bird most suited her. The falcon could fly the fastest, the vulture could glide the steadiest, and a small hawk could navigate the woods just as easily as a finch.

They raced as falcons, climbing as high as they

could go before diving down, falling like a heavy rock toward the sea of leaves. Ember arced up at the last minute, swinging horizontal to the tree-line, and she spotted Kitt alongside her.

He flashed in and out of her line of sight, dipping occasionally into the trees with a deft roll, curling around branches like water, and doing who-knew-what else among the tree limbs. At some point, he came out ahead of her and didn't look back.

Self-competition, indeed. Still a falcon, he streaked skyward, rising like a shooting star against the ocean of deep azure.

No longer trying to compete with him, Ember rose into the air as well, basking in the sun and cherishing the wind under her wings. She observed Kitt for a while, noting subtle movements, slight tilts of the wing and tail that grabbed the air, allowing him to slow, or rise, or gain speed.

The wind steadied just above the rounded mountain peaks. She soared as a vulture, and the shadow from her wingspan flooded the gorge that threaded between the feet of the mountains. The landscape below neared the heightened buzz of summer. Oaks, maples, and sycamores flushed in shades of viridian, ferns unfurled their feathery foliage, and the orange buds of sunberry shrubs studded forest openings. Pinks and sedges climbed the edge of the gorge while moss and lichens softened exposed rock. Crystalline water dashed between boulders and churned into caves and caverns.

Where the river calmed and pooled, otters swam and slinked along the forested banks, and kingfishers perched overhead to wait for fish. A black bear lumbered down a mountain slope while a nearby litter of fox kittens played on a fallen log. Further north she spotted grazing deer, porcupines tediously denuding trees of their bark, and dozens upon dozens of songbirds trilling, pecking, and swooping in the forests.

And a small flock of ducks.

Ember's vulture eyes sharpened on them as they flew beneath her. Well, not quite beneath, but they would be, flying south as they were. Eight in total. They flew too high to flee for cover, and pronounced themselves with repeating quacks. An open invitation.

Ember swirled into falcon-form, heart thrumming in her chest.

She let go.

Wings snapping to her sides, she dove head-first toward the flock, gaining speed the further she fell. Wind lashed at her but she dropped straight as an arrow, thrusting like a sword and trusting her falcon's senses as she never had before. She trained her eyes on her target duck.

They seemed to sense her and exploded in a panic. Her target shifted, and Ember struck its side, missing by a finger's width.

The duck wobbled off-course but strove to keep

close to the re-forming flock.

Without losing a minute, Ember raced back up above the flock, this time using the sun as a cover for her approach.

Panicked, the flock tightened and drove forward.

Ember picked out a new target—the duck in the center of the flock. A comfortable position to be in, with others surrounding the edge; the duck might feel a bit more secure than the others. A bit less ready to flee.

She dove.

The flock didn't see her. She struck her target with force, and the impact of the duck against her talons and chest stole her breath. The duck didn't move in her grip, but she broke its neck to be sure, snapping her wings open in the same instant.

She called out to Kitt, smiling inwardly when he emerged instantly from the gorge, a snake dangling from his hawk talons. He shrieked when he saw her, and she responded. They headed south toward camp, flying close and steady beneath the sun.

CHAPTER THIRTY-TWO

"Are you planning on sharing that with anyone?" Riggs asked later, approaching the fire that Ember and Kitt had set up near the river. Children played in the water, shrieking and splashing in shallow pools while the mutt, Jasper, leapt around them.

Sore from turning the spit and famished from watching the golden, sizzling duck, Ember raised a sweaty brow at Riggs. "Did you help cook?"

Riggs mocked hurt and grinned as he sat on an overturned log. "As I recall, I saved your life once."

Kitt snorted and pulled his snake away from the flames to cool.

"Do you always take credit for Norman's work?" Ember teased. She smiled at Riggs' baffled look, then turned her eyes back to the duck. She would give it a few more turns until the skin grew crisp.

"Where is that bird, anyways?" Kitt asked. "I haven't seen him all day."

Riggs shrugged. "I'm sure he's flying around somewhere. He'll come back, just like he always does."

Kitt cut off a steaming chunk of snake and tossed it to Riggs, who popped it from one hand to the other to cool it off.

"Ember?" Kitt offered her some, but she shook her head.

"I'll just have a bit of duck," she said, but in her mind she imagined hoarding the duck and gobbling the entire thing in minutes. When was the last time she had eaten?

She moved the spit away from the fire and restrained herself from tearing into it. As it cooled, she watched Loria splash little Vinn and chase him along the bank, Jasper galloping beside them and making them shriek as he shook water from his sodden coat.

Had they decided about whether to move the camp? She glanced at Kitt, who dug into his meat with hands and teeth, and decided to ask him later. She wondered if she should mention the boy with the dagger in the Lachian village. The oddity bothered her, but she was afraid Kitt would overreact. No, she would look into the matter herself, just as she always did.

Ember tore off a piece of breast meat and placed it on her tongue. The meat was tough, a bit crispy, but the smoky, savory flavor melted in her mouth. A moan escaped her and she rolled her eyes, ignoring Kitt and

Riggs' laughter.

"This is better than—" Ember started, but stopped herself. *Better than any of the dishes at Silverglen.* "Than anything I've had before."

Kitt smiled, a look of ruddy pleasure tinging his cheeks. "Food always seems to taste better when you work hard for it."

Ember stuffed more meat into her mouth. Hunger drove away the rules of propriety that had been ingrained into her as the daughter of a lord. The meat didn't just taste better; she found herself appreciating every bite as though it was gold. "And," she said through mouthfuls, "this is the first meal I haven't burned, or dropped, or ruined..."

She waved at Loria, who came over with Vinn in hand. The two were sodden, but grinning and breathless as they approached.

"Are you hungry?" Ember asked.

They nodded, and Ember offered each of them a duck leg. Vinn grabbed one and trotted back to the river, his hair bouncing with every stuttering stride of a three-year-old as he waved his prize overhead.

Ember laughed and clasped her hands over her heart. The image was like a gift. A gift from the hunt. *Thank you, duck. This is how I will remember you.*

Loria ate her duck leg and showed Riggs her scraped knee. He examined it and decided it needed to be cleaned and dressed. They left, and Kitt eased down beside Ember against a log. The bare skin of his leg touched hers, and his arm brushed against her, warm and solid.

He motioned to the duck. "Do you mind if I have a bite? The snake was a bit lean."

"Go ahead," Ember said, feeling heat creep up her cheeks. Even after today, she still felt the tension of yesterday's argument. How could she even begin to apologize for her reaction? "I'm sorry about yesterday," she blurted. She didn't dare look at Kitt, but was comforted by the sound of his chewing. "I had no right to judge what you've been through. And I appreciate your honesty."

Kitt stopped eating and wiped his mouth with the back of a hand. "It's what I expect when I give a blunt truth. Maybe I was a bit too blunt."

But do you expect my truth in return? She studied the silvery hair along his temple, yearning to tell him about Arundel, about the cruelty she witnessed, though she was sure her own experiences were nothing compared to his. But she couldn't be honest with him, not completely, and knowing that hurt.

Kitt tossed a bone into the fire and sank back against the log. "You haven't asked about my parents yet."

Surprised, Ember stared down at her greasy hands. Hadn't Riggs said he was an orphan? The sensation struck her again that Kitt had had a life — perhaps a very good one — in Lach before fleeing to Orion. Had his parents come with him?

She turned her gaze to the fire and clenched her jaw. "You don't have to tell me."

Kitt grunted. "I know you want to know."

Ember scowled at Kitt in accusation. "I don't want you to tell me just because I want to know. I—" She lost the words.

Gently, Kitt said, "I want to tell you anyways."

Ember dug her hands into the soil, trying to quiet her pulse of anger.

"We were hiding out in the foothills," Kitt explained. "My parents, and my sister. A patrol found us out one night, and attacked my father, who was on watch. They found my mother and sister, and..." A leaden pause. "I just sat there, clinging to a tree branch, unable to move. I remember their screams, and how the blood looked against the firelight."

Ember pressed her lips together. Why did he tell her this? Was he so open with others from the camp? She wouldn't offer him condolences, or her pity. It was too late for those things.

"Not a day goes by that I don't think about how they died and how I could have stopped it. When I saw that wizard during the attack on our camp, what he did to the mother and her babe... I couldn't stop. I've never been so angry in my life."

Odd that his story made her think of Arundel. Had he felt a similar anger while killing shifters, since they had murdered his own parents?

If she had seen Arundel killing shifters, what

would she have done? Sure, she had stopped Arundel from hurting Finn once, but that was nothing compared to what Kitt described...

Ember shook her head. "Is that why you teach the children to hide and fight?"

Kitt bobbed his head once. "They need to be ready."

The ensuing silence gnawed at her, but she stayed and held on, enduring Kitt's warmth and the heat of the fire.

Who else knows about your parents? She longed to ask. And why did he tell her?

Unable to stop herself, she glanced at Kitt and met his gaze. An assessing gaze that seemed to hold as much curiosity as she was feeling.

For a moment, she was afraid that the whole thing was a lie, a manipulation to see how she reacted. But there was honesty in Kitt's face, and a note of openness that she didn't wish to disturb. He needed this, somehow, just as much as she did.

Ember looked back to the fire.

The silence deepened.

CHAPTER THIRTY-THREE

THE EARLY MORNING met Ember with a thick ceiling of gray that rose over the mountains and loomed close to their rounded peaks. The air roved like a temperamental cat. It thrashed the sunberry shrubs below, tickled the tops of the trees, and left her in occasional pockets of emptiness, only to be buffeted by a sudden slap that made her tip and lose balance.

A heavy, wide-winged eagle form seemed to be the best she could do to handle the wind's variability. She kept above the mountain peaks, riding south along whatever steady streams she could find, and passed the half-dozen mountains that hunched between the shifter camp and the Lachian border.

The village appeared the same as before. Mud and daub homes huddled close along the river, and a few extended north to surround a small pasture where a single cow grazed.

Ember swirled into a crow and veered to approach the village from the east. One never knew who watched, and if they suspected anything, she didn't want them to see that she came from the north.

Sensing the familiar dagger spell, she landed gently on the roof of one hovel by the river and caught a whiff of rotting carcass. Her crow-side searched for the smell, but her human-side tuned in to the only sound she could hear in the small village.

A sniffle, followed by a hiccup.

The sounds came through the open window below. Ember bent toward it, clutching to the edge of the straw roof.

"Cheer up, lad," a voice boomed, causing Ember's wings to twitch. A chair scuffed along a wooden floor. "You're a man now. This is what men do. You did good. You're helping keep this country safe."

His father? Or a wizard?

A third pair of footsteps walked the floor. Methodical, rhythmic. *That* was a wizard. More precisely, an Escort. Ember could never mistake the noise of their feet, trained into submission by years of stepping into synchrony with other Escort members. But why an Escort? Fletch didn't have an Escort, or at least he never had before. Was he here now? Was Arundel?

The Escort carried his own heavily spelled weapon. She reached out with her mind, probing for other spells. Nothing.

"...the plan?" someone muttered below.

"These bitches are the plan," said the man with the loud voice. "Best sniffers this side of Lach."

Claws scratched the wood floor in a sudden rush, as though dogs—three of them?—chased something. The curiosity of the crow urged her to fly to the window or to the roof across the road. She stayed, listening to the wet sound of dogs chewing a piece of meat.

The Escort muttered something inaudible. Perhaps she should shift to a mouse—

The loud man guffawed. "Do they not tell you anything, Bram?"

"...why I'm asking you."

"Alright. They'll be back this morning. We'll see if they have anything—"

"...don't?"

"Then we'll put these hounds to good use. They'll track 'em down, no matter how long it takes. They'll find 'em."

"What about..."

"There's no telling if the shifters will come back here. That's why you're to stay—"

"I know why..." The Escort, though still partly inaudible, was growing impatient. "...expect me...fend them off myself?"

"We'll leave another with you, then. But the lord's come up with something that might help you—"

WHACK!

Ember lost her grip of the straw roof, one claw throbbing from what could only be a thrown stone. But where—?

Another stone flung at her, this time hitting her wing. Off-balance, she toppled from the roof, flapping violently to gain balance.

"Shifter!" a voice shouted. The boy. How had he gotten out of the house without her noticing?

The sound of footsteps pounded the wooden floor. Ember rose up, cawing, desperately flapping her inefficient crow's wings. She must not let them think she was a shifter. She followed the scent of the carcass, allowing her crow's mind to take hold. A plausible cover, but was it enough?

She heard the men running to catch up, and the cold of the spelled weapons pulsed closer. She rounded the corner, drawn to the scent that came from the last house of the row, the house that they had traded goods with—

Ember dropped like a stone. The carcass, the smell...

A woman swung by a noose in the door. Matted hair framed a wrinkled, puckered face. Thin legs and bare feet dangled beneath the burlap sack she wore, and around her neck hung a wooden sign reading 'TRAITOR.'

Half a moment later, the sound of footsteps rounded the corner behind her. With all her might,

Ember repressed herself and willed the crow to take over completely. She blinded herself to the dead woman's gray skin, the heavy stench that twisted to savory in the crow's mind, the way the woman's body jerked when she landed on it. Her beak sank into the flesh. She cawed again, hoping to rouse other crows to join her.

The two men and the boy halted a few paces away and gaped.

"Are you sure that's a shifter?" the loud man asked.

The boy gulped. "It was by the window. Why would a crow want to be by a window?"

"Maybe it smelled the mutton," the loud man suggested. "Would shifters eat a carcass?"

"I've seen worse," the Escort muttered. "There's only one way to find out..."

The man stepped close and reached for her. Ember burst into flight and cawed like an angered crow. She headed east and didn't dare look back. Past the nearest mountain peak, and down into the canopy before tracking north.

She focused on rowing her wings as quickly as possible. Focused on remembering what the wizards had spoken of. Their plan. Their hounds. Thought of the clouds and wished for rain. Anything to wash the taste from her beak.

CHAPTER THIRTY-FOUR

THE CAMP WAS in an uproar. People milled about, as wolves, dogs, or humans, searching through hovels, weaving in and out of the camp boundaries and sniffing the air.

Ember shifted to human form and threw on her deer-hide dress, then grabbed her makeshift spear and searched for sign of Seabird.

"...in a calm way!" Seabird's voice rang over the din of panicked voices and overturning furniture.

He stood in the center of the clearing next to Asenath, who stared stolidly at the hustle around her. A circle of shifters had begun to form around the leader, their expressions grim and fearful.

"What happened?" Ember asked a shifter as she made her way to the clearing. The man only shook his head. "What's wrong?" she asked another, stopping her as she shook out a blanket.

The woman jerked away and scowled. "You help find her."

"Find who?" Ember asked, but the woman was already striding away.

Cursing, Ember jogged into the clearing. Riggs saw her first.

"It's Loria," he muttered, "No one has seen her since last night." He was about to say more when Seabird spoke again.

"We can't have people crawling over the hills shouting. We have too many enemies and too much to risk. Kitt is leading a small search team, and the others must stay here."

Muttering broke out in the small crowd and some wandered off, giving up their search. Kitt motioned to the others to head off.

Ember pushed through the crowd. "I'm coming with you," she demanded.

Kitt stopped mid-stride and turned, his brow furrowed. Jinni and the other shifters who followed him turned as well, and for once she thought Jinni's glare wasn't quite as hateful as it usually was.

Kitt shook his head. "We need shifters out there who aren't afraid to kill wizards."

Ember scowled. "I'll kill a wizard if I have to. You know I'm the only one who can sense their spells."

Kitt's jaw bulged as he ground his teeth. "Fine. Let's go."

At once the group shifted into wolves, shedding their clothes like skin. Ember clutched her spear and jogged behind them, probing for spells as she left the camp boundary. She sensed nothing beyond impending rain.

Please don't rain, she wished at the dense clouds overhead, following the wolves around a patch of brambles as they searched for a scent trail. But rain would deter the wizard's dogs, too, who were perhaps already searching for the camp. The man said they were waiting for the others to return. Had those others been here? Had they found Loria? Did she tell them about the camp?

She had meant to tell Seabird of the men in the Lachian village, had known that their only real option was to move camp. But now the wizards might be near, and moving was no longer a viable option. The children would be too vulnerable out in the open. And Lexy.

But they must find Loria first. She quickened her pace.

They picked out a scent trail and followed it, only to lose it at the river. They searched up and down the banks, stretching further with each sweep until Jinni barked for them to come.

A light rain began to fall as Ember scrambled up the steep bank and into a clump of ferns. She considered shifting, but dismissed the thought. The dulled senses of the human allowed for easier spell searching, although whatever spells were out there might have begun to fade with the rain.

The wolves milled ahead, veering here and there as they picked up new scents. Multiple trails. Were they Loria's?

Bent oak seedlings and broken fern fronds pointed her down one trail. The duff looked disturbed at the base of a sycamore, and just past that Ember spotted a snapped sunberry branch.

Kitt raced by, snuffling with head thrust to the ground, already on the scent.

Ember reached further with her mind, straining to touch even the smallest, weakest of spells. Far away, like the sight of a torch on the other side of Mirror Lake, Ember felt a cold flicker.

She grabbed it and held it in her mind. A familiar spell.

She ran past boulders painted by lichen, over fallen logs that reached to her waist, up mossy mounds spurting with delicate orchids and fading trilliums, and skirted around a murky pool.

A potent spell. Complex. She worked through the strands in her mind, poking them and separating them, categorizing the weaves.

Her foot suddenly met resistance, and she plunged onto a grassy mat, toes throbbing.

She gasped at the pain, but scrambled up. The wolves surrounded her, all tracking different trails, ears back and tails raised high in aggression. She saw

Kitt, standing as though waiting for her, and in that moment heard a cougar's fierce growl.

The juvenile cougar rolled and lashed wildly, her paw strung taut in a snare attached to the base of an alder tree. Another part of Ember sensed that the cougar was a shifter. Loria.

Ember couldn't ignore the rhythmic pulse of the spelled snare.

"I need you to calm her," she told Kitt as she tossed her spear aside.

Kitt whirled into the form of a cougar, twice the size of Loria, his sudden purr thrumming in the air like a swarm of bees. Loria stood as he approached, and something about him calmed her.

They touched noses and he lay beside the snare, his tail hitting the ground like a rope. Loria, after another frustrated yank of her paw, lay next to him, only relaxing when Kitt started grooming her head with one wide, pink tongue.

Ember hardly noticed the proceedings. The spell throbbed in her mind, strange yet familiar. Kneeling before Loria, she peered closely at the snare.

Fine strands of metal twisted to form a loop that tucked into the snare lock to prevent slack. Arundel's work. And a strange Binding spell, most certainly not cast by Arundel's precise hand, but of a complexity that made her think it really was Arundel's creation. She had seen it before, on a collar...

The bear.

Her stomach rolled.

A Binding spell, interwoven with a bit of Freeze, a bit of Blinding, and a bit of Stupification that would dull the mind. The slight spell strands suggested mental rather than physical effects, but the Binding looked strong enough to effect mind and body.

She sat back, feeling numb. "It's a Binding spell," she said to no one in particular. "Meant to keep shifters from shifting."

A dangerous spell. And entirely unlawful. The Council, though allowing the killing of shifters, still held up the notion that it was wrong to control others through spells, shifters or not—

"So?" Jinni's voice broke Ember's thoughts. The woman stood over her with arms crossed, her figure cutting straight toward the drizzling slate sky. "Can you fix it?"

Ember bent over the snare, willing her fingers to steady. "Even if I can... Do you know how long Loria was missing?"

"Etty saw her to bed last night, but she may have left while others slept. I don't see why that matters, wizard-shifter."

Ember separated the different spells mentally, imagining the signs she would have to make to undo them, and hoped they would bend to her will. "Have you ever stayed in one form for too long?" she asked.

No one answered.

Ember pushed into the spell, twisting her fingers

to the left, then up and over the strands. She undid the smaller strands with one hand, but the dominant spell, the Binding, required two hands. Each coming from either end, unwinding, unraveling, convincing the spell to release and let go, to dissolve back into the air. She reached the center and gave a quick flick of her fingers outward. The residue burst into hundreds of silvery sparks before fading back to air's invisibility.

Grasping the snare with careful hands, she wiggled it down inch by inch until Loria's paw slipped free.

Loria pulled her paw close and licked her raw skin fiercely, ears back and tail tapping the ground.

"Loria," Ember called. How long had the girl been in cougar form? She was young, perhaps inexperienced with being an animal. Would she know enough to suppress the instincts?

The cougar gave no sign of recognition. "Loria, you are a human. Do you remember?" Ember continued. "Do you remember Kitt? And Vinn? You live at camp."

Nothing.

Desperate, Ember met Kitt's steady gaze.

"Her sister," Ember heard herself say. "What was her sister's name?"

"Evelyn," Jinni answered from behind.

Ember nodded. "Loria, do you remember your sister, Evelyn? She was with you..." Ember swallowed. "Evelyn was with you that day when the patrol attacked camp. You hid with her, but they found her. They found Evelyn."

Loria's ears swiveled at full attention, and the cougar's molten eyes froze on her as though catching sight of prey. A sudden shiver swept over fur, and it blurred, curled, and whirled, and skin took its place, with dark hair tumbling over shoulders and chest.

The girl bent over with a sob before slumping to the ground, unconscious.

Ember cursed. "Kitt—"

But he was already shifting, snapping back to human form. He scooped Loria up in his arms, worry and anger hardening his expression. "Let's go."

Ember grabbed her spear, heart thumping as she half-ran beside Kitt's long strides.

"The stench of wizard was all over that place," he said through clenched teeth. "Including that one you didn't kill."

Ember walked on, knowing that an apology wasn't enough. It would never be enough.

"The trails were old, but by no more than a day or two," Kitt continued. "They should still be near. I'm going to find them and kill them."

Fletch would slaughter him. "No. Kitt, you mustn't. You'll be risking yourself—"

"I'll take others."

"And risk them, too? Please, think about it. They have weapons and this new spell—"

"I *have* thought about it," he spat. His walk had

turned to a near jog, and he cradled Loria as if she weighed no more than a stick. "I've thought more than enough in my lifetime, and shifters died because of it. They know we are here and they won't stop looking until they find us."

"Kitt..."

He no longer listened. His jaw set, he picked up his pace to a full run, nimbly missing stones and sticks, and swiveling beyond touch of snagging vines and brambles.

Ember clenched her spear and ran after him. The raindrops thickened and spattered her cheeks with cold kisses.

CHAPTER THIRTY-FIVE

Ember pushed through the crowd gathered in Riggs' hovel to where Seabird spoke with Jinni, his arms clasped behind him in a forced stance of calm.

"I need to speak with you," she told Seabird in a hushed voice. She glanced to where Kitt sat with crying Loria to be sure he still comforted her. She turned back to Seabird, ignoring Jinni and the others. "In private."

Jinni bristled. "What you tell him is our—"

Seabird lifted his hand. "It's alright—"

Ember spun away and leapt through the hovel door without waiting for more useless chatter. The camp appeared empty, with everyone having ducked into their own hovels or gone to Riggs' to see Loria. The noise of the rising river and the sound of rain hitting leaves filled the air. It would have to do.

She strutted to the river, startling a half-dozen

doves who took cover in a sunberry shrub to burst into whistling flight. She bent to suck up water and swish it vigorously before spitting it out. The vile taste of rotten flesh lingered on her tongue. Dunking her head into the river, the cold water drove against her, beating her ears with its roar and tugging her hair downstream as it would a clump of river-weed. She let the water carry away her memories, willed it to strip her clean until the cold sank into her skull and numbed it.

But Loria wouldn't leave her, or Kitt, or the bear. The spell throbbed in her mind and she still felt Fletch's presence looming over her as it did in her dark bedchamber. *Did I really believe I could escape him?*

Water surged up her nose, and she pulled out of the water, sputtering.

"You wanted to speak with me," Seabird rumbled from behind her. "We can talk in my hovel—"

"No." Ember pressed her hair back. "I like the rain." She stood without facing him, letting the water from her hair soak whatever dry spots remained on her dress. "You mustn't let Kitt go looking for the wizards."

"I don't want him to go, but I have little sway over what he does. He'll do what he thinks is best, whether I like it or not."

Ember's chest tightened. "They have powerful spells and weapons. The one that bound Loria was dangerous. Kitt will be killed, and whoever he takes with him."

"Perhaps you underestimate him."

Ember spun around. "You are underestimating these wizards! They will stop at nothing to find shifters. They will capture Kitt or anyone else, and torture him until he reveals the camp location. Then they will end him."

Rain coursed along Seabird's scar from temple to chin. "Kitt would never give us away."

Stubborn, stupid man.

Ember swallowed her anger; she had no right to it. There only remained one way to convince him.

She took a shaky breath. "I am Ember Thackeray."

Seabird froze for a moment before taking deep, steady breaths. His nostrils pinched, and his hands remained clasped behind his back. The scar twitched.

"You mean to say that you lied to us about who you are. That you have come here knowing that you risked everyone's lives."

Ember repressed the urge to look away. "That was never my intention."

"Are you a spy for Lord Arundel?"

"No." Ember folded her arms. "I came here to escape a wizard who found me out. And to find my real father." She wouldn't admit out loud that she had failed in both those regards. Her stomach churned. "Lord Seago, I must be allowed to find the patrol on my own. For everyone here. Please, call off Kitt and the others. Do whatever you must to stop him, even if you have to Freeze him."

Seabird considered her with black eyes. "The others will be glad to see the back of you once they know the truth."

"They'll have other things to worry about," Ember said, not entirely convinced that he would try to stop Kitt and others from going after the patrol. "Some wizards are in the village where Jinni's group traded. They hung the woman who has been helping us."

"When did this happen?"

"I found her this morning. What's more important is that the wizards spoke of plans. The others in their group would come back to the village from wherever they were—presumably around here, after Loria's incident—and they would wait in ambush for Jinni's group to return. If no shifters come, they have dogs."

"They would track us," Seabird stated. His hands broke free from behind his back, and he rubbed the scar on his left cheek. "We could still move camp."

"If the patrol is here for me, they might not come. I will try to distract them, to make them think that there aren't any others. But warn the shifters of this new spell. A Binding spell that Freezes and stupifies the mind, one that will prevent them from shifting. It could kill them." *As it must have done to the bear.*

The sky rumbled.

Before Seabird could say anything further, Ember shifted into a hawk and grabbed her deer-hide dress with talons. She drove through the sodden canopy and into the rain without looking back, thinking of Riggs, Loria, Lexy, and Jinni. She wished she could apologize to them all, to tell them the truth, and to beg for their forgiveness.

And Kitt. No words would ever be enough.

With a knotted stomach, she sped southward. Her wings beat against the pummeling rain as her hawk-eyes searched the ground for sign of wizards. She cast out her mind for spells, for any slight glimmer through the dull, watery world beneath her.

I will find you, Fletch.

CHAPTER THIRTY-SIX

LIGHTNING ARCED ACROSS the sky, snapping close to the trees that hid Fletch's camp. Ember sensed the heavy Glamours stretching beneath the canopy, and as she flew closer, patches of white canvas appeared where the spells had begun to fade from the rain. Other spells pulsed down there, no doubt from weapons.

Near the camp, Ember descended to the ground and shifted back to human form, weariness stretching through her limbs. The camp must have moved recently, as she had found them in a place she had already searched, west of the burned clan village.

Ember tugged her dress on and tied a secure knot over her shoulder. Fletch knew what she was; the others in the camp might not. Or at least, they had no proof. Had Fletch told the others what he saw back in Silverglen? Had he told Arundel as well? Or was this a rescue mission because Arundel thought she had been kidnapped?

Gray sheets of rain obscured the camp and washed out the noises of horses and men. Ember curled her empty hands, straightened her back, and forced her legs to move toward them.

A man's shape appeared in front of her, probably a guard. He faced the camp, where other men milled under the white canvas. Horses and a small rickety wagon stood in the rain on the opposite side. Beneath the heavy canvas, a low, wide fire pit glowed.

"Guard," she called out.

The guard turned and saw her, but the man wasn't a guard. He was Gregory. Shorter and younger-looking than she remembered, with eyes like rain and sodden hair clinging to his temples in tight ringlets.

His mouth formed her name, inaudible beneath a pulse of thunder.

Rivulets of rain channeled down her back and curled around her shoulders like a cold snake. Her stomach hardened, and her legs trembled like the leaves overhead.

Fletch's shout rose through the noise of rain, and two men jogged toward her, one with a sword drawn and pointed at her neck.

She let them come.

Had Gregory told Arundel about her? Had he told Fletch? He seemed as frozen as her, a look of surprised dismay playing tug-of-war with his brows and lips. She remembered loving those lips.

A wizard grabbed her wrists to Bind them in front of her, while the other kept the sword leveled beneath her chin. They followed orders, with expressionless faces and the quick, efficient movements of a trained patrol member.

"Lady Thackeray." Fletch emerged from the canvas at a slow amble, unheeding of the rain as it soaked head and cloak, unblinking as it coursed into his eyes. He gave a white-toothed sneer. "I have finally found you."

No, I found you. She wanted to smack that sneer off his face. She inhaled. "You think I will escape," she said, lifting her bound wrists. "I came to you willingly." The Bindings throbbed into her mind with that spell—the same one that had caught Loria and bound the bear—dulling her senses and wrapping her in what felt like a wall made of cotton-lined stone.

Fletch tilted his head, as though curious about what she said. "It's assurance my dear. I don't want to lose you again." His fingers twitched. "And now we have two delicious prizes for all our efforts," he said, a grin pulling lips to ears.

Ember's heart thumped. She lifted her head, pushing through the spell's haze. "Who could be an equal prize to myself?"

Fletch stepped close to her, easing his mouth to her ear. "A firebird, my dear, though never so pretty as you."

Norman?

Long, spindly fingers touched her arm. Cold and bony.

She forced herself not to shudder, not to lift her arms and shove him away. "I'm disappointed, Fletch. I thought you would be smart enough not to try capturing a firebird."

Fletch stepped back, his eyes somehow dancing and empty all at once. "Hmm, you know the rhyme? 'Capture naught the bird of gold, for selfishness is freedom sold.'" His half-singing voice slithered through the rain and rumbling clouds. "Yes, it's true. But I'm testing some other ways that you might find quite clever, my dear."

KEERREEEEEE!!!

An unmistakable scream shot overhead. Not Norman, but a hawk. Familiar and strange and burning with vengeance.

A tremor swept down Ember's spine.

A burst of air hit her cheek as the hawk dove. The wizard who held her cried out and released his hold as talons sunk into his eyes like knives into butter. He flailed his hands, but the hawk was gone, and watery blood seeped down his cheeks as he fell to his knees and screamed, "I can't see! I CAN'T SEE!!"

"Damn shifters," the wizard with the sword muttered. He swiveled about, holding his weapon up to the curtains of rain.

The hawk and Fletch had disappeared. Ember's

heart thumped wildly in her chest. Had Kitt come to kill her? To kill them all? Seabird hadn't stopped him, and the fool had followed her here.

A sob lodged in her throat.

Fletch, somewhere under the canvas now, shouted orders. A shrill human cry erupted from beneath the canvas, and the camp exploded into chaos. Wizards, perhaps twenty of them, grabbed weapons and ran, stumbling, toward their horses.

A bear's roar played drums with the thunder, beating a rhythm of fury through the forest and into her bones.

The horses screamed with the men as the bear charged into the crowd. A giant paw swung out, throwing a wizard against the trunk of a tree. Another wizard was trampled underfoot, and a third crunched beneath a jaw as long as a man's face. In a blink, Kitt changed from a bear to a boar, tusks scattering men and weapons and embers as he charged through the fire and the camp's perimeter.

Thunder cracked, snapping Ember's nerves out of paralysis.

She lunged at the injured wizard and dragged his sword out of its scabbard with her bound hands. The wailing man didn't seem to notice or care.

The rough leather hilt felt good against her palms, the blade heavy and awkward as she swung. The other wizard near her stood motionless, gaping at the scene beneath the canopy. She rammed into his back, smacking his head with the flat of the sword, and he fell.

She charged into the scattering men, her arms and shoulders burning as she slashed at one man after another. They didn't see her coming, were too focused on Kitt's maddened game of chase-and-kill, and weren't suspecting an attack from a human.

How many had she slain? Injured? Perhaps none. She was only certain of the impact of her spelled blade against solid muscle, the cries of surprise, the cold wash of rain over her face and eyes.

Another wizard fell, and for a moment she stood alone.

Through dripping strands of hair, she glimpsed a cougar tearing at a man's throat. The man's limbs jerked as though he still lived and tried to get away. And she spotted Gregory standing away from her, watching the same cougar, lifting his hands to his belt to touch two silvery hilts.

The daggers rose like a pair of glinting stars. Familiar and lovely, her own gift to him all that time ago. His hands arched back, poised on the brink of a void she hadn't known existed.

Despair hurtled through her.

A clap of thunder swallowed her scream, and the stars flew from his hands.

Something blunt and heavy smacked the back of her head. Ember crumpled to the ground.

CHAPTER THIRTY-SEVEN

The stench of urine and lilies woke her.

Ember lay in dimness, her back pressed against wood that trembled and rolled beneath her. The wagon.

The cords on her wrists chafed her skin raw. Sore arms and hunger pained her body, as did the lump on the back of her skull where someone had struck her, but the physical pain was nothing against the swarm of memories. Gregory's betrayal. And Kitt...

She focused on her hands, bound to a large rod of steel bolted into the side of the wagon. The spell around her wrists, glowing silver in the dim moonlight, was too complex for her to undo, and the cords themselves too restricting to form the correct movements. She shifted her weight to see the rest of the wagon.

Two patrolmen sat opposite her, wearing their

proud violet garments, next to a third figure, nearly one with the shadows.

Fletch sat on a bench beside her, close enough that his floral stench had soaked into her own skin.

He smiled when she looked at him, and his empty, hungry eyes seemed to swallow her up.

"I'm relieved to see you awake, my dear," Fletch said. "My friend here gave you a good knocking on the head that I wasn't sure you would recover from." He motioned to the third figure who sat across from her.

The figure leaned forward, and Ember flinched. The archer. The twisting scar. The woman who almost killed Gregory at the race. How had she come here?

"I thought you might recognize her," Fletch stated, sounding amused. "My friend Ashaki is the famous winner of three Red Morning races."

Infamous winner, you mean. A person couldn't win that many races without shedding others' blood.

"Where are we?" Ember asked, ignoring the chill from the archer's gleaming eyes.

Fletch's smile widened. "On an old road used by the clans. Don't fret, my dear," he said, folding his hands over crossed legs. "We're heading back to Silverglen, as my lord requested."

A part of Ember sagged in relief. But what about the two wizards at the Lachian village? Would Fletch pick them up on the way back? Or would they all stop to search for more shifters? Assuming that he knew about the other shifters, which she was sure he did.

That boy at the village had likely told someone of the wolves he saw. Why else had those two wizards in the village planned on setting up an ambush there?

"I'm so glad," Fletch went on, "that your friend Gregory told my lord that you went missing, and that you might be in Orion looking for a faction. It seems that you found at least one other like yourself." His voice slithered into the dark, cloistered space. "He's a feisty one. And stupid. Still, I'm curious to see how you two will get along as breeders. It should be so interesting, with you half a wizard and half a shifter, and him so—hmm—*vigorous*."

Ember sat up. Searching the shadows, she thought she saw the outline of a cage, with a bulky mass within. Those shadows didn't move. Surprised, she noticed he wore the familiar Binding spell around his neck, which she hadn't seen or felt. Perhaps he was unconscious, or under a Freeze, which prevented him from moving while stuck in cougar form. Her stomach twisted.

Had Gregory missed killing him on purpose?

She turned back toward the wall so that Fletch couldn't see her expression. Willing fingers and wrists to bend at painful angles, she fought against the cords in order to get to the spell.

The wagon jerked to a stop, and she sprawled over the floor. Fletch grunted and vaulted over her, striding from bench to the end of the wagon in two quick paces. The other wizards stayed. Ember curled back against the side of the wagon and eyed them, wishing she could call out to Kitt.

A chorus of howling dogs broke out near the wagon, and a loud man greeted Fletch in false cheer. Ember recognized the man's voice from when she spied on the village.

"Sorry about the bitches, sir," the loud man apologized. A door closed, and the barking hushed.

Another voice spoke up, so quiet she could barely make out the words.

"...have her?"

"I do," Fletch replied. "She is secure."

A short pause. "...bound her?"

"She attacked us, my dear Bram. Her and another, rather interesting shifter. They are both quite feisty, if not dangerous."

The Escort scoffed, and anger amplified his small voice. "You are the one who is dangerous, treating...like an animal. Lord Arundel...to ensure the safety and comfort—"

"Lord Arundel is misinformed. And thus, so are you," Fletch said, sounding satisfied.

"I demand to see her," Bram said, his voice rising. "It is my duty as Escort to—"

Bram shouted in pain, and the sound of clashing metal rang out once, and again, followed by a grunt. After the noise, the succinct sound of a door closing.

Ember's throat constricted. Arundel had sent an Escort to take her safely home, which meant only one thing.

Arundel didn't know she was a shifter.

She sagged against the wooden wall and waited for other sounds to emerge from outside the wagon. A horned owl hooted, bullfrogs thrummed, and the river's song trickled through the wagon's canvas. Closer, horses snorted and shook their bridles, and riders creaked in their saddles. She counted four, at least. Had the others gone ahead? Or had Fletch left them behind to find the camp?

Please be gone, she wished to Seabird. *Far, far away.*

Moments later, the door opened and closed again, and Fletch strode back into the wagon, his expression hidden by the shadows of his hooded cloak. A new cloak. Velvet purple, lined in gold. A statement of powerful servitude that only the Escort could display.

Bram, dead. Arundel would be displeased.

Ember tucked herself against the wall, the cords delving too deep into her skin, feeling the odd fabrication of a spell wall around her. She drew her attention away from it. She needed to come up with a plan. There was a chance Fletch had tried to convince Arundel of what she was, and that he hadn't believed him. It might also be the case that Fletch hadn't yet told him, and that Arundel had no idea.

Closing her eyes, she listened to the passing hoot of another horned owl. *Camouflage. Fierce silence. Deadly surprise.* Her blood pulsed through her limbs, remembering the strengths of the owl.

    The night deepened.

CHAPTER THIRTY-EIGHT

"Home sweet home."

Ember jerked away as Fletch's face loomed over her shoulder. She gagged at the smell of his breath.

Fletch chuckled and used a small knife to slice the cords that bound her to the metal rod of the wagon. Beneath the cords more spelled ropes locked her wrists together. "Come now, up with you."

She eyed the small knife before it disappeared in his cloak. Fletch turned away and leapt from the wagon, leaving her with the two armed patrolmen and the archer. The rest of the wagon was empty.

Ember raised her chin and looked the patrolmen in the eyes. "My father will not be pleased with the way I've been treated."

The first smirked and waved his sword at her to stand. "Don't bother with your lies, girl. Fletch told us what he saw."

"I saw your mother myself," the second patrolman said, nodding. "Rollin' in bed with a shifter. Feathers and fur and teeth everywhere." He spat.

The archer said nothing, but stared at her in a way that made her skin prickle.

Clenching her jaw, she grabbed the metal rod and pulled herself up. Her limbs felt heavy, as though lead had been poured into her bones, and so stiff that her joints cracked like a brittle tree in a fierce wind.

She straightened her spine and ignored the bruises forming on her wrists.

Today, I am Ember Thackeray. Daughter of a lord.

One step, then another, and she climbed down the steps of the wagon. Brilliant shafts of midday sun struck her momentarily blind. The day was warm, and birds sang. It was the type of early summer day that she once would have spent with Gregory at the stables, or sneaking handfuls of fresh strawberries, or playing chase in the dappled shade of the pear orchard. She would have stayed away from the gardens to avoid Salena, and would have stayed out of the fields to avoid Arundel's hunting returns.

As Ember's eyes adjusted to the light, she saw that they stood near the edge of Mirror Lake, high up on a cliff where their road ended. The lake sprawled wide beneath them, curving around to meet the three stone arches that marked the only entrance into Silverglen. The arches were mounted by a walkway that spanned between two slender towers. Beyond this, a wall of leaded glass reflected the blue sky.

"Perhaps the lady can be kind enough to lead us to the great stair," Fletch said from behind her.

Ember whirled, and saw that Fletch stood motionless beside a great iron cage. Kitt, still a cougar, had two deep wounds in one shoulder, preventing him from putting his weight on it. Scarlet whiskers stretched back in a snarl, narrowing two gold eyes and flattening his ears. He pawed the side of the cage, and two-inch claws protruded through the iron to catch on Fletch's cloak. Her chest tightened.

A flash of orange behind Fletch. *Norman.* Fletch had secured the bird by both feet to a wooden perch, just as Ember had seen the falconers do when the birds were to sit out of their mews. But Norman's colors had already begun to fade. Even now, he didn't attempt to fly, but sat, silent and resigned, with flattened crest and drooping tail.

"Unless you would like to speak with your friend? Or is he a lover?" Fletch continued, his black eyes digging into her as he removed his cloak from Kitt's claw with an insouciant tug.

Ember suddenly found herself wishing that Kitt had wrung the vile man's neck.

She repressed a shudder and turned away.

The ancient, wide steps had been cut into the cliff-side by Arundel's father, Doune. They had been placed as a way for him and his son to access the northern forests for hunting, and for transportation of iron from the smelter to the smithies in Silverglen. Arundel had told her this once when she was very young as he helped her climb up the steep steps, and she remembered how strong and warm his hand seemed then, and how pleased he had been once she reached the top.

But that was before her shifting abilities emerged. When she was simply a lord's daughter; a blink of time in her life.

"Down we go!" Fletch scaled the first few steps before pausing. "Let's protect her from falling, shall we?"

Wordless, four patrolmen formed a tight circle around her. Ember glared at Fletch. Did he really think she would throw herself down the stairs? Or did he think she would try to escape by running across them? The Bindings made her useless for shifting, and she would only be able to run so far before the patrolmen caught up to her.

Not that she considered running. She wouldn't this time, even if she could, and it wasn't just Kitt or Norman that solidified her resolve.

Fletch continued down the steps like an impatient child, leaping down from one step to the other, as if a missed step wouldn't result in a messy, neck-breaking plunge into the water. She hoped that his carelessness would bring him down.

Ember took slow steps and focused on the guard

just ahead of her rather than the quick descent to the lake.

She allowed herself one glance back at Kitt's cage, and saw with horror that it tilted to one side as two patrolmen, white-faced and sweaty, carried it down. They clung to the very ends of two slats of wood driven through the iron grate for handles, and flinched as Kitt lashed his paw at whichever man neared too close.

To the right, Norman fared better. A single patrolmen carried his perch like a torch. The patrolman glared at the bird as a mass of white dung plopped on one shoulder.

At its base, the long staircase sank down into the murky lake. Had the water been lower when Doune's men built it all those years ago? Or had he forced his men to work underwater, slowly against the water's thickness, and playthings to a squelkin's massive jaws and suckered tentacles?

Black water lapped the steps, where three of Arundel's boats waited. A violet-clad patrolman sat in each one, except the third, where Gregory sat with a look of hardened patience.

Ember headed for the first boat.

Fletch stopped her with a wave of his hand.

"You can go in that one," he purred, tilting his head to Gregory's boat. "Ashaki will escort you."

Ember didn't wait for the archer. She strutted to Gregory's boat and stepped in, violently rocking the vessel. Gregory leapt forward to help steady her, but she lurched to the right, taking two more unsteady steps before careening into the opposite end of the boat. She gasped as the edge of a wooden seat drove into her ribs and her arm banged the side of the vessel. The boat's ledge dipped near the surface of the water, and she caught shadowy movement not far below.

A hand touched her arm.

She flinched away. "Leave me."

Gregory straightened, his expression loosened by surprise, but a moment later his features hardened again.

Ember scrambled up to her seat as the archer came on board and sat at the opposite end of the boat as her. To her dismay, Gregory sat between them and faced Ember. His hands turned white as he gripped the oars.

Without waiting for the others to board their boats, Gregory swung his boat around with quick efficiency. The oars bit deep into the water, tugging them rhythmically toward the castle. Gleaming, the hilts of Gregory's throwing knives drew her attention. Scarlet smudged their surfaces and stained the top edges of the leather sheaths. He had hurt Kitt, yes, but he hadn't killed him. Had it been intentional? Ember longed to look back, to be sure Kitt's cage had been safely loaded. Instead, she focused on the castle ahead.

Graceful curves of dark stone and ironwork. Wide windows, curving balconies, and speared towers.

For all the beauty, it appeared smaller and bleaker than she remembered. Memories lurked in those leaded windows and impenetrable walls. Her old life, her old self. A shadow. A mouse.

"I didn't betray you," Gregory said in a husky voice.

Ember froze, shooting a wary glance at the archer, whose eyes were mortared to her like stone.

Ember spoke without emotion. "You mean you didn't tell my father of my mission. I don't wish to speak of it."

Gregory stared at her for a moment, confusion overcoming the hardness of his face. His frown shifted to the oars before coming back to her.

"I didn't mean for you to be hurt. For you to be treated this way. I was worried something had happened when you disappeared, that you had done something rash after..."

"How is your lady friend?" Ember asked in a frosted tone.

Ruddiness flushed beneath Gregory's tanned cheeks, and he stayed silent, his gaze on the water.

After what seemed like an eternity, they neared Silverglen and glided beneath the stone arches. Moss had crept farther up the inside walls of the arches since she had left, but otherwise the reek of fish and squelkin hung in that damp, dark space as much as it ever had.

Their small boat emerged from an archway and pointed toward the smooth crescent steps chiseled into the castle's cliff-side. Other boats floated at the base of the steps, tied to iron rods that disappeared into the black water. Two Escorts stood waiting at the top of the steps where the path to the great hall began, their gilded cloaks stirring in a faint breeze as their hands rested on the hilts of their spelled swords.

Gregory aimed the boat at the steps and secured it to a rod. He then offered her his hand to step off.

Ember glanced at his tan, steady hand. She had loved that hand once. Surprises, pleasure, and comfort. And many times, too, she had seen them clenched in anger. He had always wanted to protect her, but couldn't; she was a shifter and very capable of protecting herself. But he had always tried, and he had tried this time by revealing her probable location in Orion. By bringing her disappearance to Arundel's attention. By helping Fletch to find her. Had he also thought to protect her by harming Kitt?

Ember wasn't sure he would ever stop trying. Did he understand the risks he posed to the faction by giving her away?

But that wasn't entirely fair. She was the one who went to them in the first place. She was the one who told Gregory, over the past few years, of her suspicion of where the faction hid based on years of rumors. She was the one who had left without a word of goodbye.

A slight tremor ran over Gregory's hand.

Lifting her chin and masking her expression with stoniness, Ember placed her bound hands in his. His firm grasp lifted her out of the boat and onto the step as though she weighed as much as a crow's feather. Gregory stepped out himself, and for a half a moment the archer's eyes left her while she herself climbed out. Ember tugged Gregory close.

"Did he leave men behind?" she whispered.

Gregory's brows furrowed and he opened his mouth to reply.

"I will escort you myself," Fletch called. His voice slithered across the lake and over the steps as his boat emerged from beneath the arched walkway. Fletch stood at the front, as steady as if he stood on solid ground.

Ember glared at him, but breathed a bit easier when she saw caged Kitt and Norman gliding in the boats behind him.

"My lord will be relieved to see you," Fletch continued, stepping from his boat to the step just as it tapped the stone. He floated up and wedged himself between Ember and Gregory, effectively pushing Gregory aside while pulling Ember close. "And your lady mother, of course." White teeth gleamed behind a charming smile as he wrapped a cold hand around her arm and guided her up the steps.

It took all of Ember's will not to shove him into the squelkin-infested waters.

"I'm not sure about your brother and sister, however," he said in her ear. "I think they've always known you are rather different. An animal, no?" He hummed a chuckle. "Unlike the others, I see you, my sweet. All your fears and longings, and your other deliciously human sensitivities, swirling and blossoming along with your womanhood." A bony thumb glided down and up her arm.

Hair on her neck prickled. She tugged her arm, and to her surprise he released her.

"Escorts," he greeted the two guards as they reached the top step.

The Escorts didn't miss Fletch's—or rather, Bram's—cloak. One scowled and the other raised a lip of disgust.

"Lord Arundel wishes us to escort her to the great hall," the scowling man said.

"Of course," Fletch replied, offering her with a wave of his hands.

Ember found herself in front of the two Escorts, with Fletch lost behind them and Arundel's iron arcade twisting overhead. Mangled shadows chilled the warm flagstones beneath her feet and chased the light from her eyes. On either side gathered the silent gardens, appearing empty of their usual visitors. Behind her, the sound of a cougar's snarl rose above the measured tramp of booted feet. Ahead lay the wide glass doors of the great hall, nearly lost in the wall of leaded glass. She glanced up at her curving balcony, where she once stood to eavesdrop, and where she had always returned after a night of spying. *And where Fletch had seen me shift.* If he hadn't, would she be here now?

The doors opened, and Ember stepped in.

Rays of sun melted through the spotless glass wall, cascaded down over empty trestle tables and pooled onto the scrubbed stone floor, filling the great hall with raw gold. Intangible and temporal gold. Did it bother Arundel that he couldn't capture it? That he couldn't melt it down and turn it into something solid and permanent that he could call his own?

Glamours on the three painted walls moved as though alive. Drogons, a boar, and a firebird. She didn't bother looking at them, but moved instead toward the dais at the left end of the great hall. The sunlight stretched there to illuminate two seated figures.

Ember steadied her breathing. *I am the daughter of Lord Arundel, and no one else shall pass my lips and eyes.*

He sat on his chair, a simple throne cushioned by purple velvet lined in gold. Dark leggings, leather boots, and a scarlet tunic lined in black gems. A matching cap offset the dark brown of his hair and softened a sharp nose and heavy brows.

Salena sat beside him, her hair like braided copper, pale skin and blue eyes ghostlike next to Arundel's dark solidity. Exhaustion etched her face like an old parchment crumpled too long in a pocket. Had Salena thought her dead? Harmed?

She shook off the impulse to reassure her mother with a smile.

A scuffle rose from behind her, and suddenly Fletch strode ahead, leaving behind a trailing stench of lilies as his cloak billowed in haste. He reached the lowest step of the dais and bowed.

Arundel frowned, and Salena waved an orange pomander under her nose.

"Fletch," Arundel greeted. "How did you find my daughter?"

"I caught her just outside our camp, my lord. Sneaking through the rain—"

"Are those Bindings?" Arundel interjected. "Remove those at once," he barked.

Ember came to stand behind Fletch. Her heart hammered her chest, and her palms sweat fiercely, but she focused on standing straight, with a raised chin and an unmoving mask.

Fletch obeyed, a sneer tugging one side of his mouth as he undid the Binding. Ember studied his careful finger movements. He winked at her before turning away.

Was he fool enough to think she would shift in front of Arundel? Gritting her teeth, she rubbed the soreness from her wrists.

"Why do you wear that cloak?" Arundel asked. "And where is Bram?" Arundel searched behind Ember, his brow furrowing deeper.

"Bram had an unfortunate accident, my lord," Fletch began eagerly, but Arundel no longer listened.

Ember knew the moment he saw Kitt. Sparking

his gaze was a familiar fire that pulled like an anchor at her heart. Norman, no doubt, caused that second wave of curiosity and a clench of Arundel's hands against the armrests of his throne. With great control, he rose to his feet and ambled down the steps. His new smile didn't reach his eyes.

"You brought me something else, too?" he asked Fletch, interrupting the man mid-sentence. "I am very pleased. The bird stays here, but you may go. Take the cat."

Fletch bowed, almost mockingly, and a metallic chain twinkled from beneath the folds of his cloak.

The key.

Ember dug her fingers into her palms. She could steal the key and free Kitt. Maybe even the bear, if he was still down there—

"Ember."

Her attention snapped to Arundel, who stood watching, too, as Fletch and his men carried the cage out a set of wooden doors. Her father—her false father—stretched over a foot taller than herself, dark and solid as a mountain. As the doors thudded closed, he ran a hand down his face.

She hadn't noticed the fine lines there. Had missed the stubble, the great circles beneath his eyes, and the way the grooves had deepened between nose and mouth. He looked haggard. Hazel eyes, bloodshot and too wide, stared at her with a mixture of relief and anger.

"Ember," he repeated, lifting her hands with his. The touch reminded her of her childhood. He stared at the bruises on her wrists. "We are glad you are home. But," he said, letting her hands drop, "we need answers."

He stepped back and clasped his hands behind him, haggardness receding behind an emotionless mask. Was this how he looked when he interrogated the shifters in the dungeon? "How did you come to be in Orion?"

Ember took a deep breath and licked her lips, not daring to look at Salena, who continued to sit on the dais. "I went of my own accord. I heard rumors of a faction there."

Arundel's expression didn't change. "Did you find any faction?"

"I found a group of shifters, yes." Behind Arundel, Salena shifted. Ember kept her eyes fixed to Arundel, her stomach tightening. "I stalked them, Father. I took them out one by one, using the methods you taught me. They were stupid creatures." It wasn't difficult to sound genuine. Lies flowed like breath from her.

Arundel's eyebrows lifted a hair's breadth. "Why didn't you tell me where you were going or what you were doing? It was dangerous and foolish of you." His spoke in a flat tone, his expression almost neutral.

It wasn't enough. She needed more. Fletch had hinted to him of what she was, planting a seed of suspicion that would no doubt gnaw Arundel alive. He wouldn't want to believe Fletch. She merely needed to provide something small that he could devour, something to quash any seedling of doubt within him.

Her head buzzed with sudden lightness, and her pulse fluttered in her temples like a moth around a candle-flame. *I am Lord Arundel's daughter,* she repeated. The web of lies stretched into her muscles until she felt as light as a moat of dust, and the sticky facade was no longer a facade but something real and solid that weighed down her stomach like stone. She did it for Riggs and Lexy and the children. She did it for Seabird and Norman. For Kitt...

His name floated away from her like a feather on a breeze. Forgotten, all forgotten but who she must be in this very moment.

Her fingers pulsed with adrenaline.

"I was afraid of failure." She let her voice crack, her head dip in shame. "If I had failed, I couldn't bear to look you in the face again. I've only ever wanted you to be proud of me." She met his gaze and held it, and the tears sprang to her eyes, as though they had been held back for too long. She hated those tears, hated the words her lips formed. Hated them for what they were, and because a part of them was true. "The cougar was the last of them. I tricked him into barging into the patrol's camp, which I discovered two nights ago."

Heat fled her muscles and she swayed.

Arundel gripped her by the shoulders, steadying

her. His gaze gleamed as he nodded and his breath resounded through his lungs like an ocean tide.

"I am proud of you," he said in a strained voice. "You were always motivated to learn more. To do more. Always striving to be better." He squeezed her shoulders. "You remind me of your mother. And of myself."

She wanted to smile and cry at once, and loathed herself for it. She despised that she should desire anything at all from him. So she stood motionless, her anger and hatred strangling a strand of warmth that curled in her chest.

He clenched his jaw, his eyes wide glassy mirrors, and released her.

Ember noticed Salena standing behind Arundel, her blue dress crumpled and her hair mussed in its coils.

"Mother," Ember croaked.

Salena pulled her into an embrace, surrounding Ember in a cloud of rosy perfume, soft damask, and silky skin. Any resentment toward her melted away. Her mother understood her, knew what she was and the secrets she kept. She knew the most important truths and forgave her the lies. "You're home now, my love. Safe and home." Her mother felt more frail than she remembered, and her voice sounded weak.

Ember pulled back. "I'm sorry I didn't tell you—"

"Sshh, now. Dry your tears." Salena handed her a piece of cloth, her own eyes wet and rimmed in pink.

Ember dabbed her face, scrambling to think of how to excuse herself. She must follow Fletch, presumably down to the dungeon. If she had convinced Arundel that no shifters remained, Kitt was her only problem. She glanced at Norman, who sat bedraggled on his perch by the thrones. *Sorry Norman. You'll have to wait just a while longer.*

She opened her mouth to ask for dismissal.

"While you were gone," Arundel spoke up, causing Salena to flinch. "A guest arrived to speak with you. He has been waiting here for days for your return." Mild irritation in Arundel's tone, but something else, too. This person was important.

"Who...?"

Arundel waved a hand toward the wooden doors, and an Escort bowed quickly before pulling one door open.

Into the light of the great hall strode a heavy young man wearing boots, trousers, and a gaudy yellow tunic lined in silver. A pelt lined his cloak as though they stood in the dead of winter, and his upper lip shone with sweat.

The man bowed long and low. "My lady. I have come to ask for your hand in marriage."

Ember's feet froze to the stone floor.

"Eawart?"

CHAPTER THIRTY-NINE

Emitting a coolness she didn't feel, Ember walked to the door and gave Eawart a slight curtsy before going out. Did the man even notice her hide dress and dirty, bare feet?

She strolled into the first corridor that began the maze of halls leading to the dungeon steps. If she ran headlong, she might lose him in the corridors. Except the daft man would probably try looking for her, and she didn't want to risk him interfering with her plan to free Kitt.

She spun around, catching Eawart's gaze on her legs before it darted away.

Ember folded her arms. "I have no wish to marry you."

Eawart gawked before giving a slight shake of his head, ruddiness tinging his plump cheeks. "Will you even listen to what I have to say?" A polite pause for an answer.

Ember tightened her lips.

Eawart released a breath and continued. "When I met you, I was astounded by your beauty, and dancing with you was like dancing with a queen. I felt myself loving you that night as I've never loved anyone before—"

Ember snorted, causing Eawart to flinch. "Did Dev put you up to this? I know you know her from the Academy—"

"Devondra told me of you, that's all," Eawart said. His blush deepened. "I wanted to meet you, and when I did... Ember, we could be great together. You and I, dancing in my castle. I could give you much—"

"Do you expect me to believe you have a castle?"

Eawart wiped the sweat from his upper lip. "I do have one. Or at least, I will, since my cousin is long gone—"

"A castle?" Ember's nails sank into her arms. Perhaps she could cast a Freeze on him and run for it. "Only the lords are allowed to own castles."

"Well, perhaps it isn't a castle outright, but it's nearly half the size of Lord Thurstun's in Pemberville. Please, you should come see it, see what you could be a part of, what I could give you—"

"I want nothing from you, Eawart, except to be left alone."

Eawart shook his head in refusal, his face as red

as a cherry. The sweat had returned to his lip and glistened along his hairline. Would the man never give up?

"I am sure there's another woman who deserves you better than I," she said, resorting to politeness.

"No, I am sure there is not." He reached for her hand, but she stepped away. Chagrined, he smoothed his palms over the pelt lining of his cloak. "I would feel better about your decision if you would agree to see the castle—ah, estate—first. You really must see it."

"Fine, I will go see your estate," she snapped. "But right now I must leave." She turned to go when he nodded. "I must be alone to think about your request," she said over her shoulder, just for good measure.

She suppressed a twinge of guilt at the hope in his eyes and dove through the corridors. Right, left, and left. Vacant, forgotten rooms lined either side of the stone walls. The last corridor had no rooms at all, only cold stone dropping down a drafty stair. A heavy iron door at its base stood cracked open, with no spells she could see or sense.

She rushed down the steps.

How long had Kitt been in cougar form? The hours had stretched to days now. How much of him remained?

Heedless, she shoved through the iron door and flew through the open room with cavernous cells. The table and chair remained in the same positions, but the moldy bread had been reduced by several bites.

Swallowing, Ember pressed on and ignored the shadowy movements from behind iron bars. At the end of the room, the small corridor with wooden doors lining each side lay as she remembered, and the sense of complex spells lingered beyond it.

Behind the stone wall.

She looked back but saw no one, and there was no flicker of torchlight this time.

No spells lined the door. No locks that she could see. Perhaps it wasn't a door after all, but just a wall with another room on the other side?

Nerves buzzing, she lay her hands flat on the stones and allowed the warmth to spread over her palms. She pushed.

Yellow light sliced into the corridor as the wall cracked open.

Too easy.

Warm air and a putrid smell of feces, urine, and rot streamed from the opening. She heard scuffling noises, rustling, and a throaty growl.

Kitt?

She forced her way past the door and froze.

Silencing and Insulating spells spanned the high ceilings and thickened the stench of the chamber. Walls brimmed with iron cages. Writhing pythons, wailing cats, and sleeping badgers. Bloodied coyotes, mangy fox, and another lying still, so scrawny and dark from its own feces that she almost didn't recognize it as a rabbit. More cages dangled from the ceiling, and others hunched in precarious piles in the middle of the room.

Each cage, each animal, bound by the spelled collar.

All of them, shifters.

Ember's stomach roiled, and she retched onto the floor, heaving up the little left in her stomach. She spit the sourness from her mouth, pushed her hair back, and stumbled deeper into the room.

A low growl from the far left corner drew her eye.

"Kitt!" She rushed to the cage, stacked beneath another cage with a sleeping—or dead—wolf.

Kitt sprawled in his cage, his leg wound matted and swollen. He panted and gave another strangled growl as she neared. "I'll get you out of this mess." She knelt to inspect the spells around his neck. The hardest part might be getting close enough to do work on the collar. "I need you to—"

In a blink, a metal loop fell around her neck and choked off her sentence.

"Your foolish friend is dead inside," Fletch said from behind her. "I hope you like mating as a cat." He tugged the loop, hauling her back.

She sprawled and kicked, clawing at the loop and restraint pole that tightened it. She tried to scream, but only a hoarse cry escaped the pinching metal. Dizziness swarmed her vision.

"We can be civil about this," Fletch suggested, loosening the loop minutely.

Ember gasped and reeled to her feet.

Fletch, still wearing Bram's cloak, stood ready at the end of the pole, knees braced and black eyes wide with anticipation. Perhaps he wanted her to shift. No spells on the loop stopped her.

Ember sneered. "You want civility? Remove this restraint from my neck."

"My apologies, my dear," Fletch replied, guiding her away from the cage. "But we lack a certain trust between us. For now I will keep you in human form—it seems to suit you best, don't you think?—because I do have so many questions for you."

"But what about him?" Ember motioned back to Kitt. "Surely he has more answers than I."

Fletch cocked his head pitifully. "You still think he can be human?" He watched her for a moment, curious, before prodding her toward a wall with hanging iron cuffs. "I've dealt with many shifters, my dear, though none were as special as you. Many lasted a long time. Months, years. I let them be a human for hours or minutes, or until they could think enough to change to something else. It is so very interesting to watch the humanity slip away, the memories melt into something much more primal. Did you know that mindless shifters will almost always change to a bear when you prod them?" Fletch held her next to the wall, and the curiosity fell from his face. "Cuff yourself."

Ember ground her teeth and flicked a gaze to Kitt's cage, still in full view. Even if she were to shift now, she'd still be useless with the pole forcing distance between her and Fletch. But perhaps if she—

Wire tightened against her throat.

"Come now," Fletch urged. "Don't be stubborn. You have nothing left to lose, my dear. Your friends are all dead, or will be soon, and your lover will stay here with us."

Wheezing, Ember grabbed an iron cuff and clapped it around an ankle, then followed with the other.

"And the wrists."

She did so grudgingly. The loop loosened again, and she sagged against the wall.

"There," he sighed. "Now you are mine."

"The Council will have you killed for this," Ember spat, hoping it was true. The iron shackles were heavy and big, almost to the point where she could squeeze her hands through. The chains attached to the shackles allowed her a bit of freedom of movement.

Fletch smiled in amusement as he tossed the restraint pole on top of a nearby cage, causing a sleeping gorret to wince awake.

"My lord *is* the Council, my dear. He knows about you, and about your little shifter friends out in the mountains. They will be taken care of soon enough, if they haven't been already—"

A bear-like moan rumbled above the other noises of the chamber, somewhere on the other side of the room. Fletch grinned and raised his thinning brows.

"Ah, I think your father recognizes your scent! You remember him, don't you? You saw him at the feast before your little escapade."

Ember's heart banged once, twice—

"Yes, believe it," Fletch sang. He reached into a pocket and pulled out a collar. "He was certainly not disappointing. We captured him up in the mountains." Fletch stepped close. "If you try anything foolish, my dear, I will not hesitate to Freeze you. I recognized him as having assisted Lady Salena with your sister's birth," he continued seamlessly as he buckled the collar onto her neck. "I prodded him a bit for answers about the faction and instead he gave me a little piece of golden information. An affair, it turns out, that resulted in you. He didn't know about you, of course. When I informed my lord, he didn't believe me, just as he doesn't believe about you now. But he will, once he sees you, and he'll let me do my experiments on you, because he always does give in after a bit of insistence. He has never understood my curiosity, but he knows how much information my experiments reveal. He cannot resist the gain of power through knowledge."

Ember's spit landed on his cheek.

He removed the spittle with a bony finger and tasted it, sucking long and hard on his finger as he closed his eyes.

Ember looked away when those black eyes opened.

"Hmmm, you are delicious, my dear," he cooed.

"I have to admit I'm a bit fond of you. Obsessed, really." His hands came back to her neck, brushing her skin as he began forming the complex spell. "You are a special flavor of woman, forged from a wizard and a shifter. And I am so very curious to learn more about you."

Ember stopped listening and focused on his spell. Binding knit with a Freeze and a Blinding. With the spells touching her skin, they started to spread like gauzy chain-mail against her mind. The cotton-lined stone wall again. A firm but invisible wall that froze her ability to change form. She watched Fletch's hand movements, or what she could see of them, scrambling to keep track of each flick of fingers, tilt of the wrist, and swirl of a thumb.

"Get your hands off of her!"

Ember's eyes flashed up in time to see Eawart, red-faced with billowing fur cloak, lunge at Fletch.

Fletch whirled to meet Eawart, both spindly hands latching onto Eawart's cloak, and suddenly Eawart was hurled against the wall.

Ember cried out as his head cracked against stone. Eawart crumpled to the ground, and blood trickled from the corner of his mouth.

Ember strained against the shackles. "He was harmless!"

Fletch shrugged. "I have no time for—"

"My daughter." Arundel's voice reverberated into the room. He stood by Kitt's cage, a tower held by a stillness that Ember knew only too well. Quiet rage lit his eyes like coals. "Why do you have my daughter?"

Ember's heart beat a maddening rhythm. Her limbs shook as she wiggled her hands, struggling to squeeze them through the shackles.

Fletch bobbed a half-bow with a look of triumph. "I have lured another shifter, my lord." He jabbed a finger toward Kitt. "That one had a lover, my lord, another shifter. Ember."

"No," Arundel said with conviction. "You've gone too far, Fletch."

"She's a shifter, my lord. I saw her change with my own eyes. She's been lying to you all the while, and so has your wife."

Arundel's hands curled to fists. "Release her from those shackles. Now."

Fletch *tisked* as though a child had said something naughty. "I can prove it, my lord. She's a shifter, and a very dangerous one at that." From behind a cage, Fletch picked up a spear. "She has a Binding around her neck."

Ember jerked against the shackles, feeling powerless, her mind screaming in panic. She needed to undo the Binding. She needed—

Fletch jabbed the spear into Kitt's cage.

Kitt's scream of outrage shuddered into her bones, rising a tempest of fury. Her muscles throbbed with the need to shift, and she tore against the walls holding her in. Her hands flew to her throat.

The pattern of spells burned in her mind, vibrant and strong but incomplete. She knew the motions to undo them, knew that they would require careful flicks and twists. Already her fingers moved the air, commanding Fletch's spells to release their hold. Every fiber within her willed the air to dissipate so that she could shift, so that she could morph bone and sinew and muscle into a cougar.

Arundel watched, frozen, but she didn't care. Kitt cried again and again, propelling her faster, and the tension in her bones sparked with hatred for the horrible man who was trying to kill him, and for all the cages towering around her, and for the awful hanging stench of dead shifters.

A left twist here, down and around while the other hand pulls back and flicks right...

The spells unraveled and recoiled like a snake preparing to strike. The gauzy wall around her burst open, and her need to shift consumed her.

Her skin melted.

Liquid movement slipped hands and feet out of cuffs and her mind snapped her body to cougar form. Instinctual fire exploded within her. Raw rage. Protection. The lust to kill.

She held back nothing.

Two leaps brought her to that vile man with the spear. Her jaws crunched around his lily-scented throat, sinking into flesh and fragile bone.

A hard jerk and he lay motionless. The spear

clattered to the floor, joining the scents of old blood and urine and feces.

"No... My daughter... I don't believe it—"

Arundel's words echoed in the chamber.

She turned to find him kneeling, his expression crumpled like the face of an old mountain. He covered that worn face with trembling hands.

She had never seen him tremble. Had never seen him look weak, or in pain.

Her chest swelled, and suddenly she was human again, and she couldn't take the sight of him hunched over, sobbing into his palms like a child.

"Father." He wasn't, really, but he was, and his agony strung her heart out on a line. "I'm sorry..." She was sorry she was what she was. Sorry she couldn't be something else, anything else.

She crawled to him, touched his hands. Cool, unsteady.

His hands moved away from his face.

Ember rocked back. His distant, sheening eyes could hardly look at her. Spittle clung to his beard as he clasped her hands.

"Ember," he whispered. "It's you. It's really you. I thought you were..." He caressed her hands, and then her hair. Nudged her cheek. "My little flame."

Her eyes grew warm, and suddenly she was in his embrace, a child again, swaddled in love and pride and all the warmth a child longed for.

He still loved her, despite what she was, and all

the pain and worry of her life had been for naught. She was still his daughter. Still a Thackeray. Still in her father's heart. And she had nearly killed him.

Arundel's grip tightened.

A pinprick against the pain of her heart. Cold metal against her back.

But it was wrong. All wrong, because her father hugged her, and they were alright—

The pain sharpened, like fire spitting into her body, a blade twisting into her spine, and she bent with the pain, morphing away from it, shifting into something small, narrow.

A deathrattler.

The mountain shook beneath her. Fury, and fear.

Snap!

She whipped around him and sank fangs into his side, terror spurring the release of venom.

He screamed and beat himself, and she fled to a dark crevice.

The mountain man writhed on the floor. His dagger lay forgotten, bloody, as the fury in him succumbed to pain.

He would die in minutes, she knew. But it seemed hours that she watched him go. With his every gasp and clutch of pain, something dark twisted in her.

"Salena," he muttered.

The woman within the snake couldn't look away from his face. Stretched in agony and sheening with tears. She didn't know this sad man.

Shattered.

Broken.

Alone.

The darkness gave another twist.

His face took on a purplish hue as he squeezed his knees to his chest. He moaned, shuddered, and went still.

Something pulled her to the cage with the cougar. Scales melted back to skin, bones grew and solidified, and her snout reformed into a mouth and nose. She knelt before the cage.

Kitt, bloody and panting, lay on his side. His golden eyes stared warily at her, but he seemed too weak to do much else.

A simple latch on the cage slid back with a metallic click. Fletch hadn't bothered locking it with his key. Ember eased inside, ignoring the blood and feces in the cage, her eyes on the collar around Kitt's neck.

The spells glowed in her mind. Similar to the one that had been around her own neck, but more complex. Fletch had known she would try to free him, and had made the spell more difficult.

A tremor shook her hands as she reached forward.

Kitt lifted his head with a growl, but rather than bite her hand, a pink tongue flicked out and licked her palm.

Ember's heart kicked. "Kitt?" Did he remember? Was he there?

The cougar set his head down and closed his eyes, his stomach shuddering with each breath.

Ember shivered as a wave of cold crept over her. Stiff-fingered, she grasped at the strands of spells to begin their unraveling. She would need to move as quickly as possible, but the chill seeping into her bones pulled on her limbs.

"Kitt, it's me, Ember," she whispered, weaving her fingers left to right, down and over. She strove to remember how she undid the Freeze before. A fuzzy memory, but her hands recalled the motions and worked the strands efficiently. She stared at them, following the intent to flick this finger and that thumb, feeling as though the hands belonged to someone else. "Kitt, it's me. Ember," she repeated. She said it again. And again. The chant brought a bit of warmth back to her muscles.

The room fell away, and her own body. The spells on Kitt's collar pulled her in and narrowed her vision. Outside, out there in the room, she was aware of footsteps and voices.

Someone touched her.

"Leave me," she said. "It is mine to undo. It is mine to undo..."

No one else touched her, and she sank more deeply into the spell. So close to the end, she no longer followed every movement of her hands but concentrated on the next step to take, the moves to make further down the strands. Her hands flew, and the spells obeyed.

Unraveling the last of the spell felt like running into a wall.

She collapsed beside Kitt, her arms numb, her mind suddenly unable to focus.

"Kitt, it's me," she repeated, her tongue and lips stiff and dry. "You're free now. I know you're in there. Please come out. Please..."

She pulled her head up from the cage floor. The cougar still slept, and his wounds continued to bleed. Too much blood lost. Too much time stuck in the same body. He was gone, just as she had feared.

Her throat burned and heat rose behind her eyelids.

"No, no, no. Kitt, please come out. I removed the spells. It's okay now. Please come back." Her voice cracked, and with it, something inside her shattered.

A wave crashed over her, and she gave into it. She let herself sink beneath the roiling surface until she felt nothing beyond the blackness and her inability to breath.

CHAPTER FOURTY

Ember jolted awake.

A gauzy wall fastened her mind and body, and the constraint caused panic to well up her throat.

"No—"

"Ember, you're alright." Salena appeared beside the bed, the bed-curtains drawn back to frame her slender form.

"What is this for?" Ember shook her wrist, which was cuffed in a golden bracelet.

"A precaution only. The Council requested it. I would suggest leaving it alone," her mother added when Ember started to undo the spell. "They also requested that you be guarded so that you are less inclined to tamper with it."

A guard stepped forward from the doorway. A wizard dressed in violet, with an expression as unreadable as stone.

Ember smoothed her palms over her face, willing away the sudden wave of heat behind her eyes. She needed to stop panicking. The spell wasn't harmful to her, not when she was in human form.

She breathed slowly, and focused on the soft sheets she sat on. Her old bed, in her old room. Her limbs tangled in her chemise and silky sheets dyed a shade of pale green.

Ember kicked the sheets off. "I must see Kitt—"

Salena gave a strained smile. "He's sleeping in the room next door. As a human," she added.

For a moment, the tension slipped from her shoulders. Her pulse beat in her temples, and her breath slipped in and out of her lungs. Relief, and something warm to replace the cold dread that had coiled around her heart the night before.

The relief nudged aside as Salena's weary, pink-rimmed eyes watched her. Unbound, her hair hung limp over her shoulders, its coppery tint dull in the dim light, and her face looked as old as Ember ever remembered seeing it.

Ember studied the silk sheet in her hand. An unbearable weight huddled in her chest. "And Eawart?"

"Recovering from a contusion to the head." Salena sank into the bed. "The others are dead," she stated.

The others. Arundel. Fletch. Ember's throat constricted. "I'm sorry," she whispered. Meaningless, frivolous words. She had no idea what Salena felt, but certainly it must be hatred toward her. With a strange certainty, Ember knew things would never be the same as they were before, and that she was the cause of it.

Salena touched her hand, then clasped it. "I'm sorry, too. For not knowing what Arundel and Fletch were doing down in the dungeon, for staying out of his affairs, for what you had to do to fix it. A part of me loved that man. But I can't help feeling relief that he's gone." A hand flew to her mouth and she squeezed her eyes shut.

Ember stared as tears fell over Salena's trembling fingers. She had never seen her mother cry.

"He would have been punished, you know," she said after a moment, wiping her cheeks. "All those spells to torture and control shifters... I remember him working on them at the Academy, but the others looked down on him for it, and by the time he was asked to leave, he promised me he would stop. I should have known, when Fletch followed him to Silverglen. He would've had both his hands taken. What would he have done then?" Salena's eyes shone, and she regarded Ember with the grasping gaze of a woman drowning.

Ember had no response, because she knew nothing she said could soothe her mother, and she knew her mother would somehow pull herself from the murky waters without anyone's help. Salena was strong that way.

She gave Ember's hand another squeeze. "You

can see your friend, but the Council will hold a judgment about Arundel and Fletch's death. They should all be here by tomorrow." Salena stood.

Ember twisted the sheet tight in one fist. "Fletch told me about my real father."

Salena stiffened. She sat back on the bed, her lips compressed into a hard line.

Ember took a breath before continuing. "Fletch found my father and tortured him until he told Fletch about your affair. Fletch drew his own conclusions about me — that I was a shifter — and kept him as Arundel's pet."

Ember forced a lump down her throat before continuing. "The bear at the feast was my father."

Salena's eyes closed. The divot between her brows deepened. "Did Arundel know?"

"Fletch told him, but he refused to believe."

"Just so," Salena muttered. "He always suspected."

Ember pushed her raven-black hair back from face in an effort to remain patient. "Why did you never tell me about him? Why lie to me, even when I knew Arundel wasn't my father?"

Salena's gaze fell on her own hands. "I suppose I didn't want things to change. I didn't want to give you another reason to hate Arundel." Salena exhaled through parted lips. "And I didn't want you searching for a man whom I wasn't even sure was alive. But of course, me not telling you didn't stop you from leaving."

Ember shook her head. "I left because of Fletch. But I did try looking for my real father."

Salena raised a brow. "Among the other shifters you found?"

Ember opened her mouth to reply, but Salena waived a dismissive hand.

"I know you didn't kill shifters. You can save your story for the Council."

"And what about the shifters in the dungeon? My father?"

"The spells have already been undone. The Council will most likely rule to free them. None returned to human form."

Ember's chest ached. All of those shifters, gone. And her own father. She had found him, but would never get to know him. He had left before she had even begun looking for him. She would never see him, never hear his voice calling her name, and would never feel comforted by his embrace.

Would he still be human if she had freed him before fleeing to Orion?

Salena rested a cool hand on Ember's fist.

"Your father was a wonderful man. Warm, kind, and intelligent. He always saw the brightest side of things, always believed in the best of others. And he was very skilled at what he did. His name was Neal, Neal Pitkin, perhaps the best healer in northern Lach."

The chamber froze, crackling, and thawed in a

blink.

Ember stared at her mother, her heart drumming. "But that would mean... He was Kitt's father, too! My friend, Kitt!"

Salena's face crumpled into a look of pity. "Oh, darling, I'm so sorry—"

Ember shook her head, grinning. "No, not Kitt's real father. He was adopted. But Kitt and Riggs were looking for him, after he disappeared a few years ago..."

Her excitement curdled. For them, Neal was gone now, too. Permanently. Any hope they had left of finding him would be erased.

But he would live on in their memories. She would make sure of it.

Salena patted her hands, reminding Ember that she still sat there. A blush crept up Ember's neck.

"What did you mean," Ember asked, though she knew the answer, "when you said sorry about Kitt and I sharing fathers?"

Salena stood and gave a cat-like smile that made her look more like Dev's age. "What did you tell that young man, Eawart?"

Ember cringed. "I told him I would see his estate before making a final decision."

Salena lifted her eyebrows and nodded, a touch of amusement on her lips. "Just so. I hope you think long and hard about that proposal."

Ember gave it a half-moment's thought before

pushing it aside. She had much more important things to do just now.

CHAPTER FOURTY-ONE

A WIZARD DECKED in armor stood inside the chamber next door. Ember moved around him and eased into the room. Kitt lay still and pale on the bed. Ember's gaze latched on to his chest as it rose and fell. The only sign that he lived.

Dim light crept from the wide glass balcony doors and scattered into the room, leaving too many shadows. Ember slipped around to the side of his bed, bare feet padding the stone floor, and lit three candles. She could feel the familiar pulse of a spell, and saw that he wore a similar bracelet to hers, only silver and slender. A small thing for such a powerful spell. A Binding, Freezing, and Blinding spell that kept him in human form, now. Safe, if restricting. Did the Council know what he did to all those wizards?

Ember knelt by him as the candlelight warmed

his stubbly face and the scent of beeswax curled around them. Bandages wrapped his arms, bulged beneath the bedsheets around his legs, and encased his torso. Dark blood spotted the white wrappings, and the sweet smell of poultice reminded her of Riggs.

She reached for his hand and stopped.

A part of her longed to wake him, to reassure herself that he was Kitt, even if he hated her for her lies and where she came from. But he needed to sleep, if he was still inside that human body.

She drank in the details of his face. A pair of steady and assured brows, thick and dark. A pleasantly bold nose above a rather nice mouth. His lips were the kind that looked on the verge of smiling, though from experience she was much more likely to get a sneer than anything else. Stubble softened a sturdy chin and darkened the subtle contours shaping cheeks, jawline, and temple.

Quiet as a mouse and soft as an owl's feather, Ember touched the silvery streak of hair above his right ear. Warmth spread over her hand, into her chest, and fanned up her throat.

She whispered his name, as light as a breeze skittering over an oak leaf. "Kitt."

He didn't stir, and his breath came and went in the same rhythm as before.

"I hope you are in there somewhere," she went on, her voice like butterfly wings beating the air. "I wish you had stayed with the others, protected them. I didn't need protecting."

Silly babble. Who had said he was trying to protect her? She had been certain, upon his arrival as a hawk, that he had been out to kill her.

But he would have, if that's what he had wanted.

She studied his eyelids, wondering if they would ever open so that she could ask him.

"I found Neal," she said. "Did you know that he's my real father? I spent all that time looking for him when he was here all the while, in Arundel's grasp. He is gone now, Kitt. He has been lost to the bear. And the Council will be coming tomorrow," she rushed on, her stream of words picking up like water over rocks. "They will make a decision about Arundel's death. They will make a decision about what to do with me. Since I was the one who..." She sucked in a fortifying breath. "Since I was the one who killed him."

Kitt didn't react. His breathing carried on, a cycle of soft waves washing over a sandy shore.

Her eyelids stung. "He was going to kill me," she explained in a strained whisper. "And he would've hunted down the others in Orion. He wouldn't have stopped. I was the only one who could've stopped him, and I did. I followed my instincts like you told me to—"

She stopped.

No amount of reasoning would ever make the darkness go away. Had Kitt felt it before? How had he learned to live and laugh with it there, twisting around his heart? How had he forgotten the memories—the metallic feel of death on the tongue, the acrid stench of fear, the raging pulse of his own blood as he waited for the kicking and shouting to cease?

Sometimes we must make painful choices for the good of others. Seabird's words rang through her mind. *Sometimes it is a matter of killing rather than being killed.* Which had it been, for her?

Power through killing. She had felt the power, the control and strength from taking those actions. But they had been propelled by fear and anger. That had been different from Arundel's killing, hadn't it? Ember wasn't so sure. She had known how much he feared shifters.

Ember rocked back on her heals and stood. It did her no good to sit there and brood. She had forgotten about Seabird, and about Norman.

She crept out of the room, followed by her own guard, and hurried toward the infirmary, which was on the way to the great hall where she guessed Norman might still be. She should give Eawart a visit.

She had put her deer-hide dress back on, and the supple leather felt incredibly free against her skin. When would she be able to shift again?

A black-clad servant scuttled by, eyes averted and hands clasping a pile of towels to her chest.

Never here, Ember realized with dismay. And if the Council imprisoned her?

She shuddered, pressing the thought away as she opened the door to the infirmary.

"Ember!"

Dev, wearing a low-cut black dress smothered in gauzy lace, rose from her cushioned seat by Eawart's bed and floated toward Ember like a queen of death. Copper hair tucked nearly out of sight beneath a black headdress sparkling with black gems, and a short veil hung just above fulsome lips painted the shade of fresh blood.

Two willowy arms embraced her as those lips pecked kisses on each cheek. The scent of roses permeated the air, but Ember didn't miss the undertone of Ekesian spice that lingered beneath it. Dev's handmaid waited like a shadow behind her, wearing a similar gown that looked a bit too small, and entirely missing the air of confidence Dev radiated.

"We were just finished seeing to Eawart," Dev said breezily, motioning to the bed where Eawart appeared to be sleeping. "But oh my, you haven't changed at all, Ember," she said, assessing Ember at arm's length. "Those dark circles under your eyes are the worst I've ever seen them—"

Ember waived a dismissive hand with growing irritation. "Did Mother tell you what happened?"

A small smile crept over Dev's painted mouth. "I know Father is dead," she stated. "And his awful pet, that smelly man who followed him like a dog. I don't mind much. Neither of them were any fun to be around, and Mother always moped about him."

Ember could never remember Salena moping

before today, but she knew Dev had a very wide definition of what constituted moping.

"Eawart should be back on his feet in no time, dear sister," Dev said with certainty, "and then you can finally be married."

"Perhaps he would suit you better," Ember suggested.

"Oh, no. I'm to marry Lord Wincel, now that Father is gone." Green eyes danced beneath the veil. "I'm not happy about it, of course, but since Father's death, Mother is allowing me to travel to Edlen with Finn before the marriage! Can you imagine? Finn and I in that place? And I'll be free to..." She thought better of whatever she was about to say, and gave Ember a smile. "There will be plenty to do in Edlen, and I'll worry about Wincel when I get back. He's an old, tarnished penny, but he does have a rather large fortune."

Ember repressed a sigh. "Where is Finn?"

Dev stepped out the door. "He's still in with Father. I tried to get him to sleep, but he's being too stubborn for his own good. Anyways, maybe later I can do something about those dark circles. Just now I feel a sudden urge to mourn."

She winked at Ember and floated like a black snowflake down the corridor toward her rooms, her handmaid following close behind her. *Mourning, indeed.*

Ember couldn't bring herself to see Finn just yet. She headed up to the third floor to find Arundel's study unlocked. The guard followed with a rustle of fabric.

The room stood as she remembered. One shadowy side devoted to weapons and traps, the other side softened by sofas and the evening light that fell from a small window onto his desk. She made her way inside, for once not closing and locking the door behind her.

She glanced at the weapons on display, remembering how they felt in her hands, how handling them had given her strength. Strange how she had never realized her own inner strengths. Claws instead of knives, teeth instead of daggers. Prowess, stealth, speed, even venom. Compared to those, some of Arundel's weapons seemed like toys to her now.

Dangerous toys, still. Made more lethal by spells.

Shuddering, Ember turned to the desk. She reached for blank parchment and cleared a space in the clutter. A quill sat in a container of ink. She pulled it out and blotted it, thinking. Then, she began to write:

Seabird,

She crossed it out.

Ryscford Seago, she wrote instead. *I am sorry for lying.* She stared at the statement, then crossed it out, too. *Lord Arundel and Fletch are dead,* she wrote instead. *Council judges tomorrow. Are you well? Did you move camp? Council does not know about you all. Did patrolmen attack camp? Kitt is here. He sleeps.*

She wasn't sure what else to say. She set aside

the parchment and pulled out another.

Riggs Pitkin: Kitt and I are at Silverglen. I don't expect your forgiveness for my lies, but I thought you should know that...

Ember chewed her lip, thinking.

...that your father is gone. Arundel had him. I'm so sorry.

Ember hesitated again before continuing.

I have discovered that Neal was my real father. I am your sister.

Would he be glad? Angry? She longed to tell him in person, but she might never see him again.

Take care.

Ember.

With a quick nod, she dried the ink and rolled the parchments together. She emptied a small leather case and pushed the tube of messages inside, tying it closed with a leather thong. The messages would have to be enough. If she didn't receive a reply...

She swallowed, unwilling to imagine that scenario. Seabird might be able to encourage Norman to return with a message, or a shifter could, though it might be a dangerous journey if patrols still scouted the mountains.

"What are you doing?"

Ember jumped. Gregory stood in the doorway, his clothes crumpled and his hair matted in one spot.

"Writing messages."

He seemed to mull this over for a moment before

a look of surprise dawned over his tired face. "There are others out there still? Is that why you asked me...?"

"I wanted to know if Fletch left behind any men to find them," Ember explained, clutching the leather case and heading for the door.

Gregory looked sick. "He left behind a few men. And three dogs."

Ember halted and stood very still, her heart hammering up her throat. She swallowed. "I must send these."

Gregory nodded, pale-faced, and backed out of the doorway.

Ember headed blindly down the corridor, down two flights of steps, and into the maze of corridors surrounding the great hall. The warm smell of fresh bread curled into her senses as a servant swept by. A platter of steaming beef came next. She had slept a night and most of a day, she realized, and she hadn't eaten since yesterday's quick breakfast. But her clenched stomach wasn't hungry.

She broke into the great hall, where a few of the castle's workers already sat to eat. Ember didn't bother looking for her family, who would likely all be eating alone in their chambers.

She spotted Norman on the dais, the leather jesses hanging half-torn and bedraggled from his feet. His great crest, once a brilliant scarlet, lay flat and dull on his head, and his drooping tail had transformed to a grayish-white.

"Norman!" Ember ran to him. The bird recognized her, but couldn't manage more than a one-eyed stare and bob of his tired head. "I'll get you out of here, don't you worry." Would tying a message to his foot be too much? Would it be a form of restriction? Ember didn't think so, but she asked Norman anyways.

"You think he will find them?" Gregory asked, coming up behind her.

Ember hadn't realized he had followed her. "Of course he will. He always does."

Norman allowed her to tie the small leather case snug against his leg, and Gregory helped her undo the jesses.

Norman shuddered, every feather puffing and shivering as he shook himself head to tail. A golden gleam returned to his eyes.

Ember held up an arm, unsure of whether he would understand, but a moment later he jumped onto it with a deft twitch of his wings. Impatient, he bobbed his head, and his crest raised an inch.

Ember stepped down the dais and to the glass doors, ignoring the gasps of onlookers in the hall. She glared toward them to warn them back, but no one tried to stop her from leaving the hall. Gregory held open the glass doors, and Ember entered the muggy evening.

Bulky shadows stretched out from the castle and flowed over Mirror Lake like a watery painting. To the north, scattered clouds played hide-and-seek with rounded mountain tops as the emerging night swallowed their wide bottoms.

Please be out there, she prayed to Seabird and Riggs and all the others. "Safe journey," she murmured to Norman.

She lifted her arm overhead, willing him speed and quick recovery, and his great wings unfolded. A few beats of those grayish wings and he sprang from Ember's arm. He rose high, nearly disappearing against the gray-blue sky, and turned northward.

Ember blinked, and Norman's washed-out tail seemed to brighten to a creamy-gold hue. Another blink, and it appeared lemon. His wings turned a shade of apricot, and in the span of a few heartbeats they became flames, and his tail blossomed into ocher tipped with scarlet.

Ember's heart swelled. *He will be strong again.* Maybe he would even find Riggs and the others. She kept her eyes locked on him until he shrank to the size of a pinhead and disappeared into the darkening green of the forested mountains.

"He saved my life," Ember said.

Gregory had stepped up beside her, silent as Norman headed for the mountains. "The firebird?"

"His name is Norman. He, and Riggs, and Kitt all saved my life."

"The cougar...?"

"Kitt."

Gregory sighed, lifted his hands, then dropped

them, as though he wished to offer her something but knew it would never be good enough. "I didn't know he was a friend. I was afraid that—"

"You had every right to be." Ember couldn't forget the way that wizard jerked with his neck crushed between Kitt's jaws. "I'm almost glad you did it, in a way. I don't think he would've stopped."

She abandoned the glint that Norman had become and studied Gregory's stooped shoulders, the violet-tinted circles beneath his eyes, and the way his arms hung limp at his sides as if they were too heavy to hold up anymore. Ember's throat cinched tight and she looked away.

"Don't blame yourself, Gregory," she said. "What happened was mostly my fault. I had the chance to kill Fletch and I didn't. I was afraid that killing him would turn me into Arundel. That a small part of me would enjoy it."

Saying her fears aloud made them feel more solid. Like a wall, but one she had already scaled; a wall that seemed smaller now than it had before.

"And do you feel like Arundel now?"

The darkness within her twisted and curled tight in her chest. *Power through killing.* Perhaps it wasn't Arundel's law, but a law of life. Inevitable. Twisted. Obscure.

"I don't think so." Arundel had had a darkness like her own now, but she thought perhaps it came in a different form. Bloodlust, a thirst for control, a desperate, terrible dream that had arisen from a desperate, broken man. Not her father, and not her. Her pity toward him surprised her. It softened his hard edges, clarified her memories of him, strengthened the boundary between them. "No," she said with more confidence. "We are nothing alike."

Gregory eyed her, his weary remorse hiding for a moment behind a glint of amusement. "You do have a few things in common, actually. You cannot be raised by someone and not pick up a few qualities. Skilled in weapon use, for instance. The way you carry yourself, head held high and back like a stone wall. Your overconfidence in yourself—"

She gave a weak smile. "Well..."

He grinned. "Admit it."

Ember rolled her eyes. "Fine. I've taken up some of Arundel's traits. But only the good ones."

Gregory's gaze sobered, and his tone grew earnest. "No, I mean admit that we are still friends."

His eyes, the hue of rain, pleaded with her. The remorse and weariness tucked themselves behind the plea and were rimmed by a strength Ember was familiar with. He could take it if she said no, if she chose to leave him in her past. He would understand, accept it, and move on.

Once, she would've clung to the memory of that lady sitting on his lap, or of his head buried against her neck, and the memories might have been a barrier between them.

But she had no interest in the lady now, only in Gregory's well-being.

Things between us will never be as they were. A pang of nostalgia, but also, surprisingly, a loosening sensation in her chest that felt like freedom. She didn't need Gregory in her life, either, though she enjoyed his company. Somehow accepting these things made her heart feel light.

She sighed. "I admit we are still friends, but only if you promise not to neck with your lady friend in my castle anymore."

"Your castle?" Gregory spluttered, a rosy tint warming his cheeks. "See, this is what I meant about your overconfidence—"

She smacked him a good one, and they moved back into the warm chatter of the great hall. Ignoring the too-familiar hunting murals and almost forgetting about the approaching Council judgment, Ember allowed herself a bite to eat with her friend and enough drinks where sleep was a comforting possibility.

CHAPTER FORTY-TWO

"Ember?"

The voice sounded so familiar, but so quiet, that Ember nearly tripped over her gown as she turned before the wide wooden doors of the great hall.

"Finn."

Her brother stood at a lanky height, sullen beneath his mop of freshly washed hair. He wore simple brown riding clothes, and his hands looked bare without his violin. Hazel eyes gazed at the ground.

"I just wanted to tell you that I'm leaving today."

Ember stared at him, the stays on her gown squeezing her chest. "To Edlen? For how long?"

"Devondra and I are traveling back with Lady Rina after your judgment. Devondra's doing." Finn managed a weak smile, and his eyes flitted up to her before casting around her dress and toward the doors.

"Mother is letting me go, but I will be tested when I get back. For lordship."

Ember's heart, already weighed down by his subdued demeanor and harrowed face, sank further. "Oh, Finn..."

"We will lose the castle, you see, now that Father is dead." His hands clenched, and his brows drew together, making his face look less boyish. "I don't care about the castle. It's for Mother's sake. What will she do now?"

Ember shook her head, eyes burning. "I'm not sure, Finn. I'm so sorry..." Again, the words sounded silly and fickle. He had gotten his wish to go to Edlen, yes, but now that the test for lordship was approaching... Finn had always dreamed of becoming a musician. He had thought—perhaps they all had thought—that Arundel would've given up on making him something he didn't want to be.

But Arundel never gave up on anything. And now he was gone and their mother was taking his place.

"But Dev or I," Ember said, scrambling to think of a way out but only coming up with Eawart's proposal, which she found herself seriously considering for the first time, "we could marry and she could come live with us—"

Finn shook his head. "She wants to stay here, Ember. I don't know why. The gardens, I guess."

Ember rubbed her hands over her face, too late

remembering the Glamours there. She had wanted to look her best for the Council. "We will think of something, Finn. Maybe lordship won't be so bad—"

"Do you realize whose shoes I'd be filling?" His voice rose in accusation.

Ember looked down and worked the tightness from her throat. "I do, Finn. And I'm sorry. And as your sister, I will do whatever I can to make things better."

Finn's shaggy head was shaking. "I don't know if that's enough," he said in a strained voice.

Ember nodded. She didn't expect him to understand her actions. Likely, he never would. "You are my brother," she stated. Had some of the tension released, just there on his shoulders? "I love you, and I believe in you. You would be replacing Arundel, but I know you, and I know you would do so much better than he ever did. You could help the Council progress. Expand. Perhaps they would even help fund a musical academy," Ember added, digging through what she knew of the Council. "Lady Rina in particular might support such a mission. They would be inspired by your passion, Finn."

A familiar light entered Finn's expression. The normal Finn, ready for adventure and brimming with positive energy. She knew her idea had sparked something inside him.

He nodded soberly. "I will consider these things. Goodbye, Ember." He stepped forward and bent as if to kiss her cheek. At the last minute, he frowned and jerked back, as though remembering what she was.

Ember didn't miss the strange look in his eyes. Fear.

Her stomach knotted, and she longed to throw her arms around his bony shoulders to reassure him that it was her, the same old Ember, and that she would never hurt him.

Instead, she watched him turn away, and the darkness tightened its grip around her heart.

Finn halted, and turned back, his gaze bright. "It was you, wasn't it? That day in the smelter. When he threw my violin into the fire... When he threatened to..." He held up a hand.

Ember nodded, unable to speak. That had been a long time ago, but the way Finn rubbed his hand now, she knew the memory had clung to him like a squelkin to flesh.

"Thank you," he said. His throat worked. "Sister."

Ember smiled. "Anytime, brother. Safe travels."

Finn's head bobbed, and he sauntered away.

Ember shook herself and tucked a seed of hope deep inside. She needed to protect it from whatever happened next.

She turned to the large wooden doors and nodded at the servants to open them. Pressing the weariness from her shoulders, she straightened her back and sucked in as big a breath as she could manage with the tight stays, and stepped into the great hall.

Lit by the late morning, the air in the hall had

warmed to stifling and clung to her face and arms like wet mud. She ignored the moving murals on the walls. Sweat prickled along her nape as she faced the Council.

An assemblage of brilliant colors mixed with dull browns spread before her, each in their own iron throne. Lord Thurstun's sumptuous body, lathered in scarlet robes, spilled out of his seat, and gilded sashes fanned out over the dais steps. Lady Rina's dark hair coiled high against the back of her throne, bones and teeth dangling from head and robes in the Zarian fashion. Lord Wincel, clad mostly in rabbit-lined garments, looked shrunken with his stooped back and baggy face. Lady Dell perched regal as always in her white and yellow silks, religious devotion stiffening her expression as she wafted a papery sun-painted fan. Strapping Lord Histion wore his pearls, starfish, and coral pieces over pants and jerkin made of sea-squelkin. Lady Ashlin and Lord Jeriel looked as dull and dusty as ever, and each of them carried hard expressions.

Ember, perhaps more than any of them, felt Arundel's distinct absence.

"Ember Thackeray," Lord Thurstun boomed, his stomach jerking under red robes.

Ember smoothed palms down her simple blue gown and bent into a slight curtsy. Did they not know who she really was? That Arundel Thackeray wasn't her real father?

"Today your fate will be judged by the Council, for committing the murder of Lord Arundel," Lord

Thurstun's beady eyes shot to Lady Dell before he muttered, "...may Yathe accept him with open arms."

The others echoed the phrase, some with less enthusiasm than others.

Lord Thurstun carried on. "As there were no witnesses to his death other than you, we see fit to hear your explanation before passing judgment."

Lord Thurstun tilted his head back, as though finished, and silence ensued.

Ember opened her mouth, unsure of where to start. "Recently, I ran away from home," she said, her voice sounding small in the great room. She wondered if the Council would be patient enough to sit through the whole story. "I ran because my life was threatened by Arundel's assistant, Fletch—"

"Who is also dead," Lady Dell interrupted with a snap of her fan and a quiet glare at Lord Thurstun. The huge man pretended not to hear a thing, and lifted a thick hand for Ember to continue.

"I left because I was sure Fletch would kill me, or worse. I went to Orion thinking to escape, but Fletch followed me there, believing I was with others like myself—"

"Shapeshifters," someone stated.

Lord Thurston cast a glare in Lord Histion's direction. *So they did know. Of course.* Someone had come into the room full of cages when Ember had been busy with Kitt's spell. Her mother, she had thought, and a few others. Likely, the whole castle knew what she was by now.

"Eventually he found me," Ember rushed on. Sweat had accumulated under her arms. "And he took me back here. He had a friend of mine who I had met in Orion. I am certain that the spell Fletch used to keep him from shifting was created by Arundel. They worked together often. Soon upon returning Fletch took my friend away. I searched for him—"

"And did Arundel not question your whereabouts?" Lady Dell put in, her face pink and sweat glistening on her taut upper lip.

"Let the girl speak!" Lord Thurstun raised a fist and hammered it into the armrest of his seat. The Council-members winced, and Lady Dell's fan flew faster.

Ember swallowed and focused on forming her words. "The hidden room I found was filled with cages. In each cage was a shapeshifter bound to animal form," Ember explained.

A gasp, perhaps from Lady Rina, and a slight shake of the head from Lord Wincel. Lord Thurstun looked mutinous, and Lady Dell's fan snapped against the air with its speed.

"He took me there and bound me to a wall," Ember went on as anger and fear crawled back from the memories. "My friend, caged as a cougar, was brought there as well..."

Ember told the rest of the story, giving as few details as possible. They might decide to hang her, or perhaps burn her, but if they believed she was Lord Arundel's daughter, she might get them to agree to excommunication. That way, she could go back to Orion. They could make a town, create a more secure space if the Council decided they still didn't want shifters in Lach.

And if they are still alive in Orion. She willed them to be alive with all her might.

"...and I bit him," Ember finished. She wouldn't tell them of the way Arundel writhed on the floor, nor of his last spoken word. *Salena.* The familiar darkness squeezed around her chest.

Lord Thurstun blinked at her. "And he died from the venom?"

"Yes your lordship." She hesitated, then added, "I knew that if I didn't kill him, he would kill me."

Lord Thurstun's eyebrows lifted. "Self-defense?" A heavy nod. "Rightly so. We discussed the matter of his death and the existence of the faction at some length."

Ember's heart thumped painfully. *But how did they—?*

"Yes," Lord Thurstun said, "we already knew about the faction. In fact, Salena told us months ago about it. She had been in contact with Ryscford Seago, the faction's leader, for some time before they suddenly lost contact. We had all grown weary of Arundel's ploys to send out patrols, but we didn't have a way to stop him. He didn't need our gold, and he didn't need our agreement to do what he wanted. Had you not killed him, we would have removed him from the Council and punished him according to law for using spell-work to torture others."

Except that you wouldn't have found out about the spell-work because you never cared enough to investigate him. Ember remained silent while Lord Thurstun continued.

"Your mother did a very good job convincing us of the need for shifters in our country, as spies, or other servants of the Council. Now that Arundel is gone, the faction may return to Lach to work for the country—"

"No."

The Council gawked at Ember, struck silent.

Sweat sprang over her palms. She steeled her voice. "The faction will not return to be forced into work. They should be able to lead normal lives, just as others in Lach. If they were payed for their services, if the laws were changed to prevent cruel treatment, and more severe punishment of the use of spells to control them, they might consider it, but not otherwise."

"Do you want a worse judgment, child?" Lord Wincel asked in a reedy voice.

Ember raised her chin. "Do to me what you will. I was protecting myself and my friend. But I am certain that your judgment today will impact the faction's decisions about returning. And the laws will need to be revised."

The Council-members shifted in their seats and

muttered indecisively to each other.

"If they are still alive," Ember added.

Lord Thurstun turned to her with a quirked brow.

"They are alive and well. The patrolmen were captured."

Together, Ember and the Council shifted their attention to the wooden doors of the great hall, where a slender young man stood bare-chested in a deer-hide skirt. Linens wrapped limbs and torso, and on one covered arm perched Norman.

Ember's chest expanded. "Kitt," she whispered, unable to stop a grin. She repressed the urge to run and hug him.

Kitt, looking pale and in pain but stubborn, gave her a grim smile and limped forward, handing her a piece of parchment.

The letter was from Seabird, but she didn't want to read it now. Knowing the others were alive was enough, and knowing Kitt was...well, Kitt, had her nerves jumping all over the place and the sweat returning to her palms.

"Council," said Kitt, limping into the room. "Although I was in cougar form at the time, I witnessed this lady's actions and can testify that she acted in self-defense."

The muttering among the Council-members increased before Kitt cut them off.

"I would like to add to her statements about

changing the laws. It has come to my attention that if shifters will be allowed to return and *thrive*, that a school must be put in place for them. There are many orphans from the rebellion, and they will need someone to teach them about being a shifter, and," Kitt paused to be sure they listened, "to live peacefully as civilians of Lach."

Ember stared. Who was this Kitt standing before her, speaking to the Council without his usual hatred of wizards? *He not only speaks, but convinces them,* Ember realized, watching as Lord Thurstun's large head bobbed once. Several others echoed his agreement.

"A fine idea, lad," Lord Thurstun boomed. His brows dug down to form a divot. "But where do you propose to build this school? Certainly not as part of the Academy?"

"My name is Kitt Shearwater, lordship. If the laws change so that shifters may own land, my return to the country means that I will have inherited an estate from my parents. My grandmother legally owned the estate, as she was not a shapeshifter. Since my disappearance with my parents at a young age, I believe my only cousin, Eawart Shearwater, is the current owner. However, I am sure that he and I can work something out..."

Ember couldn't stop her laughter from bubbling up and out of her like a spring of water. Perhaps because she felt light-headed, or perhaps because her skin tingled, she sat, crumpling her gown and not caring even a little that the Council stared at her open-mouthed.

A moment later, the laughter faded. She cleared her throat.

"We still have your fate to think over, girl," Lady Dell stated.

"There is one other matter," Kitt said, after casting a look of concern at Ember.

Lord Thurstun waved a hand for him to continue.

"A patrol, which I believe belonged to Arundel, burned one of the Orion villages to the ground. I don't know how many Orians they killed, or what was taken."

The Council shifted. "What evidence do you have that the patrol belonged to Arundel?" Lord Thurstun asked.

Ember knew Kitt would have no evidence beyond his own gut feeling. "Grey fletching," Ember announced, "on the arrows they used to kill the villagers." Only Arundel used fletching the shade of welded iron.

Kitt's jaw clenched. *He'll see it as another lie from me, that I never told him I knew.*

"I believe Arundel was trying to acquire more mining land," Ember went on. "Orians never give up their land easily."

Arundel himself had taught her that.

Lord Thurstun's sheening face nodded. Was he thinking of Arundel's bribes? Realizing that they had all likely been stolen from murdered clans?

"This is important information," he said. "We certainly don't wish to rouse the clans into war. Now, we must make a decision."

They muttered amongst themselves for a long while, and finally Lord Thurstun relaxed back in his chair, dark circles of sweat spreading under his arms and forming a crescent above his great belly.

"Kitt Shearwater, I am glad you were able to join us at this meeting. We received some disconcerting stories from wizards this morning upon our arrival. They witnessed you, as a cougar, slaughtering their patrol. Do you deny this?"

The Council glared at him, and Ember felt the blood drain from her face.

"No," Kitt said. "I admit that I killed several wizards."

"And do you admit that you killed these men and women out of bloodlust? Or do you wish to plead self-defense?"

"I admit I was mad at the time. I killed out of anger," Kitt said in a heavy tone. His tired face didn't look at her.

"No!" Ember stated, hauling herself to her feet. "He was protecting me from—"

"Silence!" Lord Thurstun bellowed, his eyes glints of ice. "We have numerous accounts that say the same thing. Ember was not in danger at that time, and Kitt deliberately killed wizards."

The flame of hope in Ember's chest snuffed out. She looked at Kitt with a solemn heart. He seemed frozen and stiff to her. A man who knew he would die. A man who believed he deserved it.

Lord Thurstun continued, his eyes on Kitt. "According to our current laws, we might burn you at the stake. Or we could behead you and any other shapeshifters who dare act the way you have acted. Such behavior is what began the long, gruesome rebellion. Do you wish to start another one?"

Ember gave Kitt a pleading look, but his stolid gaze remained on Lord Thurstun.

"No, your lordship." His throat worked. "I wish for peace between my kind and yours."

Lord Thurstun seemed somehow satisfied, and looked at Ember. "For you, we do not believe such a severe punishment is deserved for acts of self-defense."

Having said this, Lord Thurstun sighed, and the others in the Council seemed to relax a bit in their chairs.

"Your fate shall be this. Convince the faction to return to Lach—" he raised a hand before Ember could speak. "We will adjust the laws according to your wishes, with the exception of one thing. Your mother informed us of this new spell, and that it could be used safely to keep shapeshifters in human form. You must understand that in order to give criminal shapeshifters the same just punishment that we give criminal wizards, we must have a way to constrain their violence. For wizards, we remove a hand or two. For shapeshifters, we can use a spell that keeps them from shifting. You both have one now, do you not?"

"Yes," Ember said in a hoarse voice. Were it not for the strange way her hand would have to bend, she could likely undo her own.

"Very good. You will remain spell-bound and guarded for a year. Because of his violet history, Kitt will remain spell-bound and guarded for the remainder of his life, or until we see that he has improved his behavior and attitude toward wizards."

Ember forced a lump down her throat. This would kill him, as surely as him being hung.

Lord Thurstun wasn't finished. "Both of you will assist with the establishment of a shapeshifter school. We will draw up our own wishes in a document, to guide the teaching process. The school will be located at Kitt's holding, once the new laws are in place. We expect only your best behavior, to avoid a reassessment of your judgements."

Lord Thurstun fell silent. The Council looked resolute.

Breathless, Ember stood and curtsied as deeply as she could manage. She glimpsed Kitt's ashen face. "Thank you, Council, for your decision."

CHAPTER FOURTY-THREE

By THE TIME twilight crept up from the east and swallowed the feet of the mountains, they had released all the animals from Arundel and Fletch's dungeon room and buried those that had died.

The bear was the last to go.

"Do you think he remembers being human?" Ember asked Kitt as they watched the bear amble down the knoll where they sat on a moss-covered log.

"No," Kitt replied, leaning his elbows on his knees.

The bear made its way around a sycamore and nosed a sunberry shrub.

Ember's throat constricted. *I wish I had known him*, she wanted to tell Kitt, but it seemed selfish of her to talk about her own wishes when so much lay between them.

She smoothed the deer-hide dress over her thighs. "I know I can't expect you to ever forgive me, but I'm sorry I lied to you about who I was. I wish I had done things differently. Maybe people wouldn't have gotten hurt that way—"

"You can't go back, Ember," Kitt said, shrugging his shoulders. "There's no point in regretting what you've already done. We all learned from what happened." Kitt paused, watching as the bear disappeared behind a boulder and reappeared on the other side of it. "And as for forgiveness, you should only worry about getting it from yourself."

Ember frowned as the darkness wrung her chest. Forgiveness. Was it possible? She found it hard to believe the memories would fade, that at some point they would stop replaying in her mind. She had killed two people, quite relentlessly. And she would have done it the same had she been put there again. Ember wondered if Kitt felt that way about the wizard he had killed. The one he castrated and consumed.

Power through killing. But she understood now that the power had been necessary. A power of defense and survival. Without it, others would have had power over her, and she couldn't let that happen. Not then, and not now.

"Does the darkness ever go away?" she asked.

Kitt exhaled, and those moss-green eyes turned to her. "No. It stays with you. Becomes a part of you. Once you accept that, it's easier to bear."

Ember looked away and picked up a stick to whittle with her thumb nail. She scowled at the bracelet on her arm, hating the vulnerability it brought with it.

"And anyways," Kitt continued, his tone growing lighter. "I suspected you were not who you said you were. You didn't act much like a kitchen scullion. Or a washerwoman."

"Really? I suppose I don't know enough bawdy jokes."

"I get enough of those from Jinni." Kitt said, smiling. The silver streak along his temple glinted.

Ember wondered, not for the first time, what Kitt's relationship with Jinni was. Friends? Or more than friends?

"I met your cousin Eawart some time ago," Ember said. "He's rather fond of the estate. He invited me to come visit."

Kitt turned suspicious eyes on her. "A visit?" A glint of amusement, and a flash of something dark. "You aren't going to accept his hand, are you?"

Ember thought of her mother, and Finn. "Why not? He seems nice enough. And he's a good dancer." She couldn't stop herself from smiling, even if she was half-serious in her consideration.

"Because he doesn't know you're a shifter. Or at least, he didn't mention it when I spoke to him last night."

"Oh." Ember supposed she didn't need to marry anyways, now that she was to help Kitt with the school.

Her mother could come live with her, if Kitt allowed it. She glanced at him, wondering, and caught him watching her. Heat rose up her face. "I am glad you are better. I think you impressed the Council with your negotiations."

"I don't care about impressing the Council." Tart words. The normal Kitt. "I care about the future of shifters in this country."

"I know." A pause. "Why did you come after me when I left for the wizard camp?"

Kitt studied his bracelet. "When Seabird told me about you, all I could feel was anger. I wanted to follow you so I could kill every one of the wizards you found. He tried to stop me." Kitt gave a hollow chuckle. "The anger made everything hazy. I felt it toward everything and everyone, and by the time I got to the wizard camp..."

The bear pawed the ground beneath a walnut tree.

"After a while," Kitt continued, "I got lost. The anger blinded everything but my animal instincts. I don't know if I would've stopped if those knives hadn't hit me."

Gregory's knives. Ember swallowed.

"Being in that cage hadn't helped with the anger," Kitt said. "I've never wanted to kill that wizard more. But then it was the both of us who were in trouble. And now it's this." He held out his cuffed wrist. "A part of me is glad for it."

Ember wondered how much he remembered, or whether he had seen everything. Whether he had noticed that she fought and killed for him. Him and all the other shifters. She wasn't ready yet, to ask him, or to talk too much about what happened.

His distant gaze watched the bear, but his eyes shone with something she knew too well. He seemed rigid and cold beneath that gaze, pale as death and as isolated as a stone in an ocean.

As isolated and vulnerable as she herself felt.

Ember wanted to hug him, to shift into a cat and curl up in his lap, to assure him that everything would be alright. She wanted to erase the sadness in his eyes, to let him know that she would find a way to undo their spells. To tell him that she, too, would be trying to forgive herself.

Instead, she found herself reaching out to him, taking his face into her hands, pulling him close so that she could rest her lips on that silver temple.

He came alive beneath her. Slipped his arms around her and moved his lips over hers.

Sweet lips and a heat that curled into her.

"Ember," he whispered. "I'm glad you're here."

And it really was her, for once, stripped of all her silly, stupid lies. She was Ember Pitkin, a wizard-shifter. And she loved this man who kissed her, and who wanted her.

"You mean you don't want to kill me anymore?" she teased.

"I admit I was too judging of wizards before," he said, though his light words belied the sadness and guilt lingering in his gaze. His lips quirked. "The Council wasn't all bad, and your mother was kind to me."

'"You met my mother?"

"She was there when I awoke. She reminded me of how to eat, how to think again. And you, Ember," he added as the sea-foam flecks in his eyes took on a peculiar heat. "You are reminding me of how to be human."

They held each other, and for the first time since Arundel's death, the darkness inside her didn't strangle her heart. For the first time, she felt the past might be bearable after all.

Below them, the bear melded into the forest.

A NOTE TO READERS

Thank you for reading my book! If you have a moment to spare, I would really appreciate a short review (on Amazon, Goodreads, or wherever you like!). Your help in spreading the word is gratefully received.

You can sign up to be notified of my upcoming books—and to get a free short story—on my website at:
www.eaburnett.com

You can follow me on Facebook @eaburnett.author or on Twitter @eaburnett3

ACKNOWLEDGEMENTS

Ember's story would not have been possible without the long-standing support of my family and my writing group. I am eternally grateful to my mother for teaching me a love of reading, and to all of the numerous authors who inspired me to become a writer at a very young age. They gave me the courage to take that dream and fly with it. I also must give credit to my grade-school and high-school English teachers (and one substitute teacher) who encouraged me to write more and better. They had more impact than they could possibly imagine. Special thanks to David Farland, whose invaluable class taught me how to make a strong outline. Also thanks to my editor, Katrina Kittle, for her encouragement and willingness to give me more feedback when I needed it. Great thanks is also needed for my illustrator, Leesha Hannigan, whose amazing talent has given Ember's story a beautiful and captivating face. And finally, thanks to my husband Adam for suffering old drafts, bouncing around ideas with me, and tolerating my swings of doubt and elation over the years. I am so incredibly lucky to have him with me on this journey.

Made in the USA
Columbia, SC
28 May 2025